Mrs. Perivale and the Blue Fire Crystal

By Dash Hoffman

Mrs. Perivale and the Blue Fire Crystal

Written by Dash Hoffman

Published by Paris Publishing
Copyright © 2017 Angel Canann

Cover art copyright © by Angel Canann
Cover copyright by Angel Canann
Interior art and imagery copyright © Angel Canann

Also by Dash Hoffman

Mrs. Perivale and the Dragon Prince
Journey Blue
The Starling Chronicles
The Wish Weaver
Voyager: The Butterfly Effect

…and many others

WITH SPECIAL THANKS TO

@BROODINGYAHERO

AND

@DINURIEL

FOR INSPIRING THIS BOOK SERIES IN THE FIRST PLACE!

@broodingYAhero published a post that read:
"It's amazing how many prophecies involve teens.
You'd think they'd pick more emotionally stable
people, with more free time. Like grandmas."

To which @Dinuriel replied:
"…I would read the hell out of a series of a
chosen eighty-five-year-old woman who goes
on epic journeys throughout a dangerous and
magical land, armed only with a cane and her stab-
tastic knitting needles, accompanied by her six
cats and a skittish-yet-devoted orderly who makes
sure she takes her pills on time.

WISH GRANTED...

DEDICATIONS

FOR MY CHILDREN
AND MY CHILDREN'S CHILDREN
MAY THE WONDERS OF
ADVENTURE AND IMAGINATION
ALWAYS BE YOURS

FOR CAPTAIN BRADD KEADLE,
WHO HAS GIVEN ME AND ALL OF YOU
THIS WORLD

FOR MARGOT BUSH &
CECILIA SORIANO
WITH GRATITUDE FOR YOUR CONSTANT
LOVE AND SUPPORT

WITH ALL MY LOVE
DASH

FOR THOSE WHO HAVE SUPPORTED ME
IN MANY WAYS
FRIENDS AND FAMILY
WITH TREMENDOUS GRATITUDE
THANK YOU

THIS NEW WORLD BELONGS TO
ALL OF YOU

TABLE OF CONTENTS

Prelude   1

Chapter One ~ A Rainy Day   3

Chapter Two ~ Chippa Mari   19

Chapter Three ~ The Chosen One   39

Chapter Four ~ The Sea of Tranquility   61

Chapter Five ~ The Light House   77

Chapter Six ~ A Wild Ride   98

Chapter Seven ~ Along the Way   116

Chapter Eight ~ Lyria   137

Chapter Nine ~ The Unexpected   159

Chapter Ten ~ Aridan   185

Chapter Eleven ~ The Illusionary Palace   207

Chapter Twelve ~ Dangerous Delusions   218

Chapter Thirteen ~ Shattered Illusions   235

Chapter Fourteen ~ Truth   250

Chapter Fifteen ~ Full Circle   262

Chapter Sixteen ~ Realization   273

CHIPPA MARI

PRELUDE

An earsplitting clap of thunder struck, and a bolt of lightning shot from a clear blue sky where the morning sun poured out honeyed light.

The powerful javelin of electric energy ripped through the air straight down to the ground, where it pierced a large boulder, shattering it, and sending shards spraying in every direction. They pelted the ground, splashed into water, and whipped against tree trunks, not far from several tiny homes making up a small village.

The village was nestled into an idyllic spot on gently rolling hills between a great forest, and a wide lake. To the north of the village, the low mountains at the start of a massive range stood sentry. To the south, over more hills, was sea.

The inhabitants of the village; small furry creatures about two feet tall, went rushing about in chaos. Many of them were shouting, some were weeping; all of them were looking for answers, and help.

One of them, worrying over the pandemonium, suddenly turned and scurried away, heading to the woods. He picked his way skillfully through the trees and brush, nipping beneath some of the branches, and scuttling over large roots and a few fallen tree trunks.

He came to a wee space where all of the growth had been parted away from a low tree stump. The giant, leafy lord of the forest which had once reigned there had fallen long before, but its roots remained; great and knobbly, crawling over and through the ground in every direction. They connected in an intricate web to all of the other tree roots for as far as the forest grew.

The stump was slightly lopsided; one jagged edge of it, covered with soft moss and tiny flowers, rose like a shield, just a bit taller than the furry creature who stood beside it. The rest of it was fairly even, dipping down into a kind of rough bowl in the center.

The little creature bent to a nearby flower, which was filled with morning dew, and tipped it into his paw. With the greatest care, he turned his paw over the center of the hollowed out bowl of the stump, pouring the water into it. Next, he opened a small leather-like pouch on a drawstring around his neck, and picked out a pebble-sized chunk of a glowing ember. He blew on it, making it catch fire, and then lowered it into the hollow. It hovered just above the water.

Moving both of his paws together in a circular motion above the maw of the bowl, the creature concentrated and focused, staring into the space as the droplets of water, the bits of fire, and the air, along with the leaves and dust already in the bowl, began to turn and twist together, forming a translucent disc.

Shifting images appeared within the ring of elements, and the creature gazed at them; his large dark eyes searching desperately. The scenes within the circle changed, going from city to country, from mountain to sea, from one human's face to the next, and the next after that, in a seemingly endless parade.

At long last, the scenes stopped, and the creature focused the vision on one woman; an older woman, standing outside on a step, speaking to a postal carrier. At her feet, there was a cat.

Chapter One

A Rainy Day

In a prim and proper townhouse, neatly set back from a respectable street in the poshest end of the Notting Hill neighborhood of London, lived an older woman named Alice Perivale. Mrs. Perivale was widowed when her husband, the late Lieutenant General George Perivale, passed away bravely in a battle on a distant shore in the service of Her Majesty the Queen of England.

Alice left their spacious country home after George had gone, as she felt that it was too empty. Their son Edward went off to Oxford and then become an important businessman in the Central Business District of London.

He'd married and had his own child, and Alice saw them on holidays and occasionally on odd weekends. She had only been able to stand the quietness of her large home for a short while before she determined that it would be much better if she lived closer to her family in London. She wanted to be there for them whenever they needed her.

Alice purchased a lovely townhouse and settled into it with her six cats, and her butler Henderson. Henderson had vowed to remain in her service for the duration of her life. He felt that it was his duty, his obligation, and indeed his honor, to do so. He took excellent care of Alice and the cats. Alice said more than once that Henderson was the glue that kept the household together, and he did his best to live up to that bar. From making certain that tea was always served promptly at four in the afternoon to ensuring that Mrs. Perivale took the right pills at just the right time every day, he was the clockwork that kept it all going.

She had recently brought home a fluffy orange kitten with big green eyes, that she had found homeless and hungry in the park down the lane. Alice cleaned him up, fed him, and introduced him to the other older cats, naming him Oscar, and explaining to them that they were to take care of him; he was their new charge. Oscar was having a trying time learning to fit into his new place in the family, but each day he grew a bit more comfortable.

On the most unusual day of Alice's life, the morning had been gray and rainy, though at intermittent points the sun made efforts to shine at the edges of the clouds, brightening them somewhat from behind.

Alice was seated at the old wooden roll-top desk in her small library. Marlowe, the Abyssinian cat, was curled up on a red pillow cushion on a modest chair beside her, watching her through heavily lidded eyes, while he purred quietly.

Nearer to the fireplace, on a thick, soft rug, lay two more cats. Tao, the Siamese, was resting so still that she could have been mistaken for the statue of a sphinx. Her sea blue eyes were closed, her breathing slow and deep, and her tail was wrapped around her carefully. She often meditated in such a way.

Not far from Tao sat Sophie. She was picturesque, as always, with her long white hair carefully groomed, her posture elegant, her manner poised, and her slender diamond studded collar fastened about her neck. Her sky-blue eyes were set on Alice as she sat at the desk.

Lounging in a cushioned basket right beside Sophie was an old grey cat with black stripes streaking back from his bearded-looking whiskery face.

The stripes varied in size, growing wider as they reached the middle of his body, wrapping around him. His coat was long and soft, and more white hairs now mingled with the grey than before. Montgomery was asleep; stretched out lazily and happily, facing the warmth coming off of the flames in the fireplace.

In the window was another cat. She was all black, and her fur gleamed like smooth satin in any light. Though she gazed coolly around the room now and then, her golden eyes were diverted more often to the street outside, watching the passersby and the rain as it fell from the sky, rolled down the buildings and streets, and splashed in the gutters when cars swept by.

Jynx was fond of ignoring the other cats and taking in the world that existed just outside of their home, but with the arrival of the fuzzy orange kitten, that had changed. She'd taken him under her paw, and watched over him more than the other cats did.

Oscar poked his head in the door and looked around; his green eyes wide and his whiskers twitching as he sniffed the air. His fur was fluffy and unkempt, sticking out in nearly every direction. His gaze touched on Tao, Sophie, and Montgomery beside the fire, and on Jynx in the window, who turned her head and looked at him patiently, but he stopped when he saw Marlowe on the red cushion beside Alice.

The kitten padded over slowly and sat at the foot of the chair, looking up at Marlowe, whose attention was on Alice.

Alice reached her fingers to a dark cubby hole in the inner shelf of the desk, just beneath the slats of the roll-top, and pulled out a colored seashell. It was shaped like an open lady's fan, and its warm shades resembled a spring sunrise: a rosy blush at the base blended into peach and then to a soft, buttery yellow that faded into a smooth vanilla crème at the scalloped edges of the shell.

Oscar meowed at her. She smiled down at him, lowering the shell for him to examine. He sniffed at it tentatively as she spoke quietly to him.

"My husband George gave this to me. He brought it from far away and he told me that he kept the other half of it, knowing that the two halves would always make a whole, even when they were apart. We really were one, he and I. I guess we still are, and we'll always be."

She waited until Oscar was satisfied with his inspection of the seashell, and then she returned it to its place in the cubby box in her desk.

With a wistful smile, Alice picked up her phone and cleared her throat as she gazed at a photograph on her desk of the man she was calling. The phone at the other end of the line rang a few times.

"This is Edward Perivale." The man's voice came through deep and strong.

"Hello, Edward. It's mother." She smiled happily. She was always glad to hear his voice; it brought his face directly to the forefront of her mind, along with many of the sweet memories she had of him.

"Hello, mother. How are you doing?" He asked, sounding distracted.

She curled her fingers tighter around the phone. "I'm well, thank you darling. I was hoping we could have dinner soon. Perhaps tonight, if you're all free." She didn't want to use up any more of his workday than she had to, and got right to the point.

Her son sighed heavily. "Mother, this really is the worst time. Annabel has a meeting, Eddie is playing in a match, and I'm right in the middle of a deal at work that needs all of my attention."

Alice pursed her lips together, looking up from her desk to the window before her, watching as rivulets of raindrops rolled down the glass.

"Well... perhaps I could go to Eddie's game. I'd love to see him play in a match."

"No, mother, he's riding along with some of the other boys, and neither Annabel nor I will be going to this one. It's clear on the other side of the city. It wouldn't work for you to go." His tone was strained and weary.

With a deep breath, she set her shoulders back a little. "Is there another night soon when we could have dinner together? I miss you all, and it would be lovely to see you. I really did move to the city just to be closer to you, and it seems like I don't see you much more now than I did when I lived in the country." Alice willed herself not to be dejected.

He breathed out a long sigh. "I have no idea. There's no night I can think of right now. Perhaps Annabel can look at the calendar and try to find a time. We'll have to figure it out later. I really do have to go. I'm quite busy at the moment."

Alice stared at the window, not seeing anything past the rain water washing all down the pane. "Of course. I'm sorry to have bothered you."

"Bye, mother." Edward answered shortly, and hung up.

Alice sat in silence, holding the dead phone to her ear, and closed her eyes. Swallowing hard, she pushed down the emotion rising in her heart. With a shaky sigh, she set the phone back on the desk and lowered her hands into her lap, clasping one around the other.

Her hands were old, and her skin pale; the darkness of her veins showed through here and there. Her fingers, once slender and pretty, were a bit more knobbly at the knuckles. There were delicate crepe paper lines where the skin had once been smooth. She began to lose herself in the years she could see on her hands.

The subtlest sound of a cleared throat pulled her from her reverie. Alice blinked and drew in a breath, turning in her seat to look behind her. Henderson, her butler, was standing there. All of the cats looked at him. At his feet was another cat that had followed him into the room.

It was a very fat calico cat, whose fur was white, with big splotches of orange and black all over, from his nose to the tip of his tail. His face was flat and had the slightest look of being pushed in, which only served to make his cheeks look wider and rounder.

Bailey looked up at Henderson expectantly, watching him closely. The fat cat was always hungry, and he had developed the habit of following Henderson around until he was fed, when it was close to mealtimes.

Henderson's coat was black, and the longer tails of it hung down at the back while the front was cut short at his waist. He wore a white button up shirt with a small tidy black tie, set crisply at his neck. What little hair he had left was combed over to one side, and his narrow body stood at attention. His lean face was turned up ever-so-slightly in sincere concern.

"Excuse me, Madam, I was coming in to ask about your evening meal tonight. I… couldn't help but overhear your conversation. I apologize, I hadn't intended to eavesdrop." He lifted his thin eyebrows a little.

She gave her head the merest shake. "Not to worry. It's fine, Henderson. I think I'd like beef tonight, and whatever Fran wants to make with it."

He nodded and turned to go, but stopped after a step and faced her once more.

"Madam… if I may… as I understand it, there is a new group coming together at the little church beside the park, just down the lane. It's a Widows of War group. They are forming to help each other and to do service in the community where it's needed. I wonder if that might be of some interest to you. I have no doubt you'd be quite a helping hand to them, if you joined them. I think they're accepting new members until three this afternoon." He gave her a hopeful and encouraging smile.

Alice smiled back at him. "That sounds like a good group, Henderson. Thank you for mentioning it. I believe I'll go have a look and talk with them. Perhaps there's something I can do. Maybe I could be of some use."

Henderson gave a slight nod and left the room with Bailey waddling close behind him, meowing at him. The cats shared looks amongst each other, and turned to gaze up at Alice.

She rose from her chair and glanced down at the phone on the desk. "I guess since my son is too busy for me, I'll go see if this Widows of War group could use some help."

Alice reached the library door and turned her attention down to Marlowe, who was right at her heels, where he always was.

"Marlowe, dear, it's raining. I doubt you'll want to go. You'll get wet." She spoke with a tender half-smile.

He looked up at her expectantly and pawed gently at her foot.

She sighed in resignation. "Very well then, you can come, but don't complain about your fur getting soaked. You won't let me put a raincoat on you, and the best I have is the umbrella. Sure you won't stay? No? Well, maybe you'll be all right."

The corners of her mouth curved up a little more. "Come on then. Stubborn boy." She chuckled quietly and they walked to the table by the front door together.

Alice pulled on her mismatched gloves and her brightly colored purple coat. She dressed well, but she couldn't deny the flair of spice and sass that had flowed through her all of her life.

Besides, she thought to herself as she set her matching purple hat decked out with ribbons and flowers atop her head, if the Queen of England could go around dressed in every color and look wonderful, so could she.

Giving herself a peek in the mirror, she leaned in a little closer and considered her reflection, just as she had been considering her hands earlier.

When she was younger, she'd had dark hair and fair skin, rosy cheeks, and full lips. She'd been quite a belle. Time had drawn itself around her slowly and carefully, etching every moment, happy and sad, good and difficult, into her face. There were smile lines framing her mouth, and laugh lines extending from the corners of her eyes.

She had been happy for most of her life, and it showed. Her cheeks were fuller than they'd been in her youth, and the dark color in her short hair had faded to nearly all white, but her brown eyes were as warm and kind as they had always been, and she had a welcoming smile for anyone who took the time to look at her.

With a gentle tug on the edge of her hat and a nod of satisfaction, she picked up her umbrella cane with the bird's beak shaped handle, and reached for the door. She held it open as Marlowe lifted his tail and stepped out with her into the misty rain.

They walked side by side along the road. She was careful to avoid stepping into puddles so that she didn't splash water onto Marlowe. He held his head up; his eyes wide as he kept watch all around them, his ears alert and pointed sharply. She carried the umbrella over them both, though she wasn't sure just how much good it was at covering the cat beside her.

They had just rounded a bend in the road when Alice stopped short and gazed at a spot on the pavement opposite them.

She peered closely and frowned. Marlowe stood beside her, staring at the place where she was looking, and then turned his head up to her with curious eyes.

"Marlowe…" she began quietly, leaning her head slightly to the side as she spoke across her shoulder to him, "did you see anything over there… just now?" She blinked a few times and peered harder.

"I was certain I just saw some kind of little animal over there, but there's nothing there now. I could have sworn…" she trailed off and bit gently at her lower lip.

Alice finally turned away and gazed down at Marlowe, who tipped his face back up to her. "Did you see anything?" She asked again. He meowed and waited for her.

Drawing in a deep breath, she raised her brows and shook her head. "It must have been a trick of the light. Could have sworn I saw… something." Her eyes narrowed in puzzlement for another moment, but then she shrugged and began on her way again.

After a short walk, and carefully crossing one street when the cars had stopped, they made it to the church.

It was a small building made of gray stone blocks and set with stained glass windows that had been in place since before Alice's grandmother had been born. A single narrow bell tower rose from one end of the church, housing an old brass bell that rang out on Sunday mornings.

Reaching for the worn handle on the thick, old oak door, Alice eyed Marlowe seriously.

"Now, you won't be allowed in here. I'm sure they'd have a fit. Who knows if their church mice have claimed sanctuary, but you'll have to wait outside for me. I won't be long. Stay right here and don't go off anywhere. I'll be back soon enough."

Marlowe meowed and sat at the side of the doorway; his eyes locked on her as he curled his tail around himself.

The overhang above the door reached out far enough that the cat wasn't being rained on. Alice gave him one last look and stepped into the church.

Through a door to a room off the side of the foyer, she saw a small table where a young woman sat with a few stacks of papers and a cup filled with pens.

The young woman had mousy brown hair pulled back into a sloppy bun. Her thin lips were pressed together in a hard line. She lifted her hazel eyes and stared over the top of the squared glasses perched at the end of her narrow, upturned nose.

"Can I help you?" She intoned coolly.

Alice gave her a warm smile. "I hope so. I'm looking for the Widows of War group. I'd like to learn a little more about it and sign up for it. Is this where I-"

The young woman pulled her head back in exasperation, giving herself a double chin as she did so.

"Ma'am," she interrupted swiftly, "I don't really think there's anything that you could do for the group. It's designed for a younger crowd. I think you're just a little too old to try to do any of the things that we do in this group. We wouldn't want you to get hurt."

Taken aback, Alice blinked. "Well, I realize I might not be quite the same age as some of the ladies in the group, but I can certainly-"

The young woman cut her off again. "We just don't think it would be a good idea. We're only looking out for your best interests."

Alice gazed intently at her. "What is your name please?"

"Deborah." The young woman answered in a snappy tone.

"Well, Deborah, you keep mentioning this 'royal we' that you seem to be speaking for. Is there anyone else running the group with whom I might speak?" Alice maintained her decorum as best she could.

Deborah folded her hands and leaned toward Alice, glaring above the rim of her glasses and answering with a bossy, impatient tone. "There is, but she's not here right now, and I *do* speak for the group."

Alice felt the rare flickers of annoyance and frustration ignite in her. "When might I be able to speak with this person?"

"Not anytime today." Deborah smirked with satisfaction. "By the way, I just thought I'd point out to you that your gloves are mismatched."

Glancing down at her hands, Alice turned them over as she inspected her gloves. "Yes, they are. How crass of you to mention it." She answered, looking back at the young woman before her. "I'm wearing them anyway, though. It's a sign of taste, which apparently comes with age."

Deborah stood up; her cold, hazel eyes locked on Alice. "I don't think there's anything we can do for you here. I think you're just a little too old to be looking into something like this. Perhaps you should focus on acting your age and doing things that people your age do."

Alice's mouth fell open slightly as she gasped. "And just what age would that be? How should I act? Should I stay in bed? Indoors? Should I just be done with my life since I'm so old? Well I've got a thing or two to say about that, Miss Deborah! I'm a long way off from the grave, and I have a lot of living yet to do. There is quite a bit that I could do for others, especially for the Widows of War group! I'm not about to stop doing anything that I *can* do, just because someone else thinks that I shouldn't!"

She was about to go on, but Deborah went to the door and stood beside it expectantly as she gestured for Alice to leave.

"Thank you for coming in." Deborah sneered icily. "It's raining. Perhaps you ought to go home, where you should be."

Alice clamped her mouth shut and strode briskly through the doorway. As she passed the young woman, she snapped, "If the group offers a class on manners you should sign up for it!"

With her chin high and her fingers closed tightly around the handle on her black bag, she pushed open the old oak door of the church and stepped into the fresh afternoon air. The rain had stopped, though it was only a brief break. Marlowe was sitting just where she'd left him. He meowed; his brown and gold eyes steady on her.

"Well, that didn't go well at all." She grumbled in irritation as she planted her umbrella cane on the ground. "Let's find a little spot. I need a few moments to gather myself."

Marlowe and Alice walked away from the church and down a pathway that meandered into a park. After a few turns, they came to a bench beneath a tree that looked to be a mostly dry spot. Alice sat and placed her bag on the bench, and Marlowe leapt up gracefully beside her.

Blinking back hot tears, she patted Marlowe on the head and opened her bag to dig around in it.

"I guess I'm not much use to anyone anymore." She sniffed as she pulled out a dime-store romance novel and set it beside her purse, going back into the depths of the bag.

"I used to do so much. I was really active and involved with so many things." She sniffed again and pulled out a butterscotch candy, setting it on her lap before reaching in once more.

"That wretched woman in the church practically told me my life is at an end. She said they have no use for me. Perhaps she's right…"

Alice trailed off and finally pulled a neatly folded handkerchief from her bag before she pushed the romance novel back into the folds of it. She clutched the cloth in her hand and brought it to her eyes and nose.

"Maybe there is nothing more I can give to my community. My son and his family have so little time for me, and now the Widows of War group doesn't want me. I just feel so useless! I can't give anyone anything if they won't let me, can I Marlowe?" She asked in a thin voice as she worked at swallowing her emotion, and rubbed her fingertips over his head.

He moved closer to her, purring and nuzzling his face into her hand as she petted him. With a half-smile, she tilted her head and her voice softened.

"Thank goodness I have you and all the other cats, and Henderson. I don't know what on earth I'd do without all of you."

The two of them shared a long and quiet moment together, save for his loud purring. She opened her butterscotch candy and popped it into her mouth, rolling the wrapper between her gloved fingers. Eyeing them thoughtfully, she frowned.

"She didn't like my gloves. Just because they don't match. George bought one of these pairs of gloves for me when we were on our wedding anniversary holiday in Paris one summer. She didn't know that, did she? How could I toss away something as sweet as that just because it doesn't match? I was silly and I lost one of the gloves, but I still want to wear them, so I just wear a different glove on the other hand. It's not as though I'm ever going to get another anniversary gift from George again. I think short-sighted people can't appreciate the beauty and true value in things they don't understand. Last time I saw him, I was wearing this glove… he held my hand and kissed my cheek just before he left. Wearing it, I can almost feel him holding my hand again. I'm not about to give that up just so my gloves will match."

Marlowe listened carefully and watched her, and she rubbed his head once more. "Oh dear… it looks like the rain is going to start back up. We should probably head for home, my darling."

She tucked her handkerchief back into her purse and pushed herself up from the bench, taking a few steps toward a nearby rubbish bin, where she dropped the candy wrapper. She was about to walk away, but then she stopped short, staring intently at the trunk of a nearby tree.

"Marlowe," she whispered, "I swear I just saw something over by that tree… that one, just there. Do you see anything? Is there a little animal over there? I'm so certain I saw one just now… not much bigger than you, but now there's nothing there at all! Look carefully, do you see anything?"

He peered closely along with her, and a low growl sounded from his core. She gave him a sharp nod. "That's what I thought. I can't be seeing things. I refuse to go senile. It's just that… there's nothing there now."

Alice's mouth twitched, and she harrumphed softly. "My goodness. Perhaps it's time to be getting back. Tea time soon."

She opened her umbrella and glanced toward the elegant Abyssinian beside her. "Come along then, Marlowe. Let's get home." She straightened her coat and hat, and they set off together.

CHAPTER TWO

CHIPPA MARI

The gears in the massive old grandfather clock began to whir and grind, and the deep tones rang out from it four times as Alice spread her napkin over her lap.

The cats were lined up at their dishes, and Henderson gave them each a few treats before he came to the table and served tea and scones with clotted cream and raspberry jam to Alice.

"How did it go at the church?" He asked with a hopeful smile.

She furrowed her brow some. "Not very well, actually. I don't suppose I'll be joining the group. They are looking for a younger contingency."

He was genuinely disappointed. "I'm so sorry to hear that, Madam. Perhaps there is another group that might need your help elsewhere."

"Perhaps so, Henderson. Thank you." She gave him a little smile, wishing with all of her heart that it was true. "It is a great feeling for one to know that they are needed." She added, lifting her teacup for a sip.

"It is indeed." Henderson answered pleasantly. "It's quite fulfilling." He spoke as if it were the one thing in his life that made him happiest.

When tea was finished, she rose from the table and sighed, feeling the weight of the world on her shoulders. "I think I'll skip the evening meal tonight, Henderson." She told him quietly.

He frowned slightly. "Are you feeling all right? Can I get you anything?"

"No, thank you. I'm just a little tired."

Alice bid him goodnight, went to her bedroom, and readied herself for bed. Once she was in her nightgown, she sat in her chair beside the fireplace in her room, reading a book for a while as the cats all napped nearby. She tried to keep her mind off of the worries of the day. When the grandfather clock chimed eight times, she put the book down, turned off the lamp, and got into her bed.

Reading had not distracted her much from her thoughts, though she tried to push them away as best she could. Deborah's cold words had cut at her and she wasn't sure whether or not they were true, even though she felt as though they couldn't possibly be.

She didn't feel old. She still saw the world around her with the eyes of a woman less than half her age. That didn't necessarily mean that her body would let her do what her heart and mind wanted to do. She was still in decent shape, and strong enough, but her age had slowed her down a little, at least physically, much to her disappointment.

She lay in bed in the dark, pondering over all the things on her mind. The shadows and light from the dying fire danced lambent across the ebony ceiling and walls, and she watched them, listening to the ticking of the clock. Marlowe lay curled at her feet; the warmth from his body comforting her through the blankets.

He moved slowly and carefully, a few steps at a time, and she wondered at the edge of her thoughts what he was doing, as he rarely came up further on her bed than his favorite spot at her feet.

It was then that she realized Marlowe hadn't moved. He was still curled up by her ankles; his soft form and body heat against her, but his purring had stopped. Alice's breath caught silently in her chest as she realized that something else was taking very slow steps up the other side of her body, toward her arm.

She knew it wasn't one of the other cats. They never got up on her bed; any of them. They each had their own beds around the fireplace, and Marlowe had made it clear that Alice's bed was his, and nobody else was allowed there. He'd have had them off of it in a moment if it had been one of the other cats.

Her heart began to beat faster, and blood rushed through her, pulsing in her ears as the slight pressure of the moving thing inched closer. Her eyes were locked on the ceiling; motionless, while her mind was focused with magnified intensity on her predicament.

Somewhere in the vast reaches of her heart, an untapped strength took over, and she found herself feeling level-headed and in complete control.

Whatever it was creeping up beside her kept pausing, and then inching forward slowly. It stopped again. Alice waited until it began to move once more and then like a flash, her hand shot through the dark and she grabbed wildly at where she was sure the thing was.

Her fingers closed tightly over something very soft; a kind of silky fur, and just as they did, there was a loud squeak.

A moment later, Marlowe was at her elbow, opposite whatever it was that she had a hold of, growling deeply as he stared at Alice's hand.

The softness inside her grip wriggled about, but she held on tightly as she reached over Marlowe's head with her free hand and flipped on the lamp beside her bed. Blinking in the light and pushing herself upward, she saw that all of the cats were grouped together on the floor right beside her bed.

She sat up and realized that she couldn't see what was in her hand. It looked as if she was holding onto thin air, except that where her hand was supposed to be, it wasn't. There was just nothing there to see past the middle of her forearm. Whatever the thing was, she had a death grip on it, and it wasn't going anywhere, though it squirmed and pulled to get away.

Marlowe growled even louder, and in a blink all six of the other cats leapt up onto the bed, surrounding Alice's body as she pulled the soft invisible thing onto her lap and gave it a shake.

"All right now, I've got you and I'm not letting go. You come out right this minute! Do you hear me? Come out! I don't know why I can't see you, but I know you're there and I've had enough of this foolish nonsense! Now *out*!" She demanded.

All of the cats and Alice watched in disbelief as color and form began to show through a strange looking fringe just before their eyes. It was as though a feathery curtain was parting, revealing the creature behind it.

Two big, dark, round, shining eyes appeared; they were deep black, almost like portholes to the universe. Around them was a thin sliver of an ocean blue ring.

The eyes were framed with short, light brown fur, and above each eye there was a delicately arched fringy antenna in place of its eyebrow.

Just below its eyes sat a tiny nose and mouth that resembled a cats', though the mouth was wider, and shaped with an upward curve, as though it was smiling a little. It might have been smiling, Alice wasn't sure.

The rest of the creature emerged then, and Alice realized that the feathery fringe that had been covering it was actually its tail.

It was fanned out like a peacock tail, but it was all directed forward and was made of several wide, fluffy ostrich-looking feathers. There were short, dark brown feathers at the base of its tail, longer golden sand-colored ones that reached up to the creature's shoulders, and vanilla-colored fronds that draped all the way over the front of its body, touching the blanket in front of the creature's feet. The colors blended softly into each other where they changed.

The tail feathers came up around the creature like a bubble, covering all of it and making it disappear, until the animal pulled its tail back, opening the feathers like a curtain, revealing itself.

The little being slowly retracted all the feathers, and curled its tail into a nautilus spiral reaching up its back and resting snuggly just behind its neck, similar to a squirrel.

Its furry ears, like those of a large puppy, were perked up at attention. It had small paws with four fingers and what looked like a thumb, as well as toes on its feet, like a raccoon.

Alice could see that it had retractable claws, though they weren't extended. The fingers on its paws were shaded dark brown with white and tan spots on them. The thing stood upright on its hind legs.

There was a thick soft white tuft of fur in a V shape at the creature's throat, which wrapped around to the back of its neck, like a bandana. The rest of its fur was varying shades of natural browns, from tan to mahogany, and black, and all of the fur on its body, save for the white fur neck collar, was short and silky, like a rabbit.

Alice could see dark freckles of varying sizes and shapes all over the creature's face, almost like it had been splattered with paint.

The animal stood at about a foot and a half tall, but it was cowered down somewhat, making true height difficult for Alice to determine.

Its body was shaped like a teddy bear, with a gently rounded and protruding belly, but it didn't seem fat; rather that some of the roundness was an illusion of its fur.

It blinked and a quiet chirping sound issued from its throat, though its mouth didn't open.

Marlowe arched his back and vaulted up on his toes; every hair on his body standing straight on end. His eyes filled with fire as he pulled his mouth back and hissed and spat, growling dangerously.

Alice, and the creature she was holding by the arm, both jerked in surprise. Though Alice wasn't afraid, the creature was terrified. It whimpered and began to wriggle in her iron grasp once more.

"Marlowe! Now hold on! We don't know what this thing is yet. Let's figure this out. Please, try to calm down a little!" Alice reassured him gently.

Marlowe wasn't listening. His body remained rigid, ready to pounce in an instant. Alice picked up her reading glasses from the nightstand beside her and pushed them onto her nose, tilting her head back and looking through them at the creature in her hand as she shook her head almost imperceptibly.

"Well my goodness…" she spoke in a near whisper, but then her voice became sharp and strong.

"I knew I wasn't seeing things today, you dodgy little ankle biter!" She dragged the thing a little closer toward her on her lap, glaring hotly at it. "What in the world are you up to?"

It reached its front paws up and closed them gently over her hand. "Had to see 'ef 'et 'es you! I know 'et 'es you." He spoke in a tender voice not much bigger than he was, with a strange accent. It was immediately clear that English wasn't its native language.

Alice's eyes widened as she blinked at it. She hadn't been expecting an answer. She spoke to her cats all the time, but they never spoke back to her.

The cats all scowled at it, except for Marlowe, who was still on the razor's edge of a full on attack. "Never mind about me! What are *you*?!"

He held his paws around her hand still, and she could feel their softness on her skin. "I 'es Chippa. Chippa Mari. I 'es an Inkling."

Her whole face contorted as she frowned and looked at him a bit closer. "You're a what?"

"I 'es an Inkling." He answered, slowly beginning to pet his paw over her hand with a calming touch. "You 'es surprised by me?"

Alice narrowed her eyes at him. "Of course I'm surprised by you! I've never seen anything like you, but that doesn't mean you're getting off scot free! You've been following me today and I want to know what's going on! What do you want, Chippa Mari?"

Marlowe growled long and low again, and Oscar the kitten slowly padded up the side of Alice's leg, his eyes wide and his orange fur fluffed out more than usual. He got just close enough to the Inkling's tail to lean out and sniff it carefully.

Chippa Mari glanced back at him nervously, and then returned his attention to Alice. "Had to come. Had to find you. Have come from home... from Mari Village."

"I've never heard of Mari Village." Alice countered shortly.

The Inkling shrugged a little. "No. You doesn't know 'et. Mari Village 'es very far away."

"Why are you looking for me?" She pressed, regarding him suspiciously.

His eyes grew wider, though that didn't seem possible to Alice, and he continued to pet her hand gently with his paw.

"Mari tribe need your help. Need you to come to Mari Village." He pleaded, "Mari tribe 'es desp'ruht!"

"Well that's certainly true if they think they need me." Alice muttered under her breath. "What do you need me for? Isn't there someone else who can help you?"

He shook his head and the soft fringe on the antennae brows over his eyes swayed with the movement. "No one else. Only you! There 'es the prophecy. 'Et can only be you! You must come! We 'es in trouble! There 'es danger. Everything 'en danger."

"I don't need danger in my life." Alice stated flatly, but she softened a moment later. "Why are you in trouble?"

He stopped petting her hand and gripped it a little tighter. "There 'es the crystal was stolen from Mari Village, Blue Fire Crystal. Must be found. Must be brought back."

She frowned sharply. "The Blue Fire Crystal." She shook her head. "Well, I think that's just about enough of that. I'm not going anywhere with some strange creature to-"

"Inkling... I 'es an Ink-"

"-to God knows where in the middle of the blessed night. It's bedtime, just look at that! It's a quarter after eight already, and any reasonable person should be off to sleep! Now out you go! You've caused enough trouble for one day. Off with you, and don't let me catch you sneaking around here again!" She released him and sat back against her pillows, giving him an unrelenting glare.

His big black eyes shone with the beginnings of tears. "Please! You must come! Mari need you! Can't be anyone but you... 'ef I doesn't bring you back... I've failed again. Everything 'es lost." He sat his little body down on her lap and sniffed.

"Please come!" He clenched his paws, wringing them together; his soft, pointed ears directed forward, along with his imploring gaze.

Alice's heart melted, and she sighed heavily. "I don't even know where this place is. You're some strange creature-"

"I 'es an Inkli-"

"-from some strange village I've never heard of.... Goodness knows where. How far away is it? Would it take long to get there?" She couldn't believe she was considering it, but there was something about his tone and about him altogether that intrigued her.

"'Es fast trip." He replied in a soft voice, but he glanced away from her nervously.

"So this Blue Fire Crystal is missing... What do you need me to do about it?" She lifted her chin and eyed him pointedly.

"We 'es needing you to come and help us find 'et." He murmured hopefully, then hesitated. "But, 'et's not 'en thes world."

Alice crossed her arms over her chest as she regarded him pointedly. "It's in *another world?* And how am I supposed to get there? How do I even know that what you're telling me is true?" She peered sharply at him.

He blinked and pulled his head back a little. "I 'es here, right 'en front of you. I doesn't think you 'es ever seen anything like me before."

"Well I saw plenty of you today." She snapped back at him. "You'd better come up with something more than that. Some kind of proof."

He fidgeted, and his feet curled and uncurled as he thoughtfully considered what she said. Reaching his paws up underneath the long white fur at his neck, he tugged, and a small cloth pouch came into view.

It was on a drawstring around his neck. He slid it open and his eyes danced a little as he reached in and pulled out what looked like a fiery twig. It shimmered and glowed just as the embers did in the fireplace across the room.

Alice gaped at it. "What is *that*?"

Chippa Mari smiled brightly and his pointed ears perked up as he lifted it for her to see. "Thes 'es Tinder Root. Not from 'thes world. Mari eat 'et. Inklings love Tinder Root. Comes from base of Flame trees."

Alice reached her finger toward it, but he pulled it away and wagged his other paw at her. "You shouldn't touch. Might burn you."

"You're going to eat that?" She gasped.

He turned his attention to the glowing root he held, and a wide smile came over his little face as his eyelids lowered and he gazed adoringly at it.

"Yes. Mari love Tinder Root. Hot and spicy." He popped it into his mouth and the chirping sound issued from his throat again as he closed his eyes and savored it for a long moment before swallowing it.

Chippa Mari came back to himself then, opening his deep, dark eyes as he stood back up and took a few steps toward Alice, still on her lap. "Please... you has to come. Mari need your help! None 'es can survive 'ef you doesn't come and find the crystal!"

Alice sighed, crossing her arms over her chest once more. She turned her eyes toward Marlowe, who was still at rigid attention beside her, glaring hotly at Chippa Mari.

"Oh, Marlowe. I've never even thought about whether or not there were other worlds. How bizarre! Strange business; this situation, and this little one here. He's certainly the most unusual thing I've ever seen, but he does seem to be telling us the truth, even if it is difficult to believe. I'll be honest, I hate to think of anything happening to him and to his little Inkling village, no matter where it is. You know I can't stand to see anything suffer. Obviously. I do have seven cats."

Marlowe briefly glanced at her before darting his smoldering eyes right back to the creature.

Alice gave the Inkling a small smile. "All right, little Chippa Mari. I suppose I will come with you."

He was about to speak when Marlowe took a few steps closer, pressing his body against Alice's arm. Alice chuckled at the cat. "It seems that Marlowe will be coming with me. I should've guessed that."

Chippa Mari frowned, eyeing Marlowe. "…um, 'et 'esn't a good idea 'ef 'thes cat comes-"

Marlowe growled deep and loud, bristling sharply as his golden eyes pierced the Inkling.

"Oh!" He squeaked, "Okay yes, 'es fine, I guess." Chippa Mari nodded humbly, folding his paws together and sulking.

All six of the other cats on the bed began to walk toward Alice, looking from the creature to her. "Actually it appears that they all want to come. I didn't expect that. I hope that's all right."

The Inkling looked doubtful, and shook his head. "Not good. I doesn't think they should-" he paused, looking around at them, staring at him. "…uh… 'es going to make a lot harder to… um…" He shrank down slightly under their hard stares and grew quiet. "'Es fine. I guess. Have to think of some way to explain to-" He stopped himself and raised his eyes to Alice, giving her a pained smile.

"When should we go?" She asked evenly.

"Now. Have to go right now." The Inkling answered anxiously.

She nodded. "All right. Chippa Mari, how do you disappear like you do?"

He smiled, holding his paws together as he gazed up at her with his wide, round eyes. "You can just call me Chippa. Mari 'es tribe name, so we all share name Mari, because we all one tribe, but you can call me Chippa."

He lifted his tail out of the nautilus spiral against his back, and carefully fanned out all of the delicate fringed feathers, waving them almost like a fan as he turned to one side.

"All Inklings 'es having a tail like 'thes. When we 'es born 'et's small and wild, like a rooster tail, but we grow and older get, tails grow bigger, softer, more beautiful. We 'es 'en danger, or we need to hide, then we cover ourselves 'weth tail completely, like a chameleon. Hides us so we blend 'weth everything around us, and we can't be seen. We 'es staying there, but can't be seen at all."

He covered himself with his tail, arching it over his head and all the way down the front of him, until the feathers touched the blanket in front of his toes, and he looked as if he were in a feather bubble for a moment, but then he disappeared.

Chippa lifted his tail and reappeared a moment later, smiling up at Alice. She raised one eyebrow at him. "You use it when you're in danger, or when you need to hide?" She asked with suspicion.

"Yes." Chippa nodded.

"Or when you want to be sneaky." She added, giving him a meaningful look.

The tips of his ears drooped slightly, and he looked down at his paws. "Yes. Sometimes then, also."

"All right, Chippa, you said we need to leave right away. I'll just get dressed and gather a few things, and tell Henderson that we're going. I want you to stay right here until I come back for you and the cats." She asserted smartly.

He gave her a nod and moved off of her lap so she could get up. The cats circled around him, all of them studying him closely. Chippa didn't move as he gazed about at them nervously.

Oscar reached out one little orange paw to bat at the fringy feathers of Chippa's tail, and Chippa drew his tail in close to his body as Jynx gave Oscar a stern look. Oscar pulled his paw back and sat still as they waited.

Alice dressed and then went from one side of the room to the other, to the bathroom, back into the bedroom, down the hall, and returned to the bedroom again, all the while stuffing various things into her ever widening black bag.

Finally she waved at the cats and Chippa, and told them to follow her downstairs. The group of them went into the kitchen, where Henderson was putting clean teacups away. He glanced over his shoulder at Alice and his mouth fell open.

"Madam! What are you dressed for? Certainly you aren't going anywhere at this hour! Are you all right?" He worried over her.

"I'm fine, Henderson, thank you. I'm going out. I don't know how long I'll be gone." She answered simply.

He gaped at her. "What, in the middle of the night? So late? Where are you going?"

Alice stepped aside and Chippa came out from behind her; his little paws held to his mouth as he gazed up shyly at Henderson, who stood nearly two feet taller than Alice. Henderson gasped loudly.

"What in... -oh my *goodness*!" He fumbled with the teacup he held, and then shot a wide-eyed look at Alice. "Shall I call animal control at once?" He set the cup down and started for the phone on the wall.

Alice raised her hand and shook her head. "No, thank you, Henderson. This is Chippa. He's an Inkling, so he tells me."

Henderson blinked hard, overtaken with exasperation. "He... -he *speaks*?!"

He stared at Chippa for a long minute, and then looked back at Alice. "Madam, I must insist. You cannot go."

Chippa drew in a breath and turned his big eyes to Alice. "But... but Messus Perf... Pel... Peliv..." He stammered worriedly.

Alice leaned down closer to him. "Perivale. Pear-ih-vahl." She sounded out for him.

"Pevi..." he tried again and shook his head, miserably ashamed. "I 'es sorry. Can't say 'et. I has trouble 'weth big words in your language."

"Can you say Alice?" She asked kindly.

Before Chippa could utter a sound, Henderson stood straight up and gave Chippa a sharp look. "Madam, that won't do at all!"

Alice sighed and glanced from Henderson back to Chippa. "Henderson's very proper, my dear, there's no getting around that. Try saying Mrs. P."

Henderson balked, completely affronted.

Chippa wrung his paws a little and gave it a try. "Messus P." He brightened up and smiled widely when he realized he had gotten it right.

"Well that's-" Henderson began, horrified, but Alice held out her hand and stopped him.

"That's perfectly fine, Henderson. He can call me Mrs. P." She gave them both a smile. "Now it's time we were leaving."

Henderson grew greatly flustered. "You're going out? With that... -with... *Where are you going?*" His voice rang with panic.

"I think I'm going to Mari Village." Alice answered thoughtfully.

"A village? A vil... There aren't any villages around here! You certainly can't go anywhere like that alone! I'll have to come with you, of course. There's no question! I just need to pack a few-"

Chippa's mouth fell full open and his ears flattened to the back of his head as he narrowed his eyes angrily. "Heda... Henness... Hesson..." he was growing increasingly frustrated, "...now 'thes one has to come?" He finally shot out.

The cats and Alice all turned to him in shock. Chippa curled his little paws into fists and pushed them backward in defiance.

"No! 'Thes 'es very many! Chippa came for one! One! Chippa came to get one, and Chippa had to say yes to all these others..." he waved his paw wildly at the cats around him, "and Chippa didn't want to, because Chippa already has explaining to do! Chippa says no! 'Thes one cannot come! Chippa cannot explain *all* of you! 'Es only supposed to be one! 'Thes 'es... -'thes 'es many more than one!"

He was shouting, at least as much as his light voice could let him, and his naturally light tone didn't lend itself easily to his frustration.

Henderson was flying around the kitchen, shoving several things into his large, black leather shoulder bag. He spoke in half-thoughts as he bustled about.

"Tea of course... -and medicine, can't go anywhere without her pills... -must have... -cat food! An umbrella of course, and... -oh heavens, I've forgotten the-" He dashed madly out of the kitchen.

Alice lifted her chin and sniffed. "He can come if he wants to. I don't care whom you have to explain things to, he is with me, the cats are with me, and if you want me, you get them."

Chippa frowned deeply and glared. "Fine, but no more! 'Thes 'es all! Chippa already going to be 'en trou-" He stopped short and turned toward the door.

Alice followed him, and the cats trailed behind her. She picked up her umbrella cane and her black bag, and opened the door for all of them. "Why are you referring to yourself that way when you talk? You didn't do that earlier."

"Chippa wasn't upset earlier. Chippa very upset now! 'Es how Chippa talks when he 'es upset!" He snapped, marching hotly down the stairs with his tail fanned out widely, shuddering behind him.

"Well Chippa, I'm sorry you're upset, but you'll need to hide yourself so no one will see you. It's dark, but still, if you show yourself there's a chance someone might take notice of you. We probably don't want that to happen. You may be difficult to explain." Alice told him gently as they headed down the stairs to the sidewalk.

Chippa stopped and touched his paw to his mouth thoughtfully. With a nod of understanding, he looked up at her. "'Thes will work." He answered, and faster than the blink of an eye, he had vanished.

Where he had been standing, there was a small paw print that glowed like the embers in the fireplace, and like the root he had eaten. It only glowed a dark orange and red for a moment on the pavement, and then it faded away.

Alice clapped her gloved hands together and giggled softly. "That's brilliant, Chippa! How do you do that?"

He parted his tail feathers just enough so that she could see his eyes and face and nothing else. "'Et 'es from Tinder Root. Warm paws when needs. Very warm. Follow me." He replied quietly, and he vanished again.

Glowing little paw prints appeared on the pavement behind him as he hurried along. Alice and the cats trailed them as the marks disappeared quickly.

Alice looked down at Marlowe in his place by her feet and chuckled softly. "He must not be as mad as he was a bit ago. He stopped referring to himself in the third person."

They were nearly at the end of the lane when Henderson came rushing up behind them, calling out. His leather shoulder bag swung wildly against his back, and his long black coattails flew in his wake while he pinned his black bowler hat to his head with one hand as he hurried to catch up.

Huffing and puffing, he just made it to them as they crossed a quiet and empty street, and headed into the park where Alice had seen Chippa earlier that day. Chippa's glowing paw prints disappeared altogether when they reached the grass, so he lifted his tail and unveiled himself, waving his paw at them to follow him into a place where the growth was abundant.

Chippa stopped before two trees that were growing about six feet from each other. He reached his paw toward the trunk of one of them, running it gently along the bark in an upward motion.

The tree began to bend slowly, leaning its upper branches to one side as Chippa stroked his fingers in that direction, almost as if he was willing it to move, and the tree was doing his bidding.

When the tree had arced over at the top, Chippa went to the trunk of the other tree and did the same thing, going the other way, so that when the second tree arced over at the top, it met with the first tree and created a natural archway.

When the branches and leaves at the tops of both trees had connected, he looked up at what he had created and chirped, pleased.

Chippa turned, his dark eyes shining at the group standing behind him; Oscar, Tao, Jynx, Sophie, Montgomery, Bailey (who was panting), and Marlowe, who was with Alice. Henderson stood behind Alice, also panting.

With a tip of his head and a flip of his ears, Chippa waved his paw at them to follow him, and the moment he passed through the archway of the trees, he disappeared.

Alice, Henderson, and all of the cats stared at the spot where he had been. There was nothing there any longer; he had simply vanished into thin air.

Oscar padded forward and hesitated only a moment before bounding toward the archway, and a second later, he was gone, too. Jynx rushed into it right behind him, followed by Tao and Bailey.

Montgomery turned to Sophie and meowed. She wouldn't budge. Montgomery went to her, curling his body and tail around her, meowing once more as he stepped toward the place where the other cats had gone. She wouldn't move. He turned and went after the others, leaving Sophie with Alice.

Sophie tipped her pretty face up to Alice and cried, but Alice shook her head. "None of that now, Miss Sophie. Off you go with the rest of them. Come on."

Alice straightened her hat, and she and Henderson, along with Marlowe, walked through the archway and disappeared. Sophie cried again, going up to the space slowly; pawing at the air in front of her.

A dog barked in the distance. Sophie looked in dismay over her shoulder for a moment, then leapt toward the archway and vanished.

Chapter Three

The Chosen One

Alice found herself standing on a worn dirt path that wound capriciously through a wooded forest. The sea of trees; thick and knobbly, twisting in a curly and meandering fashion toward their dark green canopies, swallowed some of the light.

Small plants carpeted the ground around the trunks, and flowering vines drifted here and there among the limbs and branches.

It was a peaceful, serene place, and Alice felt the strange sensation of being contented to be there, though she knew that by all rights she should be anything but contented at that moment.

It was later afternoon; the golden hour just before sunset, and warm buttery sunshine poured over the group, and through the trees and plants, giving the forest a soft, almost daydreamy sort of glow.

Alice turned and looked about her feet, counting the cats, and then raised her eyes to Henderson. He was standing behind her with his mouth hanging open in absolute shock.

"At my age I've seen a great many things, but this is something altogether new." She spoke with a quiet voice. "Are we all here? We all made it?"

"We're here," Henderson finally blinked, "but where are we? What *is* this place?" He was completely astonished. "We were in London just a moment ago, and now we're... we're certainly not!"

All of the cats stared wide eyed at the woods, but Oscar left them and padded to the edge of the dirt path where the green grass and moss grew thick. He began sniffing at various plants and flowers. Jynx was right behind him, watching him closely and sniffing a little herself.

"More importantly, where is Chippa?" Alice asked with a note of concern in her voice.

The little Inkling popped his head around a bend in the path before them, and waved his paw. "Come on, Mari Village 'es 'thes way." His eyes looked a bit bigger than usual.

Alice lifted her chin, cleared her throat, and gave her family a determined nod. "Right then, off we go, shall we?"

She was nervous, but she knew that she couldn't let anyone else around her see it. She had to be brave for all of them, and then maybe she could convince herself of it as well.

The group followed around the bend in the path and only managed a few more steps beyond that when they stopped short again, awestruck at what sprawled out before them. They discovered they were standing at the edge of a small village, but were not far from the center of it.

The village was made up of circular homes only three or four feet high, each topped with thatched roofs built of reeds or slender branches from trees tightly bundled together. The roofs were laid so that they came over the homes in a sheltering, conical way, and rose to a point at their centers. The look of them reminded Alice of the shape of a yurt.

There were no corners or angles on any of the buildings. They were formed of a burnt orange, light brown, or cream colored clay, and featured arched doorways holding doors made of old wood from the forest.

The windows were round, and some of them had curtains, but none of them were enclosed; there was no glass or any other barrier to keep out wind and rain.

The buildings were scattered about with no particular order that Alice could see, and there were winding dirt paths that curved and twisted between them.

The village was nestled in a clearing between the woods they had walked out of, and a lake just down a lightly sloping hill on the other side.

A wide-open rounded space formed the center of the village as a courtyard, with only a lone standing, tall, marble gazebo on the lake-side of it.

Chippa went to a water well at the edge of the courtyard. He turned his face upward and trilled a loud whistle.

Alice, Henderson, and the cats walked slowly toward Chippa. Inklings all over the village stopped in their tracks and stared as they caught sight of the incoming group of strangers.

The Inklings were of varying sizes, though most of them were about Chippa's height, save for a few small ones that Alice realized were cubs, zipping around and playing until they looked up in awe at the visitors.

The colors in their fur ranged from natural browns and beiges like Chippa's to silvery grays with black, reddish, and cream hues.

At the sound of Chippa's whistle, several Inklings came out of their homes and momentarily froze in surprise. Slowly they moved to the central clearing. From the biggest home facing the courtyard, came a deep booming voice.

The wooden door of the home opened, and an Inkling a bit larger than Chippa stepped out and peered around. It was his voice that had rung out like a big bell, and he repeated himself.

"Who 'es calling gathering?" He demanded. His fur was a blend of salt and pepper colors, and his tail though shaped similarly to Chippa's, was much bigger than Chippa's, curling all the way up his back and almost rolling over his head, even though it wasn't flared out at all. He looked to be very old, and a bit shaggier than Chippa, or any of the other Inklings who were coming together at the center of the village.

The big old Inkling stepped out into the thickening group around him, and saw that they were all looking up at Alice, Henderson, and the cats. His eyes bulged, and his mouth fell open.

Alice could see fear, uncertainty, and curiosity in the eyes of all those who were gathered, hovering together as they gawked at the strangers before them.

She had never felt so out of place in her life. The cats looked around and held their ground silently, gazing at the members of the village as they came into the clearing.

Oscar took a few steps forward to sniff at some of the Inklings, and they gasped as he did so, shrinking back away from him, though he was smaller than them.

Jynx reached her head forward quickly, and closed her teeth gently at the back of Oscar's neck, pulling him to where he had been sitting near her. He grumbled quietly and looked at her with a pout, but he sat where she wanted him to, and he didn't move again.

The big old Inkling made his way through the villagers and came to stop between them, and Alice with her company.

"Who 'es 'thes?" He demanded, looking up at her, and eyeing the cats suspiciously.

Chippa, who was still standing beside the well, cleared his throat and took a few steps toward Alice.

"I 'es found the Chosen One of the prophecy; 'et's her." He pointed his paw toward Alice without taking his eyes off of the old Inkling.

The old one glared at him and then huffed, and let out a small roar. "That cannot be! 'Thes 'es not the Chosen One! What can you be thinking? You did no' have permission to go out and try to find the One! You went out into the yonder and found 'thes and all of these others, and you brought them here? You never! You 'esn't even of age yet! You still has a 'bet of time left before you can leave Mari Village!"

Another Inkling came and stood beside the old one. His fur was dark and tufted out. He was big and younger looking, and strong and rough around the edges; as if he had been in more than a few fights and come out the winner every time, though not cleanly. He held on to the shaft of a spear made of a tree branch with a stone arrowhead at the tip.

"Young Chippa 'es thinking he brought back the Chosen One?" He asked in a loud voice, looking from

Chippa to the old Inkling, and then toward the crowd of onlookers.

Alice saw Chippa shrink down somewhat, and cast his eyes downward to the ground. Her heart went out to him. Seeing him there with his tribe, she could tell that he was still a young Inkling, though not a child. He seemed nearer to being an adult, but it was clear by his size and his behavior just then, that he was not quite fully grown.

She frowned at the Inkling with the spear in his hand, as she could easily see that he was intimidating Chippa and bullying him, and she had no patience for it.

"I am Alice Perivale, and I have come because Chippa asked me to. He believes that you need help, and I have agreed to help him and all of you. What is this Chosen One that you're speaking of please?" She was polite, but to the point and determined, and her voice sounded out clearly over the village.

Every eye turned to her and the old Inkling as he took another step forward, eyeing her skeptically. "I 'es Bayless Grand Mari. I 'es the Chief of the Mari tribe." He announced, and Alice could see reverence shown to him by all the Inklings in the village who turned to regard him before looking back to stare at her and the cats.

Bayless Grand Mari nodded his head toward Chippa. "He 'es not to be out there 'en the yonder, not to be leaving the village yet, not ever to be bringing anyone to the village, especially from your world, and not to be supposing he knows who the Chosen One 'es! The Chosen One 'es the one 'en the prophecy."

~ 44 ~

Alice sighed. "Well we're past all of that now, aren't we? I'm here and I want to know about the prophecy. Can you tell me what this prophecy is please?"

Chippa cleared his throat and looked up from the ground toward her. Holding her gaze with his, he explained. "The prophecy 'es that a warrior would come to save Corevé."

She spoke in a kindly tone to him, thinking that he was already getting the hot end of everyone's tongue as it was. "What is Corevé?"

Chippa gestured at the area they were standing in. "Corevé 'es the land. All the land. All you see."

"It's your country?" She asked to confirm.

He nodded. "Yes. The prophecy says the Chosen One will come to Corevé and bring back the stolen crystal. See… there 'es the Temple of Elements." He pointed to the eastern edge of the clearing.

There stood a round gazebo made of carved buttercream marbled stone, with four columns rising from the circular floor to the roof, which arced in a gentle dome at the top.

Because the roof stood at five feet, it was easily the tallest and grandest structure in the village. Around the bottom perimeter of it was a short stone wall that encased it only to a foot in height, but to the Inklings, that was nearly as tall as they were.

Flowering vines wound around the columns, twisting and rising to the dome of it, also reaching away from the pillars toward the spaces in between them, so that there were natural arches made of vines all along the top, connecting the pillars.

At the center of the gazebo were four short pedestals grouped together, each reaching two feet in height, and sitting on three of them were colored crystals, but one of the pedestals was barren and empty. At the center of the four pedestals was a fifth stand, and on that rested a closed, peach colored seashell.

"Those 'es the Element Crystals." Chippa explained, pointing toward them. "That 'es the Red Earth Crystal, and the Green Water Crystal, and the Purple Air Crystal." He saddened as he paused, gazing at the empty pedestal last.

"That was the Blue Fire Crystal?" Alice looked back at Chippa.

He nodded and dropped his gaze to the ground before meeting her eyes again. "'Et was, 'tel 'et was stolen." Every Inkling around them was silent as he spoke.

"I had to come get you. You 'es the Chosen One… you 'es the warrior to bring back the Blue Fire Crystal." He affirmed as he moved closer to her.

Every Inkling who was gathered around them began to laugh at Chippa's final words, but none so loud as the Inkling beside Bayless Grand Mari; the one holding the spear.

"'Et cannot be! 'Thes one 'es no warrior!" He laughed so hard that he bent over at the waist.

Bayless Grand Mari held one old paw to his very round belly and laughed a bit, and then shook his head. "Chippa, you 'es wrong. She 'es not the Chosen One. She 'es no warrior."

Marlowe growled low and deep.

"Well, I never!" Henderson scoffed just under his breath.

Alice simmered inside with indignant flames, and she planted her umbrella cane sharply in the dirt.

"If I'm not needed or wanted around here, then I'm going to leave. I came to help you, but clearly you do not need my help, just like every other place where I try to be of service, so I'll be on my way. Good day!" She snapped smartly.

She was just about to turn and head back into the woods when she saw Oscar's bottlebrush orange tail up in the air as he was entering the Element Temple.

Alice called out to him, but he wasn't listening to her; his attention was solely focused on some strange flying bug. She hurried toward him as the Inklings continued to laugh and talk amongst themselves in their own exotic tribal language.

When she reached the Element Temple, she bent over slightly and went inside, reaching for Oscar to pick him up. As she did, the pedestal at the very center of the temple; the one holding the seashell, began to light up almost as if sunlight were radiating from it.

Alice turned to it with a start, uncertain what she had done to cause it to come to life. The entire gathering of Inklings became silent in an instant.

Alice froze in place as she noticed the seashell, and saw that it began to open, turning in its place and facing her. It was empty, except for a single perfect pearl sitting exactly in the middle of it.

Bayless Grand Mari rushed from his spot at the edge of the crowd toward her, hurrying into the temple, and picking up the seashell in his paws. His eyes were wide as they flicked from the seashell to Alice.

Without a word, she scooped Oscar up into her arms, then turned and walked out of the temple, back toward the other cats and the path to the woods where they had come from.

"Wait!" Cried Bayless Grand Mari, following her as swiftly as his little legs and heavy body would let him go. The entire tribe stood agape, looking from the seashell to Alice. She turned then, stopping to gaze back down at him.

"Yes?" Alice asked in a level tone. "I didn't touch it and you know that; you saw me." Oscar squirmed in her arms some, so she bent over and set him on the ground. Jynx went to him and sat on his tail so that he couldn't go anywhere.

"'Thes seashell, 'thes 'es the compass that keeps the Element Crystals balanced. 'Et centers the crystals. 'Weth one crystal gone, 'et stays closed and 'well only open for the Chosen One." His voice dropped, as did his almost overbearing stance. He had been mightily humbled.

"Can you tell me exactly what the prophecy says?" Alice asked politely. She was wondering why they weren't surer of whom their Chosen One was.

First they had said there was no way that it could be her, but then the seashell compass opened up and they were saying that it would only open for the Chosen One. She thought perhaps if she knew precisely what the prophecy was, she could help them sort it out and figure out who their champion might be.

Bayless Grand Mari shook his head. "No, I canno' tell you what the prophecy 'es. 'Et's 'en Mari language. No translation. Chippa told you as best we can."

Alice nodded. "All right then. Well, if you can't tell me more than what you've already told me, then I don't think there's anything else that I can do. Besides, you probably need someone younger; a teenager or young adult perhaps. Someone with boundless energy and a wanton disregard for imminent danger. I wish you luck. Now then, we'll be on our way. Goodbye."

Alice turned and began to walk along the path toward the woods with Henderson and all of the cats following her, but Bayless Grand Mari called out to her again and chased after her.

"Stop! Please stop!" He cried. "I doesn't know how Chippa knew 'et, but you 'es the one… 'thes 'es right, you 'es the Chosen One. Chippa was right!" He admitted loudly. Alice stopped, turning to look back at him.

"We need you to find the Blue Fire Crystal and bring 'et back to the Element Temple!" He pleaded. "We need you! Corevé needs you. All of 'thes, all of us, all of the world you see here, 'well be gone without you. You have to stay, please stay and help us. You 'es needed!" He looked like he might fall right down on his big belly and beg her if she didn't say yes.

Chippa hurried up behind him and stood near him, staring up at her with his little paws outstretched to her. "'Et 'es you, please!' He added to the chief's plea.

The rest of the entire tribe came up behind Chippa, and all of them called out, pleading with her to stay and help them.

Alice looked around at the group of about forty or fifty Inklings before her; so many ages and sizes, all of them staring at her with their big dark eyes, all of them begging, all of them meaning it desperately. She hadn't felt so needed in years. It softened her heart, and a few tears stung at the back of her eyes.

"Oh, very well then, since I'm here anyway, and you do need someone to give you a hand." She called out to them with a kind voice. "We will help you."

A loud cheer went up throughout the group of Inklings, except for the warrior Inkling, who stood at the back edge of the crowd with a sour expression on his face.

Henderson stepped up close to her and spoke. "Madam, I really must insist. I don't think that you should undertake any endeavor of this kind at all! It's really not a good idea to-"

She held her hand up and looked from him back to the Inklings directly in front of her, all of whom had worried looks on their faces as their eyes shifted between her and Henderson.

"Well, there we have it. If Henderson says that I ought not to do it, then I know for certain that I should. We are committed to your task." She gave her head a nod, and Henderson groaned behind her.

Bayless Grand Mari turned toward the tribe. "We have our Chosen One! We must have a feast! Prepare!" He called out loudly. A moment later, most of the Inklings around them scattered, rushing to and fro, bustling about and working.

Alice, Henderson, and the cats returned to the center of Mari Village. Chippa stayed with them, looking pleased and happy that things had worked out the way that he wanted them to.

Alice gave him a wide smile. "Well done, my dear." He chirped softly and curled his paws around themselves.

Three pretty looking Inklings came to the cats tentatively, eyeing them with curiosity and interest.

"What 'es 'et?" One of them asked, looking from Sophie to Chippa.

Chippa lifted his chin and puffed out his chest a little. "'Et's a cat." He answered them. He looked up at Alice then and held out his paw. "'Thes 'es Umee Mari, Channa Mari, and 'thes 'es Nubo Mari. Nubo 'es the village scribe. She 'es the writer."

As Channa drew near to them, Alice, Marlowe, Sophie, Oscar, and Jynx were surprised to see a tiny little Inkling pop up out of a pouch on her stomach. Chippa smiled and waved his paw at the baby. "Channa 'es carrying a cub." He said fondly.

"Well that's almost like a kangaroo pouch, isn't it?" Alice asked, looking pleased as she admired the tiny Inkling in Channa's pouch. "What a sweet darling you have there. Congratulations!"

Channa chirped and rubbed her paw over the baby's head, but then her attention joined that of Umee and Nubo, as the three of them gazed adoringly and wide eyed at Sophie.

"So pretty!" They exclaimed as they tiptoed near her and tentatively reached out their paws to stroke her fur.

Sophie lifted her chin and closed her eyes, purring and loving the attention of her admirers. Jynx grumbled low and turned her head away.

Another Inkling, an older one that looked only a bit younger than Bayless Grand Mari, went to Montgomery, smiling and bowing to him a few times. Chippa waved at him.

"'Thes 'es Luto Mari." He said pleasantly. "He likes the cats too." He gave a nod.

Luto looked blissful that he was engaging with Montgomery. He reached for the hidden leather pouch tucked beneath the mass of soft gray fur at his neck, and tugging on the drawstring, he opened it, pulling out a monocle. He showed it to Montgomery who was fascinated with it.

Luto bowed and gave it to him, moving close to place it on Montgomery's eye, and help him as he got it adjusted.

Montgomery turned to look at the other cats, and they stared at the glass piece over his eye; some of them admiring it. Sophie went to him and purred, sniffing at it and rubbing her face against his.

Just then there was a sweet, loud chirping sound that came from the woods, and they turned to see another Inkling coming out of the forest.

She was as old as Bayless Grand Mari, or perhaps even older, with beautiful dark fur, streaked with silver. She had a big round tummy, making her look fat and happy.

The big old Inkling slowed as she took in the sight before her. Her deep, dark eyes focused on Alice and Chippa in particular. She strode to them with a leisurely pace; her body swaying as she moved, almost as if she was walking to music that only she could hear. The closer she got, the more intently she looked at Alice, and Alice felt that the Inkling was looking right through her.

"Hello, I'm Mrs. Perivale." Alice greeted her.

The dark-colored old Inkling nodded. "You 'es the Chosen One... I see."

"I suppose I am." Alice smiled at her. She knew that the old lady Inkling hadn't been in the village when the discovery about the Chosen One had been made. It was the first that any of them had seen of her.

Alice was properly surprised that the old Inkling had said her piece so immediately and confidently. There was no question in her voice or in her eyes; she spoke it because she knew that it was indeed a fact.

Chippa cleared his throat and stepped forward, away from Channa, Umee, and Nubo, who were settled around Sophie, preening her with their paws as she purred and indulged in the attention and adoration.

"'Thes 'es Oppa Mari. Oppa 'es the village healer." He introduced her reverently.

Alice nodded. "Well it's nice to meet you. How very clever of you to know so quickly what it took everyone else some time to figure out. How did you know that I am the Chosen One?"

Oppa Mari laughed from deep in her belly as she raised her paw and waved it in the air dismissively. "I know because I can see. Bayless Grand Mari 'es blind. He can only see what 'es right 'en front of his eyes. I can see what 'esn't 'en front of my eyes."

Chippa cleared his throat a little and looked up at Alice, who was surprised. "Oppa 'es equal to Bayless Grand Mari. He 'es the chief, she 'es the healer. Equal." He explained, and Alice nodded.

Oppa Mari peered at Chippa. "You 'es finding the Chosen One…" she trailed off quietly; thoughtfully. "On your own 'en the yonder world?"

Chippa nodded in silence, looking away from her.

Oppa Mari hummed softly as she contemplated him for a long minute. She gave a nod to him, and then a nod to Alice as she turned and headed down one of the pathways in the village, disappearing from view.

Chippa's shoulders sagged slightly as he exhaled in relief, watching her go. Alice wondered at what she was seeing.

It wasn't but a short while later that the center of the village was filled with tables and small log seats, and at the edge of the clearing, there was one thick, full length log set for Alice and Henderson, along with hastily made tables that would fit them, though they were low to the ground.

Henderson pulled the cats' dishes from his black case, and advised the Mari tribe that the cats would probably best enjoy meat of some kind. The Mari complied, and the feast began.

A wide variety of unusual foods was laid before them, from savory roasted roots to fresh fruits and vegetables. The strangest of all were the edible flowers that were presented on wide trays.

There were bright red and robust violet blooms, sweet dainty pink and white petals, and some blossoms that hadn't opened until the moment they were eaten, and those were the juiciest and tenderest. Every one of them was delicious.

The Mari tribe had dark earthen bowls filled with Tinder Root that all of them were quite excited to eat, but Chippa warned the tribe that their guests probably couldn't enjoy the Tinder Root with them, for it would burn them.

After the main meal, a warm buttery drink was served in clay mugs. It tasted almost like a mix of butterscotch and ginger going down, and all of them loved it, even the cats. The drink was served with freshly baked sweet biscuits, and they enjoyed those as well, but none so much as Henderson, who tucked several away in his bag for later.

When the food and dishes had been cleared, Bayless Grand Mari whistled loudly the same way that Chippa had when he had called the village to the courtyard. Bayless Grand Mari climbed up and stood on his tree stump seat, and gazed at the whole gathering.

"Our Chosen One has come to us, and now the journey to bring back the stolen Blue Fire Crystal must begin! Messus Purfull and her cats, and 'thes one," he said, waving at Henderson, "must need a guide to show them through Corevé. Jika Mari!" He called out.

The warrior Inkling who had come forward when Alice and her company arrived at Mari Village, and who had bullied Chippa so badly, stood up and puffed his chest out proudly. "I 'es going. I 'es leading them on 'thes journey!"

A loud cheer sounded among the Inklings.

Alice frowned and studied the villagers. She didn't like the idea that Jika Mari would be going with them. She didn't like it one bit. She cleared her throat audibly. Everyone turned to look at her.

Bayless Grand Mari silenced the gathering with a wave of his paw. "Yes, Messus Peffle?"

"If it could be allowed, I would very much like Chippa to come with us and guide us. He was after all, the one who looked for me and found me in the first place. He believed in me when no one else did. I feel that he should have the honor of going, if he wants to. I'd certainly prefer Chippa to come with us if he may."

She held her chin high, except for a glance over at Chippa, who was sitting nearby. He stared at her with his little mouth open, and his already wide eyes seemingly wider.

Everyone stared at her. Not a sound was made. The cats were smug as they gazed around at the tribe. Henderson only looked on, not at all surprised. Bayless Grand Mari cleared his throat again.

"Yes, o' course. Then we 'es sending Chippa 'weth you, 'ef that's what you want. Chippa's no full grown yet..." He added, giving her a waiting look as if knowing that fact might change her mind.

She nodded. "So I understand. I'd like Chippa to go."

Bayless Grand Mari waved his paw. "Chippa goes." He announced.

Chippa squeaked with excitement and his tail fanned out in an explosion of feathers. He turned to Jika Mari, who was still standing there by his table with his spear in his hand, gaping. Chippa poked his tongue out at Jika, and Jika Mari looked away and sat down quietly, laying his spear beside him in the dirt.

Bayless Grand Mari shushed the murmuring of the other Inklings and continued his speech. "We do not know who stole the crystal-"

He was interrupted by a small Mari child who tugged on his fur. He looked down at the little girl who gave her mother a bashful glance over her shoulder. Her mother nodded to her and waved her paws at her to go forward.

"Chuna Mari, what 'es 'et child?" He asked, gazing down at her.

Her small face was turned up, and she said something quietly that only Bayless Grand Mari could

~ 56 ~

hear. He gasped loudly and cried out, "What? Why 'es 'thes only now being said?"

The leader reached down and scooped up the child, holding her carefully in his paws. "Tell them what you just told me!" He insisted.

Chuna Mari held her paws together tightly and gazed at her tribe, the cats, Alice, and Henderson. "I saw the thief. I 'es afraid to tell, but Messus Paffval 'es so brave, and she 'es a lady girl like me, I want to be brave like her. I can tell now."

Alice felt her heart go right out to the child, and pressed her fingers to her lips, blinking rapidly.

"I 'es playing 'en the trees by the temple that morning, and I saw a stranger Inkling go 'ento the temple and come back out again 'weth the Blue Fire Crystal, and tuck 'et 'en a bag. Then he disappeared!" Her eyes were wide, and she was as solemn as she could be.

Bayless Grand Mari frowned in surprise. "There 'es no stranger Inklings. We 'es the only ones. Only our tribe. 'Es you sure about that?" He asked earnestly.

Chuna Mari nodded adamantly. "I 'es sure. Strange markings. Not Mari tribe. Never saw 'em before."

"We must make a search party to 'descover 'thes Inkling! Jika Mari!" He called out, and Jika rose swiftly to his feet. "Gather the searchers and go find 'thes stranger Inkling!" Jika nodded and waved to some of the other Inklings who were still sitting at the tables around them.

The chief looked back at the rest of the group. "There 'es a balance between the four elements. The balance 'es broken because one of the crystals 'es gone! 'Weth the balance broken, each of the other three elements 'es being uncontrollable. The longer they 'es apart and unbalanced, the stronger and wilder they 'es growing. No boundaries. No limits."

The entire tribe of Inklings gasped in horror. He continued, speaking directly to Alice, Henderson, Chippa, and the cats. "You must return the Blue Fire Crystal before the next full moon, or 'thes world 'es being destroyed by the other three elements!"

Alice swallowed the hard lump in her throat. She was certain that she had just taken on much more than she ever should have. She wasn't at all confident that she had it in her to take on the task that was ahead of her and her family.

As she looked about, she caught little Chuna Mari gazing up at her with hope and idealism in her small face, and she knew that she had to try, whether or not she failed. There was no option other than to make a go of it, and do her utmost to succeed.

"When is the next full moon?" Alice asked, hoping she sounded braver than she felt.

"'Et's 'en seven days." Chippa groaned worriedly.

"Well then, we'd better hurry." Alice replied quietly to Chippa, and then she turned her attention to the chief. "Bayless Grand Mari." She called out. The tribe hushed and all eyes shifted from her to him.

"Yes, Messus Pirrful?" He asked seriously.

"How will we know where to begin looking if we don't know where this mystery Inkling thief went?"

She was completely uncertain of just how she was to go about recovering a crystal she had never seen, from a thief no one knew, who had vanished into thin air.

Bayless Grand Mari nodded and stepped carefully down off of his stump, setting Chuna Mari back on the ground. He waddled over to Alice and handed the peach and buttercream colored seashell to her.

She gasped when she took it in her hand and looked at it closely. "This looks just like the one I have at home… the one that George gave me before he left." She murmured. Henderson looked sorry for her as he gazed at it in her hand.

"'Thes 'es your compass. 'Thes 'well guide you. You open 'et and you see the pearl 'en the center…" He waited for her as she opened the shell and saw the pearl. As she watched it, the pearl moved delicately, as though it was floating on air, to the inner edge of the shell, pointing away from the village.

"'Thes pearl 'es always 'en the center of the shell, when all elements 'es balanced. 'Weth one crystal gone, the shell 'well seek out the 'messing crystal 'untel 'et 'es back 'en the temple here." He gave her a nod. "Follow the pearl."

Alice exhaled a deep breath and closed the shell, tucking it into her bag. "I'll take good care of it, and hopefully bring the compass and the crystal back to you."

Bayless Grand Mari bowed to her and called out to the tribe. "Has provisions been made for 'thes group?"

Luto Mari stepped forward with two other Inklings about his size and age. "Yes, we has them here." He showed them two big bags which were still being filled with sweet biscuits and edible flowers among other tasty foods that they'd enjoyed at their feast.

"I'll be glad to carry those." Henderson offered pleasantly as he went to Luto and tied the two bags together. He hung them over his shoulder so that one was in front and one was in back. "Thank you. I'm sure that we'll need these."

Bayless Grand Mari nodded and then turned to wave at Chippa. "You take them now. Go 'en the boat, and do well on this journey. You canno' fail."

Chippa held his paws together tightly. "Yes, Bayless Grand Mari. I 'es doing my best."

Alice picked up her bag and her cane, Henderson shouldered his own bag, and the cats followed them as they walked out of the village with Chippa, down the gently sloping hill toward the lake where a fair sized wooden boat was tied to a short pier. The journey had begun.

Chapter Four

The Sea of Tranquility

They made their way down to the pier, and as they reached it, Alice stopped and looked around at the new world she found herself in.

The land rose high as foothills and then mountains to the north of them, sloping down into the lake before them. They were the beginning of a great mountain range that stretched as far eastward as she could see.

The village was behind them, nestled into softly rolling emerald hills backed by thick leafy woods, but off to the south and the east, the land seemed to disappear into a thick mist. There was nothing at all to see but the water, the mist, and the darkening night sky above them, just as dusk faded into twilight, and the heavens shifted from lavender to violet and amethyst shades of purple.

Alice felt something pressing against her coat and her leg. She looked down to see Chippa sniffing at her pocket. He didn't notice that she was watching him; he was too intent on the contents of her pocket.

Chuckling and smiling, she reached her fingers into the deep fold, and he finally lifted his eyes to her as she pulled a wrapped candy from it. She handed it to him, and he eagerly unwrapped the little sweet piece and popped it into his mouth.

The Inkling's face contorted and a second later he turned his head and spat the candy out just under a nearby bush. Chippa reached his paws up and tried to get them into her coat pocket, searching fervently.

"You don't like peppermint?" She asked, amused.

"Terrible! Something else, something else!" He insisted, sniffing curiously at the side of Alice's coat.

She reached in and pulled out another candy and handed it to him.

Chippa eyed it suspiciously and sniffed only once. As he did, his eyelids sank nearly all the way, and his body slumped in relaxation as he stuffed the sweet into his mouth and began to chirp blissfully. It reminded Alice of the way the cats purred when they were completely happy.

"You like ginger?" Alice laughed softly again.

"Thpicy." He answered thickly through the piece of candy in his mouth.

"I'm glad you like it. Now, we are getting on this boat as I understand it, yes?" She looked at the vessel before them. It was bigger than she expected, and even at a glance she could see that they would all fit.

Her question went unanswered. She looked back down at Chippa, who was nearly in a trance, he was so taken with the ginger he was chewing.

"Chippa..." She spoke sternly.

His eyes opened wide and he raised his gaze to her without moving his head. "Yeth..." He answered meekly, still savoring the candy. He sighed happily and went to the boat, waving them all into it.

The boat was made of the same wood that grew in the forest beside the village. It was old and smooth, and gently worn. It was an open air design, with nothing in it save for wooden benches that served as seats, and a mast in the middle that stood at attention and held two triangle shaped canvas sails. The mast was taller than Henderson.

While the back of the boat seemed made of older wood in soft brown colors, the prow of the boat looked as if the wood was still alive. It was a vibrant and healthy green, reaching upward to a point where a natural sort of bowsprit had curled around like a vine growing into a spiral. Hanging at the inner curve of the spiral was a small lantern box. Inside it was a sleeping worm, wrapped around a little twig.

Oscar went right into the boat and Jynx, though she hesitated a moment giving it a nasty look, jumped in behind him. Montgomery peered at it through his new monocle and sniffed at it once, but then walked along the plank carefully, keeping his paws steady beneath him.

Bailey plopped his fat rump on the dock, moaning and crying. Sophie sat beside Bailey and turned her back on the boat, wrapping her tail around herself and pointing her little pink nose up in the air. Tao studied it thoughtfully, and entered it a step at a time.

Alice sighed and rolled her eyes. "Come on you two, into the boat." She insisted, eyeing Bailey and Sophie. Sophie refused to look at her, and Bailey stared holes in her, crying and meowing.

Henderson reached down and scooped Bailey up into his arms, taking him onboard. He found a seat and settled the cat on the bench as the calico wailed pitifully and loudly. Henderson ignored Bailey and put their bags down, arranging them for the voyage.

Alice picked Sophie up as the cat grumbled low and deep, and she got into the boat as well. Henderson helped her in, and then took Sophie from her.

They were finally mostly seated. Oscar walked the inside perimeter of the boat, looking out over the short edge of it at the water below them, and Jynx followed right behind him.

Chippa went to the front of the boat and put his paws on the prow. Just above his head was the lantern hanging on the bowsprit. He reached up and touched one paw to the lantern, and the little worm inside it began to stir slightly, and glow an aquamarine color.

Everyone in the boat except Chippa, stared at the brightly glowing worm. It lit up the gathering darkness around them. Chippa placed his hands back on the bow and concentrated, and slowly the boat began to move through the water.

After fixing her hat on her head, Alice leaned her umbrella upright against the bench she sat upon, and placed her bag on her lap. She looked back at the land behind them that grew smaller in the distance as they left it.

Mari Village was a shining jewel in the night, twinkling just as the stars above them had begun to do. She wondered if she would be able to accomplish what she needed to do, and she hoped with everything in her that she could. Though there was some uncertainty in the pit of her, it was overtaken with curiosity, excitement, fascination, and hope, and beyond all of that, she discovered that there was much more courage in her than she would have guessed.

The sound of the water washing past them in small, undulating waves, made a hushing noise, and they gazed at the vast lake they were in. The land behind them was nearly gone; not much more than a sliver on the horizon, and before them loomed a great, thick wall of rolling fog. It seemed to be unmoving in any direction, but it wasn't still; it turned and swirled into itself over and over again.

"I'm surprised that you have a boat this big, it seems that everything in your village is made for... Inkling sized creatures." Alice told Chippa thoughtfully.

"Boat 'es for the whole tribe." Chippa answered. "We all fits."

She gave him an understanding smile.

After a short while, the cats began to relax slightly as they became accustomed to being on the boat and sailing. Marlowe was right at Alice's side.

"Chippa, how did you manipulate the trees in the park when you brought us here?" Alice asked, her mind finally settled to a point where she could pour out all of the questions she had saved up.

"Inklings 'es guardians of Element Crystals. When we 'es grown, we 'es able to use the elements a 'bet. We can shape them... and use them, some. We protect them, keep them balanced."

He let go of the bow then and came to one of the benches near Alice. "I 'es using water to guide the boat out where we 'es going, but 'et's going on 'et's own now. I can't do much 'weth elements. I 'es 'stell learning and growing, but almost there. Almost soon. I can help 'weth some small things; like now, but the boat does most of 'et."

Alice frowned slightly. "But where are we going? Doesn't someone need to sail the boat?" She was somewhat concerned about leaving it all to chance.

Chippa shook his head, and the feathery antennae over his eyes fluttered as he did so. "No, we 'es going to the Light House, and the boat knows the way. I told 'et where we 'es going."

Alice raised her eyes to the sail. It was only a simple canvas, tied to the mast, with a little trailing flag at the top. There were no oars, and from what she could see, there was no rudder. Only the mast, the sails, and the bright glowworm in the lantern at the front.

"The boat knows the way." She repeated quietly, looking out as far as she could around them. She turned her attention back to Chippa. "You made the way for us to come from London to Mari Village. I was thinking that if we knew where we were going, we could just do that here as well. Are you able to move throughout Corevé the same way that you brought us here to your world? Can you go different places here through portals in trees?"

He fidgeted with the little fingers on his paws as he looked down, and then slowly lifted his eyes to meet hers. "There 'es a way, but I 'esn't knowing 'et. I esn't supposed to be going to London, but I watches Oppa Mari often, and I 'es hiding and watching and learning what she 'es doing when she 'es using elements. I learned how to go to London, but 'et's not the same as going 'en Corevé, and I esn't learning that yet." He sighed and rested his paws on the soft thick fur over his legs and knees. "You 'es right. I 'es sneaking learning."

"She didn't know that you were hiding and watching her?" Alice asked disbelievingly. Oppa Mari gave Alice the impression that not much escaped her.

Chippa gasped; properly horrified. "I hope not! I 'es 'en big trouble 'ef they knows I 'es sneaking! Already 'en enough trouble." A small sigh escaped him wistfully.

"How did you know I was your Chosen One?" Alice's curiosity was boundless.

"'Et's something I see. On the day the Blue Fire Crystal 'es stolen, I used the elements to find you. I search everywhere 'en a... 'en a..." He tried to think of the word, "...like a 'wendow from Corevé to your world. All Inklings 'esn't doing 'thes, but I 'es. Oppa Mari 'es only Inkling who sees. I doesn't tell anyone I can see; not sure I should be doing 'et. 'Et's like a waking dream. I see the crystal stolen, but not the thief. I see you 'es searching for 'et. I know you 'es the right warrior to find 'et. I sneaking away to find you, and I find you. I 'es bringing you back."

She gave him a thoughtful smile. "I think that was very brave of you, Chippa. You took a big risk finding me and bringing me here. You must be certain I'm the right one for this challenge."

"You 'es the right one." He nodded adamantly. Chippa sounded as though he couldn't be surer of himself.

Alice was going to ask him more questions, but she heard Bailey whine, and she looked up to see what was worrying him. They were nearing the wall of fog, and though Bailey was focused on that, the other cats seemed to be drawn to whatever was going on in the water around them. Oscar was half out of the boat, getting a better look than anyone else.

"You'd better be careful, Oscar! I don't want you falling in." Alice admonished him. He didn't seem to hear her; he was too fascinated with whatever was in the water.

Curiosity finally got the better of her, and she went to the side of the boat and had a look over the edge of it.

"What have you found, hmm Oscar?" She asked, rubbing her fingers over his fuzzy orange head, and she caught her breath as she took in the sight below the boat.

Swimming around as far as they could see downward, were fish and other creatures of strange shapes and varying sizes. All of them glowed brightly, just as the worm was in the lantern on the bow.

Alice stared at the different colors she saw shimmering in the dark water. There were greens and yellows, pinks and reds, silver and white and blue, and most of all there was turquoise. It was a painter's palette, come to life beneath them, shining and shimmering silently before their eyes.

Alice gazed with childlike wonder at everything glowing magically beneath them, hardly able to believe what she was seeing. "Is that bioluminescence?"

Chippa shook his head and frowned at her. "No, 'es fishes."

Alice only chuckled at him. "Speaking of things that glow, what kind of worm is that up in the lantern? Will he run out of glow eventually?"

Chippa laughed, holding his paws to his belly and closing his eyes as he rolled back and forth on his bottom. When he could finally catch his breath, he sighed. "The glowworm 'es called Matataka. All glowworms 'es Matataka. They glow when they wants to, 'es long 'es they wants to." He giggled to himself a little more. "They doesn't run out of glow." He kept giggling, though he only glanced up at Alice once more before looking away as his laughter subsided with a happy sigh.

Alice turned back to see Henderson and the cats. Henderson was sitting stiffly, his mouth in a narrow line, his bag perched on his lap, with his bowler hat pulled down snugly.

Sophie sat with her back to all of them in protest; her tail wrapped around her tightly as she stayed put on the last bench. Oscar hung over the railing, fascinated with everything beneath them. Jynx was on one side of Oscar, and Bailey was off to his other side.

Tao sat as still as a statue, contemplating the stars in the night sky, meditating with her eyes open and searching the heavens for every answer.

Montgomery snoozed beside Sophie, as if he might as well have been home in his cushioned basket beside the fireplace. Marlowe remained at Alice's side, watching everything.

They passed into the wall of fog before them, and it surrounded the boat, embracing it in silent billows. Everything grew quiet, and it was a long while before Alice could pinpoint just what it was that had changed in the sounds around them.

She blinked and swiftly faced Chippa. "It's too quiet! I don't hear the water anymore... it's gone! There's no water hitting the boat." She was stunned and leaned toward the starboard side, looking over it cautiously. The fog had become patchy, and there were slight openings in it above them, revealing the night sky, and openings in it below them as well.

Oscar stretched further over the edge and she glanced at him. "Don't lean over too far, Oscar. I'm

curious as well, but we must be careful, mustn't we."
He meowed up at her in reply.

She peered over the side of the boat, drawing in a sharp breath, amazed at the beauty that she saw. "The sky!" She marveled, "The sky is reflected in the water so perfectly! There's not even a ripple! Look at that, why it's almost a mirror!"

Smiling, she looked from the reflection of the stars on the water beneath them to the sky above, expecting to see the same configuration.

Instead, there was a thick blanket of fog that had swept over them. She frowned and lowered her eyes from the fog overhead down into the water again, and saw that the stars shining there were crystal clear; there was no fog on the water.

"Now just a moment... how can the stars be reflected in the water if there's fog above us?" She frowned, bewildered.

"'Es not water. No 'flecting. 'Es the Sea of Tranquility." Chippa answered nonchalantly.

Alice was speechless for a moment. "A sea? What do you mean there's no water?" She tugged one of her gloves off. "How can there be a sea if there's no water? How can we be sailing if there's no water?"

Questions poured from her mouth like a waterfall. She stretched her hand downward over the side of the boat, expecting to feel wetness, but there was only cool air. Tiny, wispy ribbons of fog curled around her fingers, and then disappeared, as she trailed her hand through the air that should have been water.

Beneath the boat there was a vast blackness, bigger than anything they could imagine, and in it were countless spots of glowing light; stars twinkling, spiral galaxies, and all manner of heavenly bodies.

"It's the Universe…" Alice whispered, staring at it. "It's the whole Universe…"

"'Es the Sea of Tranquility." Chippa stated again matter-of-factly.

"It's stunning." She said quietly. "I thought we were on a lake."

Chippa pointed his paw back to where they had come from. "Was a lake. 'Thes 'es the Sea, that 'es the lake."

Alice furrowed her brow and turned to look behind their boat. There in the far off distance, she could see waves of water from the lake they had been on; the lake before the wall of fog had come upon them. The water was visible beneath the fog, and it swirled up to an invisible edge where the Universe began, seemingly washing up on a shoreline, with small waves rolling in and splashing gently against the unseen barrier of the Universe, the same way that the sea tumbles onto a sandy beach.

"How in the world is that possible?" She murmured, filled with wonder. "So there's an earthen shoreline by the village, and a universal shoreline out here? That's the strangest thing I've ever seen. Will we fall through the sky?" She worried breathlessly.

Chippa blinked in surprise. "No. We 'es sailing on the air. First water, now air. All sailing. No falling."

Alice was mesmerized with wonder. Looking overboard again, she gasped loudly. "There are creatures moving around beneath us! Look at that! What are they made of?"

Creatures large and small, stranger than she had ever seen, moved around in the dark, starry space below them, as though they were swimming. They shimmered in the darkness; their variant bodies seemingly made of moving light in emerald greens, dark purples, and shades of blue and yellow.

"They… they're like the polar auroras when they're lit up. Just look at that! Each one of them! Why, see that fish just there… it's all made of stars! It's a star-fish!" She laughed at her ironic joke and gave her head a shake. Most of the cats were getting a good look by then, save for Sophie, who was still punishing everyone for making her go along. Her back was turned to the group.

Montgomery sat beside Sophie at the very end of their bench, with his tail draped gracefully over the side of the boat. He gazed down into the water, and just then a massive illuminated beast, bigger than a whale, glided slowly along beneath them, dwarfing the boat by size. Montgomery's eyes grew wide and he carefully pulled his tail back in, and moved closer to Sophie.

Oscar was fascinated with the creature, and leaned over the edge of the boat to paw at it; riveted by the long tendrils along its back that seemed to float and dance behind it. He slipped suddenly, and with a loud cry, he tumbled over the edge, but he didn't fall. His bright orange fur stuck straight out all over his body, and his tail looked like a bottle brush.

"OSCAR!" Alice shouted, reaching for him, but she didn't have to try to rescue him. Bailey had grabbed Oscar's tail in his teeth just as he'd gone over, and was pulling him back into the boat before Henderson or Alice could even get to them.

Oscar was terrified, and he looked as though he had just come out of a hurricane. His eyes were wide, and his fur was on end all over his body.

Jynx growled loudly at him and he glanced up at her once, and then went and sat on a bench; his head and tail hanging down in disappointment.

Alice clicked her tongue at him. "I told you not to go too far off the edge. Now stay there on that seat until we're out of the boat. I won't have anything happening to you while we're in this world!"

The fog above them thickened, and soon enough a gentle rain fell. No one seemed to mind it much except Sophie, who began to wail and cry, moving over to Alice to sit at her side and moan pitifully.

"Oh dear, my princess is getting wet. We can't have that now, can we?" Alice consoled the cat, pushing her umbrella open and holding it over them all.

Jynx narrowed her eyes at Sophie, but she went under the umbrella as well. Henderson opened his own umbrella and sat beneath it, glancing about unhappily, though he remained silent about the situation.

Chippa fanned his tail out and sat beneath it, and all of them stayed dry as the boat moved on through the night and the rain.

A while later, the sky began to grow lighter and the clouds cleared away, leaving only a thin veil of fog around the boat where water would normally have been.

As darkness faded, they could see the Light House up ahead of them. All of the bright colors in the sky seemed to be coming from it, almost as if it was where sunrises came from.

They sailed through the air to a worn and shabby looking wooden dock, and as they neared the dock and the Light House, Alice, Henderson, and the cats could see that there was still nothing but air beneath the boat, and that they had begun to sail over a mass of land far beneath them.

The land rose upward, forming a huge mountain covered in trees, bushes, and foliage, and at the top of the very highest peak, seeming almost to teeter on the edge of it, was the Light House and a boat dock. They had sailed through the air to the top of a mountain.

As the boat pulled up to the dock, Alice saw a small old man standing there; bent, withered, and crooked looking, as though he had been pieced together with limbs of mismatched lengths. He waved his hand slowly at them as the boat came sidelong to the rickety dock.

He wore an old cotton shirt that had perhaps once been white, and a dark brown leather vest that had softened and been worn smooth over time, though it was ripped and patched in many places. It hung on him like second skin. The trousers hanging on him were made of the same material, and they reached down to his old brown shoes. His vest was filled with pockets, and every one of them bulged with some odd thing or other.

Under thick, white, bushy eyebrows, his bright blue eyes were scrunched and narrow, as though he had squinted for so long that his eyes just stayed that way.

His nose was big, his ears round and long, sticking out from his head like car doors left open on either side of a vehicle.

There were tangled, long, wild, white tufts of hair poking out over his ears. They wrapped around the back, avoiding the top of his head, leaving it gleaming and bald, except for one tall patch of white hair that sprouted upward, like a dollop of whipped cream perched upon a sundae.

The hobbled-together man reached for the boat as it came in, guiding it to a stop and tying it up with an old worn rope. He laid a plank from the dock to the boat and when it was set in place, he held his hand out to help Alice over it.

She realized, glancing down as she took his hand and walked over the plank, that there was nothing but air below her, and if she was to slip and fall, instead of falling into water as she stepped off of the boat, she would fall into air, and she would continue falling a long, long way down the steep side of the mountain until she finally hit the earth below it. She held his hand more snugly as she made her way, until she was safely across.

He let her go and stretched his hand out to Henderson, who took it, looking pale as a ghost as he painstakingly tip-toed over the plank to the dock. The cats just hurried straight across it. Chippa was the last to leave the boat, stepping carefully along the plank until he was safe on the pier side.

"I'm Caraway." The old man announced gruffly, rubbing his palms on the front of his vest. Alice could see from the marks there that it was something he did often.

"Hello, Caraway. I'm Mrs. Perivale, and this is Henderson, my butler, and these are my cats; Sophie, Jynx, Tao, Montgomery, Bailey, Marlowe, and that small fuzzy one is Oscar. This little Inkling is Chippa." She smiled, beaming at her large company.

"Yes. I've been 'specting you. Come along, then." He replied with a gravelly voice. He turned and trudged toward the Light House, and they followed him.

CHAPTER FIVE

THE LIGHT HOUSE

"What do you mean, you were expecting us? How could you have been expecting us?" Alice shot a suspicious gaze toward the old man's back.

He chuckled. "I was 'specting you cuz I knew you was comin'. Seems like common sense to me."

She pressed her lips into a tight line, dissatisfied with his answer, but knowing somehow that it was the only answer that she was going to get. "Where are we?"

The Light House was a small, two story ramshackle place that looked as though it had known many more years than the man leading them to it. A sagging A-frame roof topped it like a hat that was two sizes too big, with cracked wooden shingles that curled up at the edges all over it, as though it was a bird whose feathers were severely ruffled. There were dingy windows dotted about the face of the house; some square, some round, some bigger, some smaller, and soft golden light glowed outward through the panes of the windows, at least where it could, visible even in the bright morning light outside. An old wooden door leading inward was propped partway open, with a long and narrow tarnished brass handle barely hanging onto it.

"Yer at the Light House. I'm the Light Keeper." The old man answered as he shoved the door open further and stepped over piles and time worn boxes of junk. "Mine' yer step." He called back over his shoulder.

The Light House was filled with endless random things; boxes of curiosities, shelves stuffed full, tables towering with stacks of odds and ends, cabinets spilling out with various and sundry oddities, and piles of anything that anyone could imagine; mostly in parts. Almost nothing that could be seen was whole.

The interior of the house looked a good deal bigger than it should have been, judging from the outside, and they found themselves in one large room that was sectioned partly by a wooden counter.

A rickety flight of stairs made of flattened driftwood wound in a lazy, uneven spiral up to another floor above them. Thick, dark wooden beams laid at intervals across the ceiling.

Sophie grumbled, delicately lifting each paw, and then tentatively placing them in the least dirty spots on the floor as she made her way through it all, step by regretful step.

"Don't you mean lighthouse keeper?" Alice asked with a wary eye as she looked around the place, and frowned darkly.

Caraway glanced back over his shoulder at Alice. "Nah. Light Keeper. I keep the light. I don't keep the house."

"That's quite obvious." Alice mumbled.

Henderson was aghast, and she wondered if he was going to faint, but he stood stiff and tall, and took it all in stride.

The old man turned to them as they stood around the room, and he spoke to Alice. "Who are yeh, and where are yeh bound?"

Alice lifted her chin and spoke confidently. "We're a group of friends who are looking for something that was lost."

He peered out from under his bushy eyebrows at her; his blue eyes sharp and keen, and she saw the corner of his mouth twitch upward in a hidden smile. "Don'tcha mean something that was stolen?"

"Touché, Mr. Caraway. Yes, it was indeed stolen." She met his knowing gaze with her own.

Caraway chuckled and turned, going to a corner in the room that was formed by a counter set off of a wall. He pulled out a large bowl as big as he could hug, and he set the bowl on top of a short pile of things.

Next he began rummaging around in cupboards and drawers, pulling out small boxes and bags. He took crusty old jars off of shelves, and opened each one, sniffing at them and then holding them up and widening one bright blue eye as much as he could, examining the contents of them.

He sprinkled a little of this into the bowl from one jar, and a bit of that. He added pinches from that box and a handful from this box, and he kept at it, adding in a dash of one thing and a carefully measured spoonful of another. He concentrated so hard on what he was doing that Alice began to wonder if he had forgotten they were there.

She cleared her throat after a long while, and he waved one free hand in the air at her without taking his eyes off of what he was doing. "Now don't rush me, missy, these things take time. You just be patient. I've nearly got it."

Alice's mouth fell open and she heard Henderson gasp. She couldn't remember the last time anyone had called her missy, but she could see that he was quite a bit older than her, and she realized that perhaps to him, she was much younger than she felt.

The cats lifted their noses, whiskers quivering as they sniffed interestedly at whatever it was that he was concocting.

Oscar poked about in the junk nearest to him, and Jynx watched him out of the corner of her eye. Somewhere in the far reaches of an unseen dusty corner, a hidden clock ticked very slowly; much slower than regular seconds are timed, and from two other hidden places, Alice could hear two more clocks ticking much swifter than they ought to have been. All of them were out of sync with one another.

"That's it! I've got it!" Caraway cackled gleefully at long last.

Taking a great wooden spoon, he stirred the dried contents of the bowl. Then he grasped a small, brown, leather sachet with a long drawstring on it. With his other hand, he picked up a little silver spoon, and carefully measuring the concoction out just so, he dropped three spoonfuls of his dried herb mixture into the sachet, and pulled the drawstring to close it.

The old man set it down carefully, and moved to make another, and then another, until there were seven done. Alice cleared her throat again. He frowned sharply at her. "Now that's enough of that young lady, you can't rush this kind of thing. Never. You just wait there until old Caraway is done. I'll be gettin' to yeh soon enough."

Soon enough he did get to them, coming back around the corner with the pouches in his old, weathered hands. He knelt down before each cat, and tied one small leather pouch around each of their necks; but not too tightly. When all seven cats had a pouch, he spoke to them seriously.

"Now, don't dig into it right away. You wait on that. You'll need it later." He advised sternly. Oscar batted at his until he noticed Caraway giving him a reprimanding glare, and he dropped his paw.

"I don't s'pose you want some tea..." Caraway asked, standing again. He looked as though he was making himself bring it up, and hoping desperately that they would turn him down.

"That's very kind of you, but I'm afraid we're in a bit of a hurry just now, so we're sorry to have to say no thank you," Henderson replied politely, "but it was quite generous of you to offer."

Alice smiled at him gratefully. He was as reliable as the day was long. Caraway sighed with obvious relief, and moved toward the door, waving for them to follow him outside.

The top of the mountain was a blend of rocks and flowers tucked into patches of grass, sprinkled with trees growing here and there. The sun was shining brightly by then, and Caraway pointed to a path that led downward away from the Light House.

"Yonder is the path yeh'll need to take to get down the mountain. It's jungly down there, and it's hot. Yeh'll be losing that coat, I 'ave no doubt." He stated with a firm nod toward Alice. "Well, good luck to yeh, and keep a watchful eye. It's not safe out there."

Alice frowned slightly and peered closely at Caraway. "Who are you?" Her voice was filled with the interest and fascination that she could no longer manage to keep at bay.

He gazed back at her and chuckled. "I'm a Mystic o' sorts. I keep the light, and I knows what the light knows. We's one, the light and I. We's all one."

She smiled then and nodded, giving him a wave. It didn't answer all of her questions, but it did answer some of them. She felt like a little girl with a head full of wonder that wouldn't stop bubbling up.

He gave them a half-hearted wave in return, and went back into the Light House, closing the door sharply behind him.

"Well… that was peculiar, wasn't it? I suppose it's time to go, yes?" Alice pulled the seashell compass from her bag and checked where the pearl was sitting, hovering at the inner edge of the shell. "I guess we go down the path." She said, closing it and tucking it back into her bag.

Chippa nodded and trekked out in front of them, taking the lead. Alice straightened her hat and coat, and followed him down the path that wound away from the top of the mountain, into the jungle below. The cats trailed along behind her and Henderson took up the rear.

The company hadn't gone far when the bushes around them began to grow thicker and greener. The trees were much taller than they'd been at the mountaintop. They stretched up to the sky and shaded the ground around them with a canopy of leaves in a myriad of shapes, from tiny to massive.

Vines wrapped around the tree trunks and hung in several directions off of the branches. Flowers grew in many sizes and colors, generously strewn over everything.

Exotic sounds filled the air, from birdsong to things that they could only assume were animals, and all of them remained unseen. The further down the mountain they went, the more intense the heat and humidity grew. It wasn't long before Alice had to stop and pull her coat off, and take her hat from her head.

Henderson carried her coat over his arm, and she fastened her hat with a pin to the side of her black bag. Turning to the butler, she heaved a great sigh and gave him a serious look.

"How are you doing, Henderson? Will you be taking your own coat off?" He was still in long black coat tails and black trousers.

A stunned look came over his face. "Oh no, Madam, I'm all right." He reached for his crisp white linen handkerchief and dabbed at his forehead. "Let's carry on then, shall we?" He gave her an encouraging smile. She nodded and began to make her way downhill again.

It felt as though hours had passed. They were about halfway down the side of the mountain, trekking through thick, lush jungle, when out of nowhere an ear piercing squall that was half wild scream, half growl, sent shivers through all of them.

It had been silent between the travelers, and the sudden caterwaul made them nearly jump out of their skin. Everyone turned sharply with huge eyes as they took in the sight before them.

Sitting on his giant rump was a very fat cat, about the size of a large horse. His fur was pink with shimmery silver-tipped ends. He stared at them all, just as surprised to see them as they were to see him.

Alice cried out and held her hand to her mouth, horrified.

Henderson's gasped, "Dear God! What in heaven's name?"

Every one of the cats went into a full arch, hissing and growling at the giant pink feline sitting on his bottom before them.

"What? It's me! It's me!" The great pink cat spoke aloud, its blue eyes searching all of them.

In an instant there was silence among the group again, as they stared at him. The rosy-blush beast blinked in confusion, as if they should all know it as well as they knew themselves. It shook its head, nearly smiling.

"Why, look at that! I'm speaking, I am!" It said brightly. It sounded as excited as a child on their birthday. None of the others dared to even breathe. "You don't know me!" It moaned with sad realization, gazing at the others earnestly.

"It's me! I'm Bailey!" He assured them. "Here, sniff me!" He held his paw out, and the other cats turned up a nose to it; all except Oscar, who tentatively stepped forward and gave a few sniffs.

Oscar rushed to Bailey; big-pink-giant-as-a-horse-no-longer-a-calico-cat Bailey, and rubbed his cheek against Bailey's huge leg. Jynx came up right behind Oscar, and after a few moments she sat down and began to clean her fur, taking special care to reach behind her ears.

Alice gaped at him in wonder. "How on earth can you be talking? What *happened* to you?" She was completely flabbergasted. Henderson could only stare.

"I was so hungry... I just couldn't wait! I ate the catnip that Caraway gave us." There were still a few bits of it stuck on his whiskers near his mouth. "Goodness, look at me... I guess it had more calories than I thought." He turned his head this way and that, taking in his massive mound of a pink body, and his eyes widened in shock. "I'm all one color! Do you see that? I'm all one color!" He laughed jovially, but then stopped short and spoke with serious concern. "Be honest... does this pink make me look fat?"

Marlowe rolled his eyes and turned to walk down the mountain, but just as he did so, a strange rushing noise filled the air; a powerful repetitive thumping that sounded almost like the heartbeat of a hurricane about to sweep them up right off the ground.

They looked around wildly, and Chippa shrieked in terror, "Quiri! 'Et's Quiri birds!" He wrapped himself in his tail and vanished. "Run! Hide! Very dangerous!"

From out of the sky and light green canopy above them, came enormous birds with a wingspan of more than ten feet; their razor sharp claws stretched out from their broad, powerful legs, their hook-like beaks wide open as they screamed a deafening, raucous cry. Pure cruelty gleamed off of their pitch black eyes.

Their brilliant and brightly colored feathers in vibrant hues of red, blue, yellow, green, and purple, pounded against the air; war drums in their attack.

The Quiri birds dove downward, directly toward them. Bailey threw the hulk of his pink back up high in the air and growled menacingly. The force of it was greater than the roar of a lion. The sound waves of his growls reverberating off of the trees around the group moved through them, shaking even their hearts.

Marlowe shrank back for a moment, his fur on end, his ears laid back flat, his wide eyes set on Bailey. Bailey, startled by his own tremendous outcry, scrambled suddenly backward into a tree, scattering branches and causing leaves to rain out over the group.

Marlowe immediately got into his bag of Caraway's catnip, and ate it in one lump swallow, nearly choking it down. An instant later, he had blown up to about the same size that Bailey had become, though his fur changed to a dark blue color with silvery spots that made him look like the world's most exotic leopard.

He staggered a moment and looked briefly at himself in amazement, but in the next second he lifted his chin and glared at the gigantic birds diving straight for them. He growled as loud as he could, making the jungle around them tremble.

Alice stared in disbelief at her beloved kitties as one by one, they quickly downed their catnip; all of them shifting into massive horse-sized cats, all of them with wild and colorful fur coats.

Oscar, who had grown to the size of a large pony, turned bright red and orange; striped like a tiger. Sophie's coat became undulating swirls of silver and lavender, Tao's fur shifted into a mix of sky blue and white that seemed to change back and forth as she moved. Montgomery's coat transformed into a glittering sea blue and green patchwork of circles, and Jynx remained black, though her fur took on a bright cobalt blue tint in the light.

Every one of them roared, and Alice shook her head, gathering her wits about her as she reached for her umbrella cane. She held fast to the bird beak handle and jousted it into the air above her just as the Quiri birds reached them.

"Right then!" She cried out to them, "You'll do nothing here! Clear off! Be gone with you!" She shouted, though her voice was drowned out in the snarls of the cats. The mighty feline beasts slashed their claws through the air, leaping at the Quiri that attacked them relentlessly.

Alice bashed and jabbed at the birds left and right with her umbrella cane in one hand, while flinging her black purse wildly in every direction with the other.

Henderson ran in circles, swinging his shoulder bag all about him as he held tightly to his hat, pinning it to his head. Every one of the cats rallied against the onslaught. Chippa was nowhere to be seen.

The birds came at them like hailstones; more than a dozen of them swooping in hard and fast, and though they were beaten back as much as they could be, it was a long and fierce fight before the birds began to fly off, injured or reluctant to become so.

Just as the last of the Quiri birds was leaving, one of the largest of them darted in with another bird right at its side, and the bigger one grabbed Henderson by the shoulders, closing its claws around his arms and lifting him rapidly up off of the ground.

Henderson cried out in horror as he was flown up out of the canopy. The other Quiri bird came straight at Alice, but Tao leapt up in front of her to block the attack. The bird wrapped his talons around Tao, and snatched her right out of the air, flying heavenward. Tao wailed loudly, growling and flailing, but to no avail.

Bailey leapt up just then and closed his teeth in a death grip around Tao's tail, and Tao erupted in the loudest shriek that any of them had heard. The sheer weight of Bailey's body pulled the bird and Tao back to the ground. All of the other cats went straight for the bird as soon as it was in range.

There wasn't anything left of the downed Quiri bird by the time the cats emerged from the bushes where they had pulled it back. Tao pushed herself up off the dirt floor of the jungle and shook her head to clear it, looking gratefully at Bailey, who was worrying over her.

"Thank you." Tao spoke for the first time in a calm and serene voice. "I've never been so thankful that Bailey eats so much."

The other cats chuckled slightly for a moment, but then they looked about and cried out piteously as they discovered that Henderson was gone. Alice held her hand to her mouth as tears began to fill her eyes and roll slowly down her cheeks.

"Henderson is gone! Whatever will we do now? We're done for!" She plopped down on a wide fallen log and pulled her handkerchief from her partially tattered bag, holding the delicate cloth to her face as she wept.

The cats encircled her, looking on her with sorrow. Chippa reappeared and waddled up to her, standing beside her knee. He patted her leg gently and sniffed a few times.

"Why are we even out here?" She began to weep, dabbing at her eyes. "Why are we even bothering? Here we are muddling through this bizarre adventure with no real experience at all between the lot of us, trying to find our way through this strange world with our strange guide…" At that, Chippa huffed and frowned.

"Well we are!" She added, glancing down at him and then looking up at the cats beside her. "Everything has gone asunder! What on earth are we going to do now? I can't do anything like this. George did all of the brave things. George was the hero; the warrior. This is far and away the most rash, reckless, irresponsible thing I've ever-" She cut herself off.

"I never should have done this. I never should have even considered it! I don't know what I could have been thinking. Obviously I wasn't thinking at all when I said I'd do it." She lowered her chin and closed her eyes.

Marlowe leaned his dark blue and silver spotted head toward her, and nudged her gently. "Alice, you chose this adventure because you were needed. I know that you've felt very unneeded as of late. You talked to me about it several times. The last time you talked to me about it, we were in the park… just yesterday." His voice was deep and kind, filled with wisdom and patience.

She stared up at him. "I can't believe you're able to speak to me, and I can't believe that you were listening. I never realized that any of you actually heard me and listened to me." Alice shook her head in astonishment.

"Of course I was listening. I always listen to you. We all do. This trip wasn't just your choice either; every one of us wanted to come along with you. We love you. You're our family. We are all in this together." He nudged her with his nose again.

Bailey spoke gently to her. "We are going to work together, and we'll find Henderson and save him; we're a family, all of us, and we're not going to lose him."

Tao purred and the rumble of it reverberated off the trees around them and the ground beneath them. "We believe in you. We believed that you could do what you said you would do; find the stolen Blue Fire Crystal, and we still believe that, perhaps even more than we did at the beginning. We followed you because we have faith in you and in all of us together. There is nothing that can break the bond that we share. That bond exists because of you. It is your strength and determination; your compassion and kindness that compel us to commit ourselves to you. We follow you and love you because of who you are. You must remember that our truest bravery and courage; our most self-defining moments come when we are faced with our greatest challenges. It is then that we see who we truly are, and this is your time to discover that. When you do discover that, you will see what all of us already know about you. You can do this."

Oscar sprouted up on his feet and lifted his chin. "I'm the newest member of this family, and I agree with everything that Tao, and Bailey, and Marlowe said. We are all in this together, and together we're going to give it everything we've got. We're going to get Henderson back, and we're going to find that Blue Fire Crystal and save Corevé!"

A smile spread over Alice's face, and she wiped at her eyes one last time before she pushed her handkerchief down into the depths of her black bag.

"I'm so glad that I have you all! I love and cherish every single one of you. I couldn't do this without you, either here or back home in London. Goodness me... it might take a little while for me to get used to you looking the way that you do, and certainly to hear you talking with me, but you're mine no matter what, and I love you."

She pushed herself up off of the log, and looked around at all of them, hanging her umbrella cane on her arm. "You're right. George wasn't the only one who was brave, and he told me so when he was home with us. He always said I was braver than I knew, but I rarely saw it in myself. Now I see that he was right. We are going to go out on this quest, and we will triumph!" She hoisted her small fist in the air. "Right then. Shall we be off? Let's go rescue Henderson!"

Oscar stopped short and whined. "Wait! Henderson is gone! Who will give Alice her pills?"

A worried look came over Marlowe's face. "I don't know. None of us can tell time. I know she takes them around dinner time, which means maybe she could take them when we get hungry."

Bailey perked up interestedly. "I'm hungry!"

"You're always hungry." Sophie scoffed.

Marlowe's voice grew serious and low as realization overtook him. "Oh no... we can't help her."

Alice waved her hand in the air. "I can't take my pills anyway, Henderson has them in his bag, wherever he is, unless he dropped it when that wretched bird took him."

"Then we must go in the direction that the birds went right away, if we can figure out which way that is." Marlowe murmured thoughtfully, looking up at the canopy for any clues.

"I can try to see where they went." Chippa piped up, looking up from the pocket of Alice's coat, which was laying on a log where Henderson had dropped it, along with their sacks of provisions as the attack came on. Chippa's arms were both elbow-deep in the pocket that held her stash of sweets.

He shoved two ginger chews in his mouth, and Alice gasped when she saw that all of the peppermint candies she'd had in her pocket were scattered haphazardly on the ground all around Chippa's feet.

"I 'beh 'might 'beck..." He mumbled through a mouthful. A moment later he was scurrying up the nearest tall tree, and a moment after that, he had disappeared entirely into the branches and leaves above. They saw a wide section of the leafy tree canopy above them part as though the trees had fallen away from each other, though none of them had moved on the ground.

For a moment there was a swath of clear blue sky above them, but then the canopy swooshed shut again, looking as it had all along, and Chippa scurried down the tree, bottom first, until he was nearly at the roots. He tried to look over his shoulder as he came close to the ground; his feet and toes reaching out, searching for earth to stand on. Oscar leaned over, and with his teeth, picked Chippa up carefully by the scruff of the neck, setting him down on the ground.

Chippa growled a little and smoothed his paws over his fur, giving Oscar a dirty look as he turned to face them all.

"Quiri birds went toward Ring of Fire volcanoes. We 'es going to base of mountain to find path to volcanoes. You follow me." He waved his little paw in the air, and hustled down the path that led toward the foot of the mountain.

Marlowe carried the sacks of provisions over the back of his neck, with Alice's coat laid underneath them. They followed their Inkling friend down the mountain through the thick jungle once more for a long while.

Ambling along in their crooked, unorganized line, Montgomery groused about the bugs, and the heat, and the journey. "I'm getting to be much too old for adventure."

Sophie snapped at him. "If our Alice can do it, you certainly can. You might be an old furball, but you've got four legs and a tail, and Alice hasn't, so you're already ahead of the game over her. Stop complaining!"

Jynx's voice was level and calm, though that only served to emphasize her indifference. "She also speaks without magic catnip, so be a cat Sophie, and close your mouth."

Sophie glared at Jynx. "Well, I see your coat didn't change. It's still just as black as your soul!"

Jynx continued to look straight forward, never making the effort to even glance back at Sophie. "You'd better remember that the next time you irritate me."

Sophie couldn't think of a comeback, and instead flipped her tail sharply and looked away, sulking.

Montgomery chuckled. "Why do you fight with her Sophie? You know she's going to win every time."

Sophie stopped in her tracks and narrowed her eyes at the backs of the cats in front of her, walking away from her with their tails pointed up in the air. "Not every time!" She called out to Montgomery. "Not every time!"

Oscar sniffed at everything they passed, and Jynx was right behind, keeping an eye on him as they traveled.

Alice laughed a little. "It's so extraordinary to hear all of you speaking. I have always wondered what you thought and what you talked about, and it looks as though I wasn't too far off the mark!" She gazed back over her shoulder at them; her eyes falling on each one, and slowly her smile faded to a look of panic.

"Oh no… oh dear! Where's Chippa?" She searched around all of the cats' legs and tails. They all began to look for the Inkling then, and Marlowe was the first to spot him.

"I think we've worn him out." He said stifling a laugh as he lifted his nose to point back up the trail a short way. Chippa was curled up, sleeping in a fluffy little ball on a soft bed of grass.

"Oh for heaven's sake." Alice mumbled in annoyance. She made her way back to him and shook him awake. He sat up on his bottom, his legs poked out in front of him, and frowned up at her.

"You waked me!" He grumbled irritably.

"Well I'm sorry to disturb you, but we're on a mission, and we are in a hurry! You were supposed to be leading this group! What on earth are you doing back here sleeping?" Alice gave him a sharp look.

He whined with a thin, sad voice. "Chippa tired! Inklings 'es up 'et night mostly. We wakes up midday, goes to sleep just after dawn. Chippa 'es up very late right now. Chippa tired!"

She sighed and planted her hands on her hips. "You're telling me that Inklings are nocturnal?"

"Yes, partly." He yawned widely and curled back up on the ground, turning his tail to them and going back to sleep.

Oscar leaned close to Alice's shoulder. "He can ride on me. As long as we know what direction we're going in, maybe he can sleep on my back as we go along. Then he won't be so tired and grumpy."

Alice smiled proudly at Oscar, and reached up to scratch him behind his ears. "You're such a good boy, Oscar. Thank you."

The great orange and red striped cat knelt down, and Alice gently scooped up the sleeping Inkling, and placed him tenderly between Oscar's shoulder blades.

"You won't drop him?" She asked with concern, making sure that Chippa was secure.

"I'll be my most careful." Oscar promised, and Marlowe looked at him approvingly as they all started back down the mountain again.

The group trekked along the path, and the further they got, the thicker the plants and foliage grew. The trees stood closer together, and the canopy became low and dense. The heat had them all sweating and panting, wishing that there was some water nearby, but when they got their wish, it wasn't at all what they had hoped for.

The path ended abruptly at an aquamarine colored river of moderate depth, that was meandering through the jungle. They searched each other for a solution, but none of them knew what to do. Alice went to Oscar and gently woke Chippa from his nap. He pushed himself up and blinked in surprise.

"What 'es I doing on 'thes cat?" He worried, wrapping his little paws tightly around Oscar's fur as he stared down at the ground some six feet away.

"You were napping. Oscar was good enough to let you sleep on his back, and he carried you while we walked down the mountain." Alice answered, wishing he'd be a little more gracious. "Now we've come to this river, and there is no more path. We aren't quite sure what to do next."

Chippa let go of Oscar's fur, which the cat was grateful for, and he slowly shimmied down Oscar's leg, alighting on the ground. He went to the water and studied it, pressing his paw to his mouth in a thoughtful way. He gazed down the river, eyeing the direction that it was flowing, and then he turned and gave consideration to everything that surrounded them.

"I 'es having an idea." Chippa nodded with a note of confidence. "We goes 'en the direction of the river, we gets to the birds."

"How are we going to go in the direction of the river? The growth here is much too thick for us to try to get through. There's no path, and we can't hack our way through the jungle." Alice moved to a large rock and sat on it, resting herself as she watched Chippa.

The little Inkling scratched his fingertips over his fuzzy chin. "I can 'fex 'thes." He replied happily as he waddled over to one of the nearby plants. It was filled with massive leaves of evergreen with bright red veins on the tops, but which were completely silver on the underside. They were easily eight feet long and six feet across.

Reaching up, he touched his paw to one of the leaves. It slipped off of the plant and down to the ground right before him. A long, thick stem rose up off of the back of it, where it had been attached to the plant it was growing on. The stem stood rigidly at five feet tall.

Chippa began to walk around the leaf, stroking his paws over the edge of it, bending it upward as he went. Everywhere that he bent the leaf's rim, it stayed solidly in place. By the time he had walked the perimeter of the leaf, the entire edge was turned up to about a foot tall, solidly formed, and he grinned at it proudly as he pointed his paw at it.

"'Es a boat! I 'es making one boat for each of us. We float along river to Quiri birds!" He was as pleased as he could be about his idea, and about successfully molding the massive leaf into a watercraft.

"I'm not getting into another boat." Sophie stated coolly, turning her nose up at it.

Alice peered suspiciously, poking at it with her umbrella cane. "Chippa, it's a leaf. I'm not sure that these leaves will hold us. Don't you think they'll sink?"

He furrowed his fluffy brows and shook his head. "No, 'es a silverback leaf. Silverback leaves doesn't sink. We safe. We float!" He beamed again.

Sophie narrowed her blue eyes at him. "Have you lost your furry little mind?"

Chapter Six

A Wild Ride

Oscar moved forward and sniffed at the silver leaf boats that Chippa was making. "I'll try it!" He said with brave interest. Jynx growled softly in her depths.

"I don't know about that, Oscar." She gave the leaves a dark look, and sniffed at them as well.

"I'll go!" Bailey piped up. "I'll do anything to save Henderson!" He padded up to one of the boats as it lay on the shoreline, and sat down beside it.

"We're all anxious to save dear Henderson." Alice replied gently.

"Then we get into the boats and we go. It's the only way, right Chippa?" Bailey asked, watching as the little Inkling finished up the last of their leaves. There was one for each of them.

"'Es the only way." Chippa answered, pushing the boat over to the water's edge. "Come on, we go." He shuffled over to where Bailey was sitting near a boat, and told the cat to get in.

Bailey gingerly stepped over the short rim of the leaf and settled himself carefully inside it. "How are we going to get me to the water? You can't push me, I'm too big."

"You 'es too big, but I can push the leaf." Chippa curled his paws around the edge of the leaf and walked it toward the river just as easily as if it was already on the water.

The silver leaf boat slipped into the river, and a moment later, Bailey was drifting lazily away; his eyes wide, and a smile on his face. "Look at me! Look at me go! I'm sailing! Really sailing!"

"I want to go too!" Oscar shouted, pushing one of the silver leaf boats into the water with his nose and springing into it from the shore. He landed on it with such force that it spun quickly in place, and he dug into the bottom of it with all of his claws to hold on tight.

"WHOA!" He shouted as he grew dizzy and nearly fell over. Jynx went racing after him, pushing another of the boats into the water and leaping skillfully into it.

"Oscar!" She called out, trying desperately to get nearer to him.

"Oh my stars and whiskers!" Alice gasped as she watched three of her cats floating down the river on big silver leaf boats without her. "Hold on! I'm coming!" She cried out, hurrying toward one of the leaves and delicately getting herself settled into it.

"All right Chippa, ship me off down the river!" She held fast to the edges of it with a vice-like grip. Chippa pushed her into the water, and Marlowe took up the next leaf, going into the river right after her. He was silent, though his eyes were wide, and his hair was on end.

Montgomery looked at Sophie. "Come on, Soph, let's go." He spoke with a gentle voice.

She turned her head away, snubbing him. He gave her a nudge, but she wouldn't move.

"Suit yourself." Montgomery shrugged. Both he and Tao got into their boats and were pushed into the current.

Sophie was the only one left. She looked back to where the others had been so she could smart off about finding another way, when she saw Chippa standing beside a leaf waiting for her, and everyone else already gone.

"We 'es 'en a hurry. You goes now, or you stays, and I goes now." He frowned at her impatiently.

She gaped and stared down the river, seeing her whole family gone without her. Looking back at the boat, she wailed desperately. "I don't want to ride a leaf boat!" Her downturned mouth formed an angry pout.

Chippa waved a paw at her. "Bye." He said simply, hopping into his boat and pushing away from the water's edge. Sophie realized that she was in fact left alone on the shore, and she called out to the others who were already gone, but none of them could hear her.

There was nothing for it; she was going to have to join them, or be left behind. She pushed the last boat into the water with her nose, and leapt into it as gracefully as she could. The leaf rocked and swayed, spinning around a couple of times slowly, but it finally settled into the current. Minutes later, she was much closer to everyone, though very put out about it all.

The water swirled and moved with a pleasant pace, carrying them past all manner of unimaginable and curious plants and creatures. From slender flowering vines hanging from ancient trees that stretched their limbs and leaves over the river, to big and small bushes and blooms of every color, size, and shape.

Peculiar animals and flying things watched them from the riverbanks, staring at the spectacle of Mrs. Perivale, the cats, and Chippa sailing along.

Oscar was wide-eyed, filled with no end of excitement. He stared down into the brilliant aquamarine depths at the wide array of things swimming beneath them. The massive kitten reached out and patted the water, then shook big droplets of it from his paw.

They sailed beneath one of the flowering vines, and he reached up and batted at it. When he hit it, everyone was showered in a blizzard of tiny flower petals that shimmered and changed color as they spun and fluttered through the air. They were white on the vine, but as they twirled downward around the company, they turned light, glittering shades of blue, pink, green, yellow, orange, purple, red, silver, and gold.

The other cats and Alice watched in amazement as the petals fell softly all about them. Alice held her hand out and smiled as they filled her palm, and covered her body and her boat. When the petals touched the water, they lost their color and became translucent, seeming to vanish.

"It's magic!" Oscar called out excitedly.

Chippa laughed and held his paws to his belly. "'Es nature; nature 'es elements, elements 'es magic."

Bailey grinned. "I don't care what it is, look at this! I'm covered in them! It's fabulous!" He lifted his chin and showed off all the rainbow of petals covering his shiny pink fur.

Sophie smiled at the petals that had landed all over her, and her boat. She admired herself with delight, and purred.

Tao was positioned in her leaf like a sphinx, gazing about as she relaxed. She lifted her chin and sniffed at the petals as they drifted around her.

Montgomery sneezed, and did his best to swish his thick furry tail all over himself and his boat, sweeping it clean. "You're making a mess, kid!"

A naughty look came over Oscar, and he got his boat to turn just enough that he was facing Jynx as they went along. He curled his paw into a cup shape and scooped it through the water, launching the entire pawful at Jynx in a shower of silvery drops.

Jynx gasped and stared at him with her jaw open. "Why you little…" She began, but Oscar rolled onto his back laughing. She narrowed her eyes and shot water right back at him, covering him in it.

Sophie roared with laughter. Jynx looked over her shoulder darkly, and with every ounce of strength she had, she swiped her paw through the water again, sending a solid arc of it back behind her, right over Montgomery, landing squarely on Sophie.

Sophie shrieked a high pitched growl and dug her claws into her boat. "Oh, you're going to get it now!" Sophie swatted at the surface of the river and sent a poorly aimed measure of it meant for Jynx, landing directly on Montgomery, who was still between them.

The old cat howled and twisted around in a flash, glaring at her. A moment later he had splashed Sophie in return, and by then Oscar was back at it, and the whole lot of them were zinging pawful's of cool water at each other.

They were all getting wet and laughing, and having such a good time, that they were nearly at the base of a huge mountain looming up ahead before they noticed it.

"STOP!" Alice cried out, wiping the splashes from her face as she drew in a big breath and pointed to the behemoth before them.

The water did not ribbon around the mountain in front of them, it went *into* it, and Alice's heart began to pound in her chest as she stared at the great black cavern that seemed to swallow the entire river.

"Chippa! Where does this river go?" She called out to him as she reached for the edge of her boat, holding tightly to it.

He looked straight ahead, and his big eyes grew even wider. "'Et goes East." He answered in a low voice.

There was nothing but silence among them as they all locked their gazes swiftly approaching maw; each of them still dripping here and there, all of them feeling the cold grip of fear.

Breathless with uncertainty, they could do nothing as they entered the mouth of the cavern and the light quickly grew dim. It was only a few moments before the river curved, and the brightly lit opening behind them vanished from their sight, leaving them all coursing through the base of the mountain in total blackness.

A few of the cats meowed thinly, crying in dismay. "Jynx?" Oscar's small voice called out, echoing off of the cave walls right back to him. "It's too dark!"

"I'm here!" She answered hollowly. "I can smell you! You're not far in front of me. Don't you worry... I'm... I'm right here." She mumbled softly, "Somewhere..."

"I can see 'es all. We all here." Chippa told them quietly, searching through the blackness with his wide eyes.

A few long, soundless moments of terror passed, and Oscar's voice trembled again. "I… I think I can see something! I'm not sure. It's green, or blue…" He spoke with some uncertainty and a modicum of hope. "Can anyone else see it? Are you there?" He murmured quietly.

"I'm here." Jynx replied reassuringly.

"We're here. Smell the air. You'll find that with our sight reduced, our other senses like hearing and detecting scent are increased. Can you smell us? You know each of our scents. Try to find those, and you'll know we're here." Tao's voice was a calm and steady comfort to all of them.

Oscar sniffed loudly in the dark. "I can smell you all!" He called out with a little more confidence.

"I can see the green too!" Bailey chimed in. "It's a strange sort of light… a glowing light."

"It looks like the bioluminescent sea life we saw in the Sea of Tranquility, but it's definitely different." Alice considered curiously. "I saw it on the walls first… there are long strings of it all around us, on the walls and the ceiling, in fact… my word… we're totally surrounded by it!"

"'Es Matataka worms." Chippa told them, staring in amazement. "I never know there 'es so many!"

Filling the dark cavern on every side and across the full length of the jagged ceiling, were countless Matataka glow worms. They covered the entire interior of the cave tunnel, their light giving it volume and shape in the darkness. Though it wasn't bright, their soft aquamarine glow gave off enough light that the cats and Alice were finally able to see each other.

"I can see you!" Oscar cried out, awash in relief as he sighed, and his body relaxed somewhat. He was curled up in a red and orange striped ball on his leaf; his big eyes taking in everything around him. Even his fuzzy tail was wrapped tightly against his body.

"The fish in the river are glowing!" Montgomery gasped in surprise as he looked down into the black water and saw the illuminated forms slipping in and out of the current.

"There are vines and moss in here that are glowing as well!" Marlowe added quietly, taking in everything that he could see.

The water carried them along swiftly, and they were in awe of the cave and the wild, beautiful glowing world inside of it.

"Almost all of it is bioluminescent..." Alice trailed off, looking from the plant life to the glow worms, and then to the fish and other creatures swimming and living in the water beneath them.

"I'd glow too if I lived in a place this dark." Jynx's voice echoed back to her as she gazed about.

"You always live in a place this dark." Spat Sophie from the last silver leaf boat in their floating train.

"Home sweet home." Jynx replied with level indifference, and Sophie grumbled.

They gazed with wonder at the unique life forms throughout the darkness as the boats drifted through the cave. It was quiet again for a few minutes, but then Alice looked back at the cats and Chippa.

"Is it me, or does it feel as though the water is beginning to move faster?" She asked, reaching to hold on to the edge of her boat with a strong grip again.

"It's not you." Marlowe answered; his eyes darting here and there as he studied the cave and the surface of the water. "We're moving faster."

All of them looked then, and dug in a bit tighter, to secure themselves to their boats.

"Not to worry any of you, but I think it isn't just that we're moving faster. The water level is rising, wouldn't you agree?" Montgomery spoke in a voice, thick with carefully controlled panic.

"The water level is definitely going up." Marlowe replied gravely. "Quickly. Thanks to all these glowing Matataka worms all over the place, I can see where the walls and the ceiling and the stalactites are, and we're losing space in here."

"Uh-oh…" Chippa moaned worriedly, moving from one side of his boat to the other swiftly.

The water level in the cave they were traveling through had risen sharply as they floated along, and the glow worm covered stalactites hanging from the ceiling of the long cavern were coming closer to them as the river moved upward at an alarming rate.

"Chippa…" Alice called out to him. "What's going on?"

His voice was filled with fear when he answered her, his little paws clutching his boat. "'Es not good. 'Es the water crystal. Elements out of balance. Elements growing wilder 'weth passing time. Less control!"

"We don't have much room left! If the water keeps rising like this, we're all going to crash into the stalactites or the ceiling of this cave!" She cautioned sharply.

"Or we'll drown!" Worried Sophie from the back, as her leaf began to twist and spin in the accelerating current. The water level went up another foot in the matter of a few minutes, and all of them cried out.

"We're going to crash! We'll hit the hanging rocks and be dashed to bits!" Montgomery declared, pressing himself as low into his boat as he could. "We're already too close to the top of the cave, and we're running out of air as well as space!"

Marlowe turned to the little Inkling. "Chippa! You have to do something! The water isn't going down!"

The Inkling cried and wailed, shaking his head. "Chippa can't! Chippa doesn't move elements 'thes big yet! 'Es too much for Chippa!"

"Everyone duck down!" Marlowe commanded as they began to fly along the surface of the river, careening into the walls on either side of them and bouncing off of the stalactites that reached down from the roof of the cave. Everyone flattened as much as they could, holding tightly to their silver leaf boats.

"There's a light up ahead!" Tao called out; her voice just barely louder than the sound of the rushing water around them.

"This is no time to be philosophical!" Sophie shouted at Tao.

"No! Look, Tao is right! There's a bright light up there!" Bailey marveled joyously. "It's the other end of the tunnel! We're going to make it out!"

There was a tiny, brilliant pinpoint of light far off in the darkness ahead of them, and it grew larger as they sped toward it.

"We're not going to make it!" Marlowe growled deeply, "Look up! We're already too close and the river is still rising!"

He was right. The ceiling had finally gotten so close to them that it was scraping the stems of their leaf boats; stems that only stood five feet tall, and if any of the cats had been sitting up, they'd have hit their heads at that narrow height.

"Chippa!" Alice called out to him as he cowered in his boat. "You can do it! I know you haven't done anything like this before, but I believe in you, and I know that you can do it! Try! Be brave! You have to try, or we're all going to drown before we can get to that opening! You *must do it*!"

"Chippa 'es very afraid, but Chippa 'well try!" He groaned feebly, moving to the front of his leaf where it pointed together, and raising his body up enough so that he could reach over the edge of the boat.

He began to speak in a strange language; nothing that any of them could understand, and he placed his paws on the surface of the water, smoothing it outward away from his boat. He brought his paws back to center and smoothed them outward again along the surface of the water.

As he moved his paws over it continuously, the water began to roll up the walls of the cave on both sides as if it was spilling upward, until the rolling waves of water on both sides finally met at the top, creating a water tunnel, and an air pocket that they were all safely traveling in.

Their boats did not slow as the current kept its pace, and indeed began to go even faster, but there was nothing to harm them in their long, narrow air pocket that moved through the water tunnel.

"How extraordinary!" Alice gasped, awed at the walls of water flooding past them, rushing around the air tunnel they suddenly found themselves in. "Well done Chippa! So very well done!" She cheered to him, looking back at him, but it was then that she saw every single cat's face, and Chippa's, as they stared past her shoulder to what was ahead.

She turned to see for herself, and her mouth fell open. Panic shot through her veins. No sound could come at first, but a yell soon escaped her, just as it did from the cats. The opening of the cave was coming at them like a speeding train.

The brilliant light blinded them as their eyes had grown so accustomed to the darkness, and they all held on for dear life as their air pocket reached the opening.

"Oh-" Shouted Oscar.

"My-" Bailey cried out.

SPLASH. The long air pocket hit the end of the tunnel and all of their boats shot out of the cave like bullets, flying high over the waterfall that burst forth from the mountain.

Every one of them screamed as their silver leaf boats sailed through the air and finally came crashing down on the river several feet below them. Each boat twirled and spun recklessly as the speed of the water began to slow, and they lifted their heads to look around.

"Oscar! Oscar, are you okay?" Jynx called out desperately.

"I'm gonna throw up!" He moaned back with a weak voice.

"I'm not feeling too well either!" Bailey added thinly.

"The river 'es flooding!" Chippa yelled in a panic. "We has to get off of 'et!" He turned in circles, looking for a solution.

"We make a chain! A cat chain! Messus P, hold your cane to me!" He waved to Alice who was nearest to him. She held onto the pointy end of her umbrella cane, and pushed the bird beak curved end of it toward Chippa.

He grabbed onto it and hooked it around the stem of his leaf, guiding the stem with his paws until it curled around the handle in a full loop, locking it in place. "All cats!" He directed them. "All cats bite another cat's tail, make a cat chain!"

Alice, seeing what he was trying to do, turned and looked behind her. "Tail to mouth! We must connect! Marlowe, can you reach your paw here and hold on to the side of my boat?"

Marlowe stretched as far as he could and finally got a hold of the edge of Alice's boat, holding fast to it as he stuck his tail out and let Bailey bite down on it. He growled quietly and narrowed his eyes, but said nothing as Bailey held tight.

Oscar bit onto Bailey's tail, Jynx connected to Oscar's carefully, Tao closed her teeth on Jynx's tail, then Montgomery to Tao, and finally Sophie took hold of Montgomery's, bringing up the end. They had indeed made a cat chain.

Chippa went to the front of his leaf again and leaned forward, running his paws over the water as he had in the tunnel, gently and smoothly. He was able to guide them painstakingly to the flooding bank, thick with grasses that had only just gone underwater.

He took them in as far as he could, and they all began to leap from their boats. Marlowe went to Alice and let her hold onto him as she clambered out of her boat and stood in calf deep water. Once she had steadied herself, she made her way to Chippa's boat, where she plucked him up out of it and cradled him in her arms.

"You did tremendously well. I'm so proud of you, Chippa. You were brave, and smart, and so very clever. No one else could have thought of an air tunnel so quickly like that. You are the very best Inkling in all of Corevé, and don't you ever doubt that." She hugged him tightly and his pointed ears flopped forward as he sniffed and hugged her in return.

"Thank you, Messus P." He gave her a humble, sweet smile, and reached his paw up to stroke her cheek softly.

Just as they were getting out of the river, a shriek came from the boats. They all turned back to see Sophie half in the water, scrambling to get up into one of the silver leaf boats as it began to drift into the current. She'd been leaping from leaf to leaf, and as she landed on one, she'd slipped on the water in it and fallen out, just as it had come loose of the grasses that barely held it secure in the rising river.

The leaf turned and the current took it, with Sophie clawing at the edge as water whirled about, pulling at her, dragging her downward.

"*Sophie!*" Oscar shouted, and he rushed back to the boats, jumping into the nearest one. Reaching his paw out and cupping it so that he could paddle toward her, he worked hard against the current. She cried out to him loudly; her fur soaked, and her eyes wide as she slipped further from the edge of the leaf down into the wild river.

Oscar guided his boat as carefully as he could, and managed to get it next to hers as they coursed further away. "Climb on!" He yelled, struggling to paddle in the swift flow.

"I can't let go! If I let go I'll drown!" Sophie sobbed, craning to push her head up as far as she could out of the water while she flailed and grappled with the edge of the leaf.

Oscar searched to see if there was anything else for her to hold on to. There was nothing. "I'm sorry about this Sophie, but there's no other way!"

He turned his leaf further and dunked his whole head down into the water, closing his sharp kitten teeth tightly on the nape of her neck.

She let out a shrieking howl as he dragged her up out of the water and into his own boat. The leaf she had been holding tightly to zipped away on the river, with no weight to hold it down.

There was barely enough room for them both, and the leaf they were on began to sink lower from their weight into the river until the water around them was only inches from the edge of it.

"Paddle Sophie! Paddle to shore as fast as you can!" Oscar entreated as he curled his paw and dug it into the water over and over again, trying to draw them out of the current and into the grasses. She paddled just as hard as he did, and finally they made it to the bank where all of the cats and Alice had hurried to wait for them.

Marlowe and Montgomery pulled Sophie out of the boat and helped her to dry land. Jynx was a foot deep in the water and grasses, waiting to get Oscar out and help him. The moment he was on the dry bank, she began bathing him with her tongue, cleaning off the water and bits of grass and earth that had stuck to him. He sat still and silent for her, but his ears were flat against his head.

Montgomery stayed with Sophie and fussed over her. She was furious. Sophie tried to shake the water off, but she was soaked from her pretty pink nose to the tip of her lavender and silver tail. "I can't believe this! Look at me!" She grumbled, trying to lick the water off and not getting anywhere with it.

"You should keep that look Soph... it's a lot more apropos a style for you. Drowned Rat." Jynx taunted, taking a momentary break from bathing Oscar.

Marlowe went to the overgrown kitten and smiled at him. "That was a very brave thing you did, Oscar. You're much braver than most of the cats I know, and you're a fast thinker. She'd be gone now if it wasn't for you. You saved her life. You kept our family together. Well done, young one, well done."

He winked at Oscar and walked away. Oscar swallowed a lump in his throat and looked at Jynx, who was working on his front paws.

"Did you hear that?" He whispered in awe.

"I certainly did, and it was well deserved." Jynx smiled at him and continued to bathe him.

"I'm so glad that both of you are all right!" Alice cried out, wiping a tear from her eye. "I was so afraid that I'd lose you!" She wrapped her arms around a sopping wet Sophie, hugging her tightly, and then she went to Oscar and rubbed his ears just the way that he liked. "So well done my darling. We're all very lucky to have you in this family."

Finally tidied, they took in their surroundings to see where they had landed.

"Where are we, Chippa?" Bailey asked, waddling over to him and sitting beside him.

They were standing at the edge of a meadow; the river behind them, the huge mountain they had just passed through was to their left, west of them, and to their right in the east, they saw gently rolling hills blanketed in green grasses and scattered with stands of trees. Beyond that, off in the far distance eastward, was the beginning of a forest so wide that they couldn't see the end of it. Along the northern horizon stood a towering line of thickly smoldering volcanoes.

"We 'es 'en the right place, but 'et's not good." Chippa answered with a worried voice, staring northward.

"Why isn't it good?" Alice eyed him warily.

"Volcanoes should not be smoking. Earth crystal 'es losing control." He grumbled. "'Es not good."

He put his paw to his mouth and looked around thoughtfully. "Quiri birds came 'thes way, but not sure where they 'es now." He frowned and furrowed his fluffy antennae eyebrows.

"How can we know where they are, if we don't even know where we are?" Sophie scoffed in irritation, still licking at her wet fur.

Tao sat perfectly still, her eyes half closed, her voice calm. "We are here and now, and that is the only place we can be."

Sophie was about to say something smart back to Tao, but Montgomery shook his head at her, and she stayed silent and sulked, going back to grooming her coat.

"We 'es near Lyria." Chippa affirmed quietly, looking to the eastern horizon.

"What is Lyria?" Oscar asked interestedly, finally breaking free of Jynx's bathing.

Chippa reached up and scratched his ears with both paws at the same time. "Lyria 'es the White Song Forest. We 'es having to go through 'et because the river 'es flooded the path 'round 'et. No other way. Quiri 'esn't here, they 'es outside of here."

Oscar tilted his head as he looked off at the forest along the horizon. "Why is it called the White Song Forest? It's green!"

Chippa's eyes were closed as he rubbed and scratched at his ears. "White Song Forest 'es a big circle forest inside green forest. 'Es sacred place."

"Why is it sacred?" Oscar asked, continuing with his barrage of questions.

"'Es protected, Lyria. White Song Forest 'es where fairies live." Chippa replied quietly.

CHAPTER SEVEN

ALONG THE WAY

"Fairies!" Several of the cats and Alice turned sharply to Chippa who had only just opened his eyes.

"There are real fairies?" Oscar brightened excitedly.

Chippa blinked. "Course 'es real fairies! You 'es not seen fairies before?" He was astounded at them.

"Not yet. Will we see them in the White Song Forest?" Oscar grew breathless.

Chippa frowned thoughtfully. "Not sure, they keeps to themselves mostly." He looked up at the sun in the sky. "Must go. Try to be 'en forest by dark."

With that he turned and headed down a lightly worn path; his steps a little quicker than usual, his pointed ears which flopped forward at the tips, were bouncing as he went along.

The cats fell in line after him with Alice and Marlowe bringing up the rear.

The path beneath them was so new that it was still grassy, though the grass was pressed to the ground, and the earth under it was only showing through in some places. There were trees that grew alongside the way here and there, and short squat bushes dotted about, but the greater part of the land around them was formed of gently rolling meadows and low hills.

They took in the strange new world they were traveling through, and spoke very little to one another, focusing instead on just enjoying the warmth of the day.

Sophie took her time sidling up to Oscar, and she ignored the dark look that Jynx shot at her as she did so.

"Oscar," She began in a voice not much above a whisper, "I know I can be a little... hard on you from time to time, but I do love you, and I care about you."

He blinked in surprise, letting her continue.

"I just wanted to say... I'm glad that you're in our family and... and thank you for being so brave and coming out to save me in the river. I haven't ever been that scared in my life and you just... you came right out to get me. You didn't even think about it." Her blue eyes glistened with humble gratitude.

Oscar gave her a smile. "I didn't have to think about it Sophie, 'cause I love you too." He leaned his head over and rubbed it against her cheek, and she smiled and nudged him back.

Bailey stepped up close to Chippa, whose pace was slowing as he yawned and sighed tiredly.

"So what do fairies eat?" Bailey asked with keen interest.

"Don't know, but I 'es hungry now." Chippa answered distractedly as he gazed about and rubbed his paws over his little round belly.

"Me too." Bailey moaned. "I think we aren't getting into the provisions until we settle in for the night though."

They were strolling along quietly when Oscar started to play with the other cats a bit, flicking them with his tail, and batting his paws at them lightly, but none of them played back; they only ignored the kitten's antics and kept on walking.

He eyed them mischievously and began to sniff around at the edge of the path, checking out everything he could.

A few moments later his ears and whiskers went stiff and he nestled down, wiggling his bottom a little before vaulting up in the air and over a grassy reed-filled spot. He vanished behind the massive growth, and some of the others looked over to where he had disappeared.

"Oscar?" Jynx asked, looking cautiously after him. There was no answer, but a moment later, Oscar came strutting out of the grasses with his head held high and his teeth clenched on the solid green stem of the biggest dandelion any of them had ever seen. It had passed its flowering stage and had gone to seed. The sprouted bloom of it was just a little bigger than Oscar's face.

He shifted his eyes around subtly, looking at the other cats, and began to bob his head with a dance in his step as he walked, flipping his tail back and forth. The other cats gave him silent looks, and then focused on the path before them.

As he swayed along, moving his head, the seed helicopters on the dandelion began to come loose and float away. He saw the first few and immediately turned to Jynx, giving his head a good shake.

Jynx was showered in seed helicopters, and she closed her eyes, letting them fly around her; rolling and bouncing off of her black and cobalt blue body.

The other cats were enchanted by the flurry, and as Oscar shook his head and pranced onward, they were engulfed in the flying seeds.

Tao and Bailey batted at the fluff floating past, as did Sophie. Even Montgomery looked up from his pensive silence to watch the wonders swirling everywhere in the breeze that moved around them. He reached his paw up and swatted at the helicopters, catching several of them, playing right along with the rest of the cats.

Oscar laughed at him, and Montgomery chuckled and lifted his paw to adjust his monocle. "Well, I am a cat, after all." He winked at Oscar.

Finally, the floating seeds had blown away and the cats were in a lighter mood; their tails swaying and flipping, their steps lighter, with smiles on their faces.

Alice giggled and grinned, watching all of them. She had managed to catch a few of the flying seeds as well, and she loved seeing all of them play together.

Oscar stopped short for a moment. "Is it… is it okay to play with Henderson gone? Should we be sad instead?"

Alice went to him and rubbed her hand over his large forehead. "Darling, we are going to get him. Between now and then, we have a choice in our attitudes and perspectives. We're all concerned for him, of course, but worrying and fretting about it won't bring him back, and it won't help us. In fact, it only makes the journey all the harder. These cats know that I do my best not to worry, most of the time. No good can come of it. As no good can come of it, then we could use the time to ease the sorrow in our hearts and make the journey easier. There is a great deal of good that can come from that. So if you want to play, then play. If you want to laugh, then we will laugh with you. It's only going to help us as we go on, keeping our spirits up as we search for Henderson and the Blue Fire Crystal."

Oscar beamed. "I am so curious about this place! There's so much to see here, and discover! I'm really glad that I can be happy about being here, and have fun on our trip."

"I'm glad too, darling. You enjoy yourself." Alice patted him once more, and started down the path again.

Chippa suddenly squeaked and went rushing off into a grove of the strangest looking trees any of them had ever seen. "Hungry! Hungry!" He chattered as he stopped at the base of one of the largest there.

The cats and Alice followed him, looking on incredulously at the tree that Chippa had run to.

It was about fifteen feet tall with black bark all over the trunk and the roots that showed through the soil around it. Throughout all of the black bark were ashen gray cracks and crevices. The leaves weren't leaves. Instead, where thousands of leaves would have been, there were single flames burning; each of them fat at the bottom and tapering upward about two inches.

They were white at the center, becoming yellow, and then orange and red at their outer edges. They flickered and wavered in the breeze, but never blew out. Heat radiated from the tree, and the closer they got to it, the warmer the air and earth around them felt.

Chippa was tucked in right at the base of the tree, digging furiously with his front paws, flinging dirt off to the sides and over his shoulders. He squeaked again when he got to what he was digging for.

The little Inkling pulled out a foot long root that glowed bright orange and red, shimmering as though he had just plucked it from the heart of a fire. He sat back on his bottom and broke the root into several smaller pieces, cramming most of them into the little pouch under the white fur around his neck.

When the bag was full, he stuffed the rest of the pieces into his mouth and chewed slowly, savoring them as his eyelids fell half-closed and he began to chirp.

Alice laughed at him and rubbed her hand on Marlowe's ears as they watched. "Is this a Flame Tree? Is that the Tinder Root that you like so much?" She asked, already sure of the answers.

"Tinder Root." He answered as he rolled onto his back and settled his paws on his fat belly. "Chippa so happy." He chirped blissfully, and a moment later his eyes were closed, and he was fast asleep.

"Oh dear." Alice sighed, placing her hands on her hips as she gazed at the sleeping Inkling.

"I'll carry him." Bailey offered, coming forward and laying down so Alice could put Chippa on his back.

"Thank you Bailey." Alice gave him a proud smile and scratched his ears for him. "You're such a good cat."

She lifted the little creature and nestled him into the soft pink fur on Bailey's shoulders, and the cat walked slowly and carefully out to the path again.

The sun was warm, and the breeze that drifted past them was cool and pleasant, carrying on it different sweet scents that were unfamiliar yet exhilarating to them.

Alice drew in a deep breath and let it out slowly, beaming from ear to ear. "I don't think I've ever felt more awake and alive!"

"Agreed!" Montgomery purred.

"I agree as well." Tao closed her eyes and inhaled, savoring the sweetness. The other cats concurred.

The group headed toward the forest in the distance. Montgomery and Sophie walked side by side, talking about old stories; teasing and nuzzling each other now and then.

Alice began humming an old song, and soon enough she was singing it as they ambled along. When Sophie, Bailey, Tao, Montgomery, and Marlowe began singing with her, she laughed in astonishment.

When the song was done, she shook her head. "How do you know that tune?"

Marlowe smiled at her. "You used to listen to it all the time."

She gasped. "You're right! I did. I just didn't realize that you were all listening too. I guess I should have known that. This is so wonderful, and so strange. It's like meeting old friends for the first time. There's no way to describe it."

He leaned close to her and lowered his voice a little. "Don't worry, it's like that for us too. We talk to each other all the time, but we don't get to talk to you, and it's a great change. We love it."

"So do I." She answered him with a heartfelt smile, and light in her brown eyes.

Oscar walked beside Alice and gazed at her. "I don't know that song. I haven't heard you play it. What was it?"

Alice petted the side of his head. "It's an old song that George and I used to sing and dance to. Would you like to learn it?"

Oscar was delighted. "Yes, please!"

"Okay troupes, let's do it again, shall we!" She began to sing it from the beginning. and the rest of the cats joined in; all of them bobbing their heads as Oscar and Alice step-danced down the road.

Chippa woke up and raised his eyes to have a look about. He slid down Bailey's leg and joined them in their happy jaunt, walking and swaying his furry bottom and fluffy tail as they went along; his ears flopping and bouncing as he enjoyed the song. When it was done, Alice started another newer song, and they all joined in.

They had come around the curve of a low hill, their voices clear and strong as they sang, and Oscar saw that there was a big field thick with the strangest flowers he had ever seen. They grew in almost every color of the rainbow, and each color had differently shaped petals. The blue ones had oval shaped petals, the green ones had round petals, and the red and orange had long slender petals, among many more shapes and colors. He went to the edge of the path and leaned close to one of them, sniffing at it.

The bloom shivered as he breathed in the scent of it, and it suddenly fluttered, lifting off of its stem. The little green flower flew around a bit and hovered in the air a moment before flying back to Oscar and seeming to sniff at him.

He sat on his haunches and pulled his head back, staring cross-eyed at the blossom that fluttered around his nose and face. He didn't move. He didn't barely breathe as the thing moved around his head and his ears. It finally came back in front of his face at a short distance, where he could look evenly at it.

One at a time, other blossoms lifted off of their stems and flew to him, joining the one that was already there. All of the blooms, in every color, shape, and size, sniffed at Oscar.

Chippa looked up at them, floating and sailing around the cat, and he smiled, pressing the tips of his paws together. "They likes the singing!" He laughed lightly.

There was a moment of silence, and then Alice, who was watching in fascination, started another song. More blossoms drifted toward them from the field, leaving wide patches of it with barren stems. They encircled her as she sang, landing on her here and there, dancing and bouncing through the air.

"Delightful!" She exclaimed, lifting her hands up and letting the flowers settle in her palms and on her arms. She began to walk along the path again singing her song, and the group went with her. Everyone sang and walked, and as they did, the blooms danced and swirled among them.

Jynx only hummed, but she did flip her tail back and forth, with a bounce in her step and a smile on her face. Oscar walked beside her, loving every moment of the floral delights dancing about them.

When they reached the next hill, the field of flutter flowers ended, and all the different blossoms came close to the faces of the group, gently brushing their petals against them like soft kisses. In an undulating wave of rainbow color, they flew away back to their stems, alighting, and shivering their petals in farewell.

Step by step the group went on, their pace slow and steady. All of them had become much more curious about Corevé, and the cats were drinking it all in.

Another hill was behind them when Alice stopped suddenly and held her hand to her heart. "Wait! Where are Chippa and Bailey?"

The other cats turned in surprise. None of them had noticed that Bailey and Chippa were no longer walking with them; they had been so interested in all the lush flora and fauna; so strange and unusual, growing all around.

Marlowe lifted his head and sniffed at the air, looking about and listening closely; his ears perked fully. He turned his head. "They're behind us."

He was a streak of dark blue and silver spotted fur as he rushed back down the path and disappeared around the last curve they had passed. The rest of the cats joined him, while Montgomery and Sophie walked with Alice as she made her way back around the bend in the road.

Sitting beside a large bush were Chippa and Bailey; neither one of them aware that the entire group was standing behind them, watching them. They were stuffing their mouths with fat red berries that hung all over the bush.

"Chippa! Bailey!" Alice called them firmly.

Chippa's ears perked up, and he and Bailey turned to looked over their shoulders. Both of their faces were covered in red berry chunks and juice.

"What are you two doing?" Alice asked, planting her hands on her hips. Chippa burped and covered his mouth with his paw. Bailey leaned back on his bottom and hiccupped.

Tao laughed. "We are most satisfied when we are full of happiness!"

"I'm happy!" Bailey answered with a sheepish smile on his berry covered mouth.

"All right you two, time to go. We've got to reach that forest by dark, right Chippa?" Alice asked, looking at the little Inkling pointedly.

He scurried away from the bush and back onto the path. "Yes." He answered, wiping his paws over his face and then licking them clean. He began walking, reaching up to rub and scratch at his ears as he yawned and stretched.

Tao leaned her head down close to his. "If you're tired, you can ride on me for a while."

"Yes please, I 'es so tired." Chippa nodded. Tao knelt down close to the ground so the Inkling could grab onto her fur, and crawl up to the hollow between her shoulder blades. Nestling in, Chippa fell fast asleep, and Tao stood up carefully, padding gently down the path with the others.

They went a long way further, and when the shadows began to grow, Alice saw a fallen log not far from the path. She called out to the cats. "I'm going to sit. I need to rest a little. We've been going all day. Shall we have a break?"

"Yes, please!" Called out Bailey, finding a patch of grass and rolling onto his back.

Jynx woke Chippa, and he slid down Tao's leg to the ground. Looking around, he frowned a moment and flattened his ears. "You waked me so we could stop and rest?"

Grumbling quietly, he went to the spot where Bailey was watching clouds, and stretched out on the grass; rolling around and rubbing his fur against it.

Tao sank into her sphinx posture and closed her eyes, meditating peacefully as she loved to do. Marlowe settled in beside the log where Alice was relaxing. He peered about with half-closed eyes. Alice reached up to pet her hand over his cheeks, just behind his whiskers.

Oscar, Jynx, and Montgomery went to the sweet smelling grassy area where Bailey and Chippa were lounging, and they too stretched out and rolled in the green. Oscar laid beside Chippa, and looked up at the blue sky above them, gazing at the clouds that were sailing overhead.

His gazing turned into staring as his eyes widened. "Chippa…" He said in a serious and quiet voice, "I see such clear shapes… there's… there's a pirate ship, and a dinosaur. There's a teddy bear, and a dolphin… but they all look like they're… um, like they're alive. They look like they are moving and playing leapfrog or some kind of chasing game."

There was a mix of uncertainty and confusion in Oscar's tone. Chippa drew his little paws up over his head into the grass behind him and pushed his toes out as far as they could go.

"Well 'et's what they 'es doing. You see 'et. They 'es doing 'zactly what you see. 'Es another part of Corevé." Chippa answered him matter-of-factly.

Oscar was astounded. "You mean… you mean they're alive?"

Chippa eyed Oscar curiously. "Everything 'es alive. All you has to do 'es look around. You see 'et. You feel 'et. Everything 'es alive."

Tao spoke without opening her eyes. "That is a wise truth, Chippa."

All of them stared up into the sky then, watching as the shapes in the clouds moved and played, changing and morphing into other shapes as their games went on and on. Chippa finally stood up and yawned again.

"We go." He said simply, waddling back to the road. Everyone got up and followed him.

Sophie and Montgomery walked side by side, talking a little here and there, when she stopped suddenly; her blue eyes growing round as they locked onto something in the meadow beside them. The land was filled with grasses of varying lengths, and several pointy looking bushes.

"Montgomery…" She said quietly as she stared hard the subject of her fascination. "What *is* that? Is that a butterfly of some kind?"

"What are you looking at? I don't see a butterfly." He lifted his chin and widened his eyes, trying to use his monocle as best he could. When he had grown so big, his monocle grew along with him, fitting him as well as it had when it was given to him in Mari Village.

"That little thing right over there, floating in the air." Sophie pointed her nose toward it.

He blinked and sniffed a couple of times. "Hmm. I don't know, Sophie. It looks like a piece of a rainbow or a drop of translucent color to me."

She lowered her body down closer to the ground as she watched it, prowling slowly step by silent step, completely enchanted with the rainbow drop. The end of her tail flicked back and forth, and in a sudden single bound, she leapt out toward it, where it hovered over a bush.

The rainbow drop vanished, and Chippa turned and gaped at the lavender and silver cat. "Sophie no!" He shouted to her. "You can't be on that! 'Es a Popper tree!"

Alice looked at him. "Do you mean a Poplar tree?"

He shook his head swiftly, waving at Sophie like she might be out of her mind. "No, 'es a Popper tree!"

The words had barely been spoken when the bush Sophie was standing atop suddenly sprang straight up out of the ground, shooting toward the sky as if it had been blasted from a cannon. It stopped at a dizzying height; its roots in the ground looking like any other tree as it towered over them with Sophie clinging desperately to its highest branches.

"Good heavens!" Alice cried out. "Sophie! Sophie, are you all right?"

Sophie was more than fifty feet from the ground. Just then another of the bushes went flying up from its diminutive spot and stopped at about forty feet in height. Sophie eyed the tree and then called out to Alice. "I'm all right… I think."

Sophie concentrated hard on the shorter tree and then jumped to it just as two more of the bushes sprang up to nearly the same heights as the first two.

"Sophie! Please be careful!" Montgomery called up to her.

"Watch out Sophie!" Bailey added, looking around at the trees as they shot out of the ground intermittently. One by one, the different bushes zoomed upward, stayed tall for a few minutes, and then they sank slowly back down to earth, just as others were flying toward the sky beside them.

Jynx gazed up stoically at Sophie. "I'm sure the view is good up there, princess. Why don't you stay there and enjoy it?"

Alice watched in amazement as Sophie leapt to a slightly shorter tree. She was still some twenty feet off of the ground.

"Those look like Cypress trees." She murmured to Chippa and Marlowe, though she didn't turn to look at them. "Except they're not like any Cypress trees I've ever seen. They're certainly sturdy. Sophie is quite a big girl now, and those branches at the tops of the trees aren't bowing in the slightest! What a curious thing!"

Sophie called back to the others then as she landed on another tree that was rocketing upward, "This is thrilling! I've never had such excitement!" She began to jump from tree top to tree top as the Popper trees came up and sank slowly back down again.

"I don't want to come down yet, I'm having too much fun!" She sang out as she arced through the air and landed delicately on another tree top.

Alice sighed quietly. "All right. Well, it seems we aren't going anywhere for a few minutes." She walked over to an old tree stump and poked it a few times with the tip of her umbrella cane to make certain that it wasn't going anywhere. When she was sure that it was stable, she sat down on it and watched Sophie hopping around on the trees far above them.

"She is a spoiled cat. I suppose that she must have her way sometimes." Alice chuckled softly and rested her hands on the top of her cane.

"A cat nearly always lands on its feet, doesn't it!" Sophie bragged, and the other cats on the ground looked at each other and realized that she was right.

Montgomery was the first to join Sophie, grabbing on tightly as he landed on a bush top that raced toward the sky, and he was soon followed by Oscar and then Tao.

Bailey tried, landing on a short squatty bush, but nothing happened, so he leapt as daintily as his ample body would allow, to another bush, and it flew straight up with him clawing at it hastily and trying to keep his balance.

Marlowe gave Alice a sidelong look as she sat there, and she smiled at him. "Oh go on! Go do it." She snickered quietly.

He nodded subtly at her and shrugged out of the bags of provisions on his shoulders. Alice took her coat and slipped it on. In one graceful leap, he landed atop one of the bushes and in the next moment, he was forty feet in the air with the other cats, streaking from tree top to tree top, playing right along with them.

Alice eyed Jynx curiously, but she didn't say anything. Jynx rolled her eyes. "Well I can't let Oscar go up on his own, can I?" The black and cobalt cat sighed. In a blink she was up in the tree tops with him and the others, bounding around.

Alice felt a gentle tug at her coat pocket. She looked down to see Chippa digging around for a candy. She reached in and pulled out a ginger chew for him, handing it to him with a laugh. He stuffed it into his mouth and his eyes narrowed blissfully as he savored it. He sat down beside her, and a soft chirp sounded from him.

After waiting another ten minutes or so, Alice pushed herself up from her tree stump and waved at the cats, who were still playing in the tree tops.

"Come along now, we've got to get busy rescuing Henderson! Let's go!"

Each of the cats began to jump to lower trees until they were finally all on the ground, except for Bailey, who rode one of the slow sinking trees until it was bush sized again, and then he hopped off of it.

They caught their breath; all of them had been panting and most of them laughing. Sophie preened her fur with her tongue, and they started off again down the road.

As they neared the edge of the forest, Montgomery walked beside Chippa and spoke to him.

"Chippa, would you please tell us about your life in the Mari tribe? It seems a fascinating place with all of you Inklings looking after the elements as you do. It's quite a responsibility, isn't it?" He asked in a gentle voice.

Chippa tipped his head slightly. "'Et 'es a big 'sponsibility. I 'es not very good at 'et. I makes lots of 'mestakes. Most o' the time." He sighed and his small shoulders drooped. "I tries to do everything right, but I seems to get things wrong so much."

He had been looking down at the ground as he answered, but then his little ears perked up a bit, and he raised his big, dark eyes to Alice. "'Cept for you. I 'es taking a big chance on you 'es the Chosen One, and I know I 'es right. I 'es sure of 'et."

He looked out ahead of them thoughtfully. "I 'esn't 'posed to do 'et, but I knew I 'es right, so I did 'et. I went to you, and got you, and brought you here. So, I 'es right… once." Chippa was somewhat saddened that he was wrong so often.

Tao leaned her head down closer to him. "We all serve a purpose in our lives in different ways. We all have value, though we are all very different. Bailey saved me because he was heavy enough to pull me out of the bird's grasp but also because he was brave enough to try. Oscar saved Sophie from drowning because he is loyal and dedicated no matter what. Jynx watches over Oscar because she loves him, and she knows he needs someone to care especially for him in his new family. Marlowe is always at Alice's side watching over her and caring for her, though we all do to some extent, but none of us as much as he does. Even Henderson is an important part of our family; he cares for all of us as though we were his only priority. Alice cares for us all too, and she is the warrior you needed, just when you needed it. She's fighting to save your world. You have great purpose, Chippa; you followed your instincts about Alice even when you knew it might get you into trouble, and you have been leading us and guiding us along this journey, saving us in the river and helping us as we go. You are bright and clever, you are strong of heart and brave, even when you don't know you can be. We all have an important purpose, though all our purposes are different."

Chippa turned and stared up at her in awe. "Ohhhh!" He beamed happily as if the morning sun had just risen in his mind. "What 'es your purpose?" He asked curiously.

Tao gave Chippa a little smile. "My purpose will be revealed when the time for it to come arrives. It may be once, or it may be many times, but I do not try to find my purpose, I allow my purpose to open itself to me."

Sophie, who was walking ahead of them, glanced back over her shoulder and frowned dejectedly before looking away. She had not heard Tao say what her purpose might be.

"I makes lots of 'mestakes because I 'es young, I think." Chippa added as his step picked up a little, and his sadness faded. "I 'es only seven hundred and forty-one years old. When I 'es seven hundred and forty-two, then I 'es all grown up. Then I 'es adult. Then I think I won't makes 'mestakes anymore."

Alice smiled at him. "I am an old woman in my world, and I still make mistakes. I don't think anyone living ever stops making mistakes, Chippa. That's how we learn. We make a mistake, and we learn, and we go on."

Montgomery's eyes were wide. "My goodness... seven hundred and forty-one! How old is your chief; Bayless Grand Mari?"

Chippa's fluffy eyebrow antennae raised slightly. "'He 'es over two thousand years." He looked at Montgomery and waved his paw a little. "Our days 'es shorter than the days 'en your world. Our time goes much faster here."

Montgomery grew thoughtful. "You know, you're right. I haven't felt tired or that I needed to rest, and we haven't slept since we got here."

Alice agreed. "I'm feeling a little tired, but it looks like the sun is going to set soon, so hopefully we can rest in a bit." She turned back to Chippa then.

"When you are an adult in the tribe, what will you do? Will you have some kind of work or job that you'll do, other than guarding the crystals?"

He shrugged. "All Inklings 'es choosing work 'en the tribe when they 'es reaching adult age. Most of them 'es already learning what they wants to do. I esn't really learning mine yet, but I 'es having to choose soon."

"What would you like most to do? What is your dream work for the tribe?" Alice asked interestedly.

He was quiet a moment, folding his paws together in front of him before he raised his big, dark eyes to meet hers.

"Mostly I 'es wanting to be a healer. Like Oppa Mari. She 'es best connected to the elements. She does 'mazing things. She 'es very strong. Lots of control 'weth elements. I can't be healer though." His gaze fell to the ground and his small mouth turned downward.

"Why can't you be a healer? Can there only be one in your tribe at a time?" Alice asked, keeping her tone light.

He answered her softly. "Can be one 'weth a helper. She 'es needing help, but 'et 'esn't being me. I 'es making too many mestakes. I 'esn't doing much right. Can't be doing best, most 'emportant work 'en the tribe when I 'esn't doing anything right."

Alice lifted her chin; her voice filled with faith and encouragement. "So you want to apprentice with her. You can try, Chippa, and you must. If you never try, you'll never know, and then you'll be wondering all of your life if you ever could have done it, had you tried. I know that better than just about anyone. I waited to do many things in my life, and now I look back and I know that if I'd just had a little faith in myself; if I'd only given myself a chance no matter if I succeeded or failed, my life would be quite different now. I wish that I had taken risks much more often than I did. I lived too safely, and now I know that I've missed out on much. Don't do that, Chippa. If you learn anything from me at all, learn this. Take chances. Take risks. Failure is not the worst that can happen. Regret is much worse than failure, and it doesn't ever go away."

He stared at her as every word she had spoken soaked into his heart and soul. "But what 'ef she says no?" He began, but she held her hand up and stopped him.

"But what if she says yes?" She gave him a tender smile. "You must give yourself and your future a chance, little one. You must try, and only then will you know for certain. You'll have much more peace with that, and with yourself."

He nodded subtly and looked forward again, walking in thoughtful silence for a long while.

The trees around them grew denser, and Chippa pointed out to them that they were coming into the deeper green woods. The daylight began to fade, and Chippa found a small clearing for them on a flat grassy bank beside a large silvery pond. The clearing was encircled by a thick stand of trees; some looked like pine trees and some had wide, round, dark green leaves nearly as big as their leaf boats had been.

"We 'es sleeping here tonight." He said resolutely as he gave the area a sweeping look.

CHAPTER EIGHT

LYRIA

Alice and the cats watched as Chippa went to the trees that formed a semi-circle around the clearing. He ran his paws over one of the largest, low hanging leaves on a tree near the pond. With gentle movements, he coaxed it outward, shaping it just as he had done with the leaf boats.

When he was finished, the leaf was shaped into a wide sort of hammock, about two and a half feet from the ground. He turned and looked at Alice, folding his paws together in front of him as he spoke.

"'Thes leaf 'es working as a bed for you." He said, looking hopeful.

Alice gave him a sweet smile and walked over to it, bending to touch it with her hand, and test it for stability. She was surprised to find that it had only a little give to it, and that it felt soft and smooth to her touch, yet strong and sturdy enough to hold her. She turned and took a deep breath, silently praying that she wouldn't fall as she sat down on it.

Grinning at Chippa with relief, she giggled, and bounced on the leaf-bed a little.

"This is perfect! Chippa, you have such wonderful talents and you do amaze me. Why, this is even more comfortable than my bed back at home!"

Alice examined it from top to bottom. "I think this will do quite nicely! Thank you, little Chippa."

The Inkling beamed and looked downward in a passing moment of bashfulness. "'Thes leaf 'es giving you sweet dreams." He told her, walking over to the edge of it; touching it lightly. "'Es 'en the spirit of the tree. 'Es 'en the leaves, too. Smells good." He closed his eyes and breathed in the scent of the leaf with a pleasant smile.

Alice ran her hand over it, and then brought her fingers to her nose to breathe it in. "It does smell very good." She said quietly as she tried to place the scents. "Almost like lavender and… there's something else, but I just can't place it."

"Starlight." Chippa answered quietly. "You 'es smelling starlight. Trees soak 'et up, fills them. Starlight and time."

Alice pondered the small creature. "I know you're young, Chippa, but I think you're also very wise."

He smiled wide again before turning to the cats. "You need beds?"

"No, we're fine sleeping in the grass. I'll sleep beside Alice." Marlowe replied easily. Chippa nodded to him.

"I don't need a bed, but I am so hungry!" Oscar groaned.

"Me too!" Bailey chimed in.

"You eats fishes?" Chippa asked brightly.

"We all love fish." Montgomery answered.

"You 'es finding fishes 'en 'thes pond." Chippa pointed his paw toward the large pond beside them. "We can keep provisions for needs later, 'en have fishes now."

Tao padded to the edge of it and stared down silently into the water. In a flash, she dipped her paw beneath the surface and brought up a large fish that was colored with brilliant red and orange hues. She glanced over her shoulder and tossed it to Oscar, who caught it in his teeth.

She slipped her paw in again and again, bringing out fish one by one until everyone had enough to eat. Chippa disappeared into the forest and soon brought back the same sort of flowers and fruits that they had eaten at the feast in Mari Village. Alice enjoyed every bit of it for her evening meal. Before long, they were all satisfied and relaxed.

A gentle, warm breeze began to stir around them, and the light of day softened and faded as the sky above dimmed with twilight. The breeze drifted through reeds along the bank of the big pond, and as the air moved within the reeds, sounds like the strings of violins being played whispered forth from them.

Alice and the cats watched the reeds as they bent and played, and the violin tones which were subtle at first began to build, increasing in volume and musical range.

A veiled mist formed thickly over the pond, and droplets of water in varying sizes began to fall from it, though only a few at first. As each drop of water touched the silvery surface of the pond, a note resembling that of a key being played on a piano could be heard.

They watched in silent awe as more droplets began to fall and each size that hit the water made a different note. The largest drops made deeper sounds, and the smaller the droplets were, the higher the notes that were heard. They became tinkling water pianos playing right along with the violins from the reeds.

The breeze shifted slightly then; the tall grasses near the water waved and twisted, and as they moved, the air was filled with the resonance of several kinds of wind instruments. They heard echoes of oboes, bassoons, flutes of many different varieties, and some tones that none of them had ever heard before.

The breeze swept into flowers with deeply centered petals, and a band of many sorts of horns joined the melody, so that in minutes a symphony of nature had swelled all around them in perfect harmony.

Alice was entranced, listening to the beautiful music as it played, but her attention was drawn to something else.

"What are those? The little lights? Are those fireflies?" She asked in a hushed voice, not wanting to disrupt any of what was going on around them. She was spellbound by the wide stream of tiny glowing bugs that were sailing over and around her and the cats.

Chippa looked up at them. "They 'es fireflies."

"They're all going in one direction!" She whispered in wonder as she watched them. "Where are they going Chippa?"

He turned to her in surprise, almost as though she should know. "They 'es going to the Fairy Sway."

She blinked and the corners of her mouth turned up a bit. "A Fairy Sway? What's that?"

Chippa nodded. "Oh… yes. You doesn't have fairies." He seemed to have forgotten the fact. "Well," he reached a paw up and rubbed the end of one of his ears that was flopped over forward, "a Fairy Sway 'es a dance party for fairies."

Alice's hand went right to her mouth, and she nearly squealed; feeling as if she was suddenly nine years old, just having discovered that she was in a magical realm filled with all of her girlhood daydreams.

Chippa raised his feathery eyebrow antennae. "You 'es wanting to go? I 'well take you." He offered lightly.

"Oh yes, please! That would be wonderful!" She bubbled enthusiastically as she stood up from her leaf bed.

Alice followed Chippa, and the cats walked with her. They'd only gotten to the edge of the clearing they were in when Chippa looked back, stopping in his tracks.

"Cats can't come." He stated with a resolute shake of his head. He waved his paw in the air before him to emphasize the point.

Alice planted her hand on her hip and frowned. "Why ever not?"

"Fairies won't like cats. Fairies 'well be afraid of cats." He crossed his small arms over his chest. "Fairies 'es small. They flies. Cats 'well chase them."

Alice had to admit that Chippa had a point, though she wasn't pleased about realizing that he was right. Turning to look at the cats, she eyed them all seriously. "Will you give your word that if you come you won't chase any fairies or do them any harm?"

Her gaze met that of each cat, but she looked longest at Oscar. "Otherwise he's right. It might not be best if you go."

Marlowe was completely affronted. "I'm going. I won't bother the fairies."

The rest of them promised as well, including Oscar, who got a stern look from Jynx and Sophie.

Feeling sure that they were all going to be true to their word, Alice turned back to Chippa.

"They've given their word. They're going to behave, and the fairies will be fine." She promised pleasantly.

Chippa, his arms still crossed over his chest, shook his head. "They won't like 'et." He announced flatly. "Cats can't go."

Alice lifted an eyebrow defiantly. "I'm going, and the cats go with me."

Chippa saw that he wasn't going to get her to change her mind. He dropped his paws to his sides and his ears went back flat against his head. "Fine, but cats has to stay hidden. No showing of selves to fairies."

Alice turned and eyed the cats. "Agreed my little ones? You'll stay hidden?" They agreed, and Oscar snickered at being called a little one.

With a quiet grumble, Chippa turned and led them out of the clearing and into the trees. There were several kinds of trees, but the most abundant were tall thick trees that closely resembled pine.

The group walked beneath them, and as the last light of day disappeared, a bright, bluish-white moon came out, shining brilliant light throughout the forest. It was luminous enough that each of them could see their shadows slipping silently along the path before them.

Alice was watching her shadow with amusement when she noticed something small and furry moving over the forest floor in the moonlight. She was going to ask Chippa about the little animal, when another one seemed to drop out of nowhere and land with ease on the ground not far from the first one.

Her breath caught, and before she could speak, another one fell practically from thin air. It was curled up in a ball until it made contact with the earth; rolling a few inches and then uncurling and lifting its little head.

Each one had a diminutive pointy face with beady black eyes that glittered in the moonlight. They stood on four bitty paws, had a short, thin tail, and dainty round ears that were the same shade of pink as their tiny noses.

Blinking in confusion, Alice peered around at the ground. More emerged, and she raised her eyes, looking upward into the pine tree beside them. It was then that she saw what was happening.

The branches were dotted with the forms of the animals, and Alice gasped as she watched them. "Chippa!" She whispered sharply. He stopped and looked up at her.

"I thought those were pine cones! They're not! They're… they're little animals! What are those?" She puzzled over them.

One by one they dropped from where they were hanging by their tails on the pine tree branches, falling slowly to the ground. They rolled once or twice, and then uncurled to stand on their feet; scuttling around and chirruping to one another.

Chippa reached his paw up to his chin and scratched at the bottom of it slightly. "'Thes 'es Pinyans." He waved his paw up toward the branches in the pine tree. "They sleeps 'en trees all day. At night they wakes up and comes down to eat and play."

"Pinyans…" Alice repeated quietly as she watched them falling and landing. "What do they eat?"

"They eats Night Berries." Chippa walked a few feet over to a bush twice as big as himself. There were periwinkle colored flowers all over the bush. Alice followed him and watched in awe as the petals began to open slowly when the moonlight touched each of them.

"See, 'en each flower 'es one red berry. Berry grows 'en daytime 'enside petals. Moon comes, petals open, one berry 'enside. Pinyans comes and eats a berry. They eats 'et very slow; one Pinyan, one berry, for whole night. Then they plays 'en the forest. When 'es time for sunrise, then they 'es crawling back up to branches 'en tree, and they 'es hanging and sleeping all day. 'Thes Pinyans." He was pleased at getting to tell her about them.

Alice chuckled as she watched them coming to the Night Berry bush and pulling the little red berries out of the center of the blooms. "I like them. They're quite adorable!"

Chippa nodded. "We 'es going. Needs to get to Fairy Sway."

Alice agreed, and continued after him as he walked under the slow flowing stream of fireflies above them that weaved and bobbed their way along through the forest, all meandering in one direction.

The cats stayed near enough behind them to follow them, but also gave them some distance to stay hidden.

They went deep into the forest until they came to a place where the trees and indeed everything that grew, and even the earth, turned white. Alice and the cats stopped and stared; their wide eyes blinking as they took in the incredible sight.

Chippa realized that they weren't walking with him, and turned back to them. "What 'es 'et? Why you stopped?"

Oscar was the first to speak. "Everything is white! All of it! Every bush, every tree, every leaf, every bit of grass, even the ground! It's all white! What happened?"

"Oh!" Chippa understood. "'Thes 'es the White Song Forest. 'Es where the fairies live. 'Es sacred. 'Es protected. I thinks the Fairy Queen 'es using magic to makes 'et white."

"It looks like it's winter here; like everything was snowed on!" Alice marveled, reaching her hand out to touch a nearby leaf on the white tree in front of them. "It's not cold though!"

Chippa shook his head. "No, 'es not cold. 'Es magic. Les go." He turned and walked a short distance.

"Chippa!" Alice cried out, gaping at him worriedly.

"What?" He turned again to look at her, and she pointed to him.

"You're white, too!"

"We're all white!" Montgomery gawked at his fur incredulously. "Every one of us!"

He had spoken the truth. All of the cats as they entered the White Song Forest, had turned white; just as Chippa had.

Jynx smirked and looked at Sophie. "I guess my soul isn't dark after all. I hope you aren't disappointed."

Sophie just lifted her nose in the air and turned her head away from Jynx.

Bailey pouted sadly. "Oh, my lovely pink fur is gone! Just look at this… no more sass to me!"

"You're nothing but sass, no matter what color your coat is." Jynx gave him a wink.

"Sass and constant hunger." Sophie shot over her shoulder at them.

"Better than an ice cold heart." Jynx licked her paw and rubbed it over her ear to clean her fur nonchalantly. Sophie growled and stalked away.

Bailey smiled at Jynx, and Oscar rubbed his face on Bailey's shoulder.

Chippa looked at all of them sharply. "You can't fights! You must be cautious and gentle 'weth all the forest here, and 'weth each other!"

They nodded silently, and Sophie made a point of ignoring Jynx.

Alice was the only one of them that kept her natural color. The fur on all of the rest of them became white, and they blended into the forest around them like ghosts.

They weren't even fifty feet into the new area of the forest when Montgomery sidled up next to Oscar and flipped his tail at the younger cat playfully.

Oscar laughed at him in surprise and flipped his in return. Montgomery stopped where he was and crouched down, swirling the end of his tail back and forth, his head close to the ground, his eyes wide and locked on Oscar. Oscar stepped back in astonishment and then grinned wickedly, crouching down opposite Montgomery, ready to pounce.

They leapt at the same time, both of them rising up suddenly and meeting in the air, hugging and wrestling together, biting each other gently as they played. They toppled over and rolled around on the ground, and all of the rest of the group stopped and stared at them.

Sophie's mouth fell open. "Montgomery! What on earth are you doing? You're much too old to be doing anything like that!"

Alice held her hand to her mouth, wondering what was going on with her oldest cat. He hadn't acted so youthful and playful for years.

Montgomery and Oscar tussled a bit longer, and then he pinned Oscar to the ground and the kitten finally gave in.

"You win!" He gasped with a laugh, as Montgomery let him up with a hearty and happy growl.

The old cat turned to look at the rest of them, and saw them all gaping at him. He shrugged a little and licked at the fur on his right front paw.

"What? I might be a little older, but I can still take on any one of you. I'll tell you this, too. I don't know what it is, but I haven't felt this healthy; this strong and exuberant, since I was Oscar's age. The difference is that now I have the know-how to take him down, along with the energy."

Sophie laughed and nudged the side of his head. "You're sure this isn't too much?"

He gave her a wink. "It's the best I've felt in years. Never better. Must be all this exercise we're getting."

"'Es the forest." Chippa replied, giving them all an impatient look. "We must go!" He turned and headed deeper into the wintery looking growth around them.

"Chippa!" Bailey whispered loudly.

Chippa glanced over his shoulder at the massive cat behind him. "What 'es 'et?"

"What are all these blue and green lights around us? Are those fairies?" Bailey asked excitedly as small clusters of softly glowing lights passed all throughout the trees around them. They hovered and flowed, sailing through the air.

Chippa waved his paw. "Not fairies. 'Thes 'es fireflies. Different colors. Les go." He hurried them all along again.

"They come in colors?" Bailey blinked in wonderment.

"Course they comes 'en colors! You comes 'en colors too, doesn't you?" Chippa answered without turning to look back.

"Well, none of us has any color right now." Oscar stated, looking with some disappointment at his paws, which gave off a soft bluish shine in the brightening moonlight. "So why are the fireflies colored?"

"They 'es part of the fairy realm. Not changing here. Fairies doesn't change here either." Chippa answered as he hustled along.

The symphony being played by the forest sounded with more volume than it had before. There was a little swing to Alice's step as she smiled and listened to it, watching the leaves and trees as they orchestrated the most beautiful melody she had ever heard and seen.

They finally came to a clearing where all of the trees at the perimeter stood tall and wide in a great circle, and within the clearing, everything had color just as it did outside of the White Song Forest.

The company stopped just at the inner edge of it, still within the forest growth. A crystal clear creek bubbled through the space, winding here and there, slipping over multi-colored stones and pebbles, and disappearing again at the other side of the round.

There were white vines growing on the trees where they stood. The vines grew the same all around the clearing; outward from the circle, along the ground, and up and around the trees, reaching out over the branches.

Alice knew that if she could fly above the forest and look down at it, she would see the vines stretching outward from the clearing like a star.

Dotted along the vines were white flowers just a little bigger than the palm of Alice's hand. Each flower had five petals; wide in their centers and tapered at the ends. They gleamed brightly, shining with a brilliance none of the cats or Alice could believe. Oscar leaned close to one.

"What *are* these?" He whispered as he sniffed at it.

Chippa smiled and reached out to touch one gently with the tip of his paw. "'Thes 'es a Star Flower. They 'es drinking 'en starlight and then 'flecting 'et out again. That's why they shines at night. They 'es giving off starlight they takes 'en."

The cats and Alice admired them, and Sophie purred. "I wish I could wear them. They're so beautiful. I love things that sparkle and shine."

"You mean you love things that make you sparkle and shine." Jynx gave Sophie and her diamond collar a narrow, sidelong glance.

Tao sat back and closed her eyes. "True beauty comes from within, and shines with the radiance of a thousand suns and moons."

Oscar looked from Tao to Alice. "Like our Alice! She shines that brightly. She's beautiful within."

Alice chuckled, reaching up to rub behind his ears.

"I'm standing in the stars!" Bailey grinned blissfully as he looked at the shining flower petals all around them on the ground, and in the trees and branches. "I'm in heaven!" He purred and wiggled a little.

"You must all stands 'en the bushes. Don't be seen. You 'es cats. You can do 'et. Hide!" Chippa waved both of his paws at them as he whispered.

They found places behind trees and bushes where they could still see what was going on. Each of them looked into the clearing where just about every firefly they had seen floating to the center of the forest seemed to have ended up.

In the middle of the clearing was the biggest tree that they had seen in the entire world of Corevé, and even in their own world, back home in London.

It was a natural wood color with medium tones, and it rose like a tower, spreading out far and wide at the top; filled with branches and silver leaves. Every bit of it was covered with Star Flower vines, making it glow like the full moon on a dark night.

The Star Flower vines on the tree weren't white; they were varying shades of green, but the Star Flowers glistened and shone with the same brilliant light as those in the white part of the forest.

Soft golden light glowed from within the tree, pouring through notches and cracks, and openings here and there, revealing that it was hollow; though far from empty.

Peering through the bigger openings, they could see several small beings floating about, the way that butterflies do, going from one place to another; wings aflutter, pausing a moment, and then going on again. They were illuminated with a warm light, like that of the flame on a candle.

Oscar gasped and leaned forward; his eyes wide as he stared hard. "Are those f-"

Chippa glared up at him and waved his paws frantically. "Shhh! You must be quiet! Go hide!"

Oscar ducked his head back down, but his silvery colored eyes stayed locked on the tree.

The music that the forest played grew a little louder, and the fairies began to stream out of the hollow tree; many of them dancing together and laughing as they twirled and drifted gracefully through the air.

Chippa took Alice's hand and walked with her into the inner edge of the circle where they could both be seen.

"'Thes 'es the Fairy Sway." Chippa watched with wide, curious eyes. "I 'es knowing about 'et, but I 'es never seeing 'et." He said quietly. He was just far enough inside the circle that all the color in his fur had returned.

Alice made herself look away from the Sway for just a moment as she turned her gaze to him. "Thank you for bringing me, Chippa. This is easily one of the most beautiful things I've ever seen. What a gift."

The fairy celebration was really getting under way. Trails of golden sparkles shimmered through the air, spiraling down from the branches of the tree and vanishing before they touched the ground. As the fairies danced through them, the sparkles shifted in undulating waves, cascading in lightfall. The fireflies in all of their colors, buzzed about the lower branches, and came down near the fairies as they danced.

The fairies wore petal gowns in multitudes of shades, shapes, and sizes, or silvery iridescent sheaths spun of silkworm thread that covered them to the middle of their thighs. Each fairy's wings were a different color, and Alice could see more colors than she knew existed. The loveliness of it was breathtaking to her.

Out of the twirling fairies that filled the sweet air, one rose away from the others, coming to the outer edge of the party. She was slightly larger than the rest, with a grand and flowing silver gown. Her hair shone like the light coming off of the Star Flowers, her eyes were periwinkle colored, her skin darker than the tree, and her wings were opalescent; showing many different colors as they moved.

She was grinning with delight, and in her hand she held a shining white twig. She directed it back and forth in careful and concise movements, dancing a little herself, as she did so.

Alice gazed up at the trees around them, noticing that all of their branches were swaying, and then she turned her eyes back to the biggest fairy. She leaned down close to Chippa and whispered. "Who is that?"

"'Es the Fairy Queen." He replied simply.

"Is she conducting the music and the forest?" Alice continued, fascinated with all of it.

"Yes." He answered, swinging his little body slightly to the rhythm.

"Are the trees… dancing?" Alice looked up at them as they moved in time to the sounds.

Chippa nodded. "Course they 'es. Everything 'en the world 'es alive. Trees, plants, animals. They live, and talk, and dance, just like anyone else. Just like clouds."

Chippa dipped his head back and forth with the music, and the tips of his ears that flopped forward bobbed along with the notes.

Alice grinned. "That makes perfect sense."

Sophie was entranced with the fairies, and she hadn't realized it, but she'd crept closer and closer to get a better look, and to try to be as near to them as she could. Her eyes moved from one fairy to the next with fascination, and her whiskers twitched. She edged forward more, and at last some of the fairies saw her, and flitted away instantly.

Sophie ducked her head down to try to hide behind a big white fern leaf, but the Fairy Queen had seen her, and turned to look straight at her.

Chippa saw the Fairy Queen's gaze and followed it, noticing that Sophie was too far out of the deep bushes. "Now you done 'et!" He grumbled at her.

Sophie hurried to Alice and stood behind her, trying to hide, though she couldn't possibly do it being the size of a full grown horse.

Alice bit at her lower lip as the Fairy Queen came toward them, floating through the air gracefully. She was the picture of elegance, stopping just before them and regarding them with a pleasant smile.

Sophie exhaled and stepped out from behind Alice, bowing so low that she touched her forehead to the mossy ground. She waited a long moment and then slowly raised her eyes to look up at the Fairy Queen.

The Fairy Queen nodded to her. Alice reached out and touched Sophie's shoulder reassuringly. Raising her wooden wand, the beautiful fairy extended it toward one of the dark green vines of Star Flowers from within the circle, and as she did, that part of the vine which was thick with the blooms, lifted off the big tree and rose in the air. She drew her wand in a circle, and the flowering vine entwined in midair until it formed a garland chain.

Using her wand again, the Fairy Queen directed the garland through the air and set it carefully around Sophie's neck. Drawing her breath in deeply, Sophie grinned and bowed her head again. "Thank you so much, it's the most exquisite gift I've ever received."

The Fairy Queen smiled. Chippa and Alice bowed to her, and the rest of the cats came forth and did the same.

"Welcome to Lyria." The Fairy Queen spoke. Her voice was as melodic as the sounds of the natural instruments being played around her. "Tell me why you are in my forest."

Alice's heart pounded faster than it ever had. She could scarcely believe that she was speaking with a fairy. Even if she was the largest of them, she still would have fit in Alice's hand and only stood at six or seven inches.

Alice sensed that it would be best to be truthful with the little being in front of her. She might have been subtle with Caraway, the Light House keeper, but she knew instinctively that it would be better for all of them if she was completely honest with the Fairy Queen.

"We're on a journey seeking the stolen Blue Fire Crystal. I was curious about the Fairy Sway, and Chippa offered to bring us." Alice answered with a wide smile.

The Fairy Queen nodded. "Yes, I do know about the journey. I'm glad you've come to see me." She raised her wand in the air again and drew another circle. As she did, a silver metal cord began to appear, trailing behind her wand. When it was completed, it was about one foot in diameter in the shape of a narrow ring. It shone as brightly as the full moon.

"This is a Mystic Ring. It is made of stardust and sealed with fairy light. It cannot be broken. If you find the crystal and return it to the sacred temple in Mari Village, place this ring around all of the stones. It will grow wider to encompass all four of them within it, and then it will protect them so that they can never be stolen again. You must keep it safe." She implored Alice and the cats earnestly.

Alice took the ring, and as she did so, she felt it vibrating slightly in her hand as though the energy in it was alive, and she remembered what Chippa had told them over and again about everything being alive. She looked at Marlowe who was standing right beside her.

"Will you carry this on your collar please, so that it will be safe and not get lost?"

The cat nodded. "I'd be honored to carry it." He looked to the Fairy Queen who was watching them. "I'll keep it safe." She gave him a smile, and Alice clipped the ring to his collar.

"Thank you for your help." Alice bowed to the Fairy Queen.

The Fairy Queen inclined her head, smiling sweetly. She looked at all of them, taking her time and regarding each of them in turn, then she flew to Montgomery and eyed his monocle with interest.

"What is your name, please?" Her voice wove perfectly into the music that still played on around them.

~ 155 ~

"Montgomery, your majesty." He answered a bit shyly.

She peered at the monocle set against his eye. "What is this strange looking piece that you wear?"

"It's… it's a monocle, your majesty. It was a gift from one of the Inklings. From Luto Mari." He answered, trying not to bumble his words.

"I like it. It makes you look quite distinguished." She grinned at him, and even though they were all white, his cheeks turned a faint shade of pink.

"Thank you, your majesty." He replied quietly.

"Why are we all white?" Oscar piped up, staring in fascination at the Fairy Queen. He saw Jynx give him a sharp look. "Uh… your majesty." He added quickly. Jynx gave him a nod.

"The moment you entered the White Song Forest, you came under the protection of the fairies. You aren't really changed; only shielded." She answered him. "You see that everything here in the center of our home is its natural color. Step closer into the circle."

He looked skeptically at her, but put his paw forward, and as his paw left the whiteness of the forest he was standing in and crossed over into the center of the clearing, the vibrant red and orange stripes that he'd changed into reappeared in the fur on his paw. The rest of him remained white. He stared, moving his paw in and out of the circle, watching it change back and forth from white to color.

Oscar frowned after a moment, and looked back up at the Fairy Queen. "But Alice didn't turn white." He stated defensively. "Why isn't she protected?"

"She is protected, but she is the Chosen One, and nothing here in this woods changes or affects her. She is safe while she is here, as are all of you. Evil cannot enter; only good. Evil perishes at the border of the forest. Anything good is protected." The Fairy Queen allayed his fears.

He moved back to sit beside Jynx and Tao.

Alice spoke up again. "We are trying to save our friend. He was taken by Quiri birds. Do you know where they might have taken him?"

A vibrant fire flashed in the Fairy Queen's eyes, and her voice grew sharp as she answered, seeming to echo off of the woods around them; reverberating even in their hearts.

"The Quiri birds are evil. They cannot come to Lyria, or even fly over it. They live in the dark woods beyond the far eastern border of the forest you are in now. Pass through the forest, and when you come to the edge of it, go around the side of the mountain and you will find the dark forest. Your friend is imprisoned there."

Before Alice could respond, another fairy flew up to the Fairy Queen and bowed low to her. He was dressed in the iridescent silvery tunic that many of the others wore. There was a quiver of arrows and a bow on his back, and he looked a little bigger and stronger than most of the other fairies that Alice and the cats could see.

"Your majesty," he began with a serious tone, "the northern edge of Lyria is under lightening fall, and a fire has started there. It's burning the trees."

Chippa moaned worriedly. "'Es the Blue Fire Crystal! Fire element 'es growing out of control!"

The Fairy Queen nodded. "It is indeed." She looked back at the warrior fairy. "Take all of the Protector

Squad in your command to the north, and if you need more help send a message. We'll be ready."

He bowed and zipped away instantly. She turned back to the group and Alice gave her a warm smile as she spoke to the little Queen.

"Thank you for your help and kindness. We've enjoyed being here, but I think it's time for us to go."

"Safe journey to you all." The Fairy Queen bid them farewell.

With one last pleasant look toward them, she turned and went back to the Fairy Sway, and the music began to change. The piano sounds of raindrops landing on water were joined by the sounds of raindrops touching on leaves and flowers, on the ground and on the trees. It changed the music, and Alice and her company turned and headed back the way that they had come.

Sophie glanced back and took it all in once more before she joined the rest of them; looking down at the glowing garland around her neck, and lifting her chin in pure joy.

CHAPTER NINE

THE UNEXPECTED

The rain fell everywhere, and Alice opened up her umbrella cane and walked beneath it. The cats went on their way, most of them using their tails to try to cover as much of themselves as they could.

Sophie noticed with astonishment that Montgomery was stepping lightly; his tail straight up in the air, almost prancing and dancing as he went along. He had a smile on his face that was turned up to the sky and the rain.

"Montgomery! What has gotten into you?" She asked curiously as she shook her head and laughed.

Chippa smiled and held his paws out, upward and open to the rain as he let the raindrops soak into him. "'Et's healing… Clears the mind. 'Liven's the senses. 'Et's nature connecting 'weth all of us and giving us what we needs."

Tao lifted her face to the rain, as did Oscar, and even Jynx. Alice closed her umbrella and tucked it back under her arm, enjoying the droplets of water that found her. Bailey stuck his tongue out and tried to catch raindrops on it; tasting them as they walked. Sophie let it sprinkle all over her coat. She even nudged a few leaves to bring down some extra drops.

All of their brilliant colors and patterns came back to their fur as they left the White Song Forest and entered the Green Forest. Not long after that, they reached the clearing beside the pond where they would be spending the night, and Alice sank onto her wide leaf bed. She set her bag down on the ground beside her, and Chippa guided a wide leaf over her to keep her warm and dry.

The rainclouds drifted away, and the night sky above them was clear, and endlessly deep. The cats began to stretch and yawn; some of them finding a place to sleep. Marlowe curled up at the side of Alice's leaf, and tucked his chin into his paws.

Oscar was still buzzing from all of the excitement of the day, and he wasn't interested in sleeping. He went to the edge of the pond and looked into it, sniffing at the water and the growth of grasses and flowers there.

He stared at the surface of the pond. "What are those shining lights in the water?" He asked as he tried to lean forward for a closer look.

Montgomery went to his side to see what he was talking about. Then he lifted his chin and looked up. "They're stars in the night sky, and they're being reflected in the pool below."

Oscar looked up and discovered that the night sky was flooded with countless stars of nearly every color in many sizes. "Wow…" He sighed as he tried to take it all in. "I've never seen anything like that." He said quietly and thoughtfully.

The stars above twinkled and danced just as much in the sky as they did in the water. Alice sighed and looked at him.

"Well my dear Oscar, you don't see them in London because there's something called light pollution. There are so many lights in the city that we are blinded by them, and we can't see the stars in the night sky. We used to live in the country where there was no light pollution because there weren't many electric lights, and we could see more stars, planets, and objects in the sky than anyone could ever count. It was quite a show every night, when it was clear and there were no clouds."

Montgomery gazed upward at the night heavens above them. "I remember that."

"So do I." Sophie added. "It was beautiful. Real diamonds… fire in the sky that blazed all night long."

"It was beautiful indeed." Tao agreed, and Bailey, Marlowe, and Jynx nodded as well.

Alice watched the kitten as he star-gazed. "I'll take you to the country someday Oscar, so that you can see it as well. In the meantime, we have this, and this might even be a little more incredible than what we had out away from the city. This looks like the whole universe right above our heads, sparkling and twinkling just for us!"

The sounds of the night surrounded them, but then out of the mix came a singularly haunting and strange song that sounded as if it was both far away, and yet very near to them. The cats all pricked up their ears and looked around. Alice leaned up on her leaf bed and listened.

Oscar moved close to the water's edge and sniffed. "I think… I think the singing is coming from…" He sniffed again and turned his head this way and that to listen, "from the pond!"

Chippa launched himself at Oscar and wrapped his little body around Oscar's tail as it hung to the ground. He held tightly to it and slowly began to slide down it like a fireman's pole, until he landed on the grass, where he dug his small feet in and yanked and pulled as hard as he could.

"Oscar no! 'Es not safe! No! You must…" He strained and tugged on the cat's tail with all his might to no avail, "get away…" he wriggled, and panted, and puffed, "from the pond!"

Marlowe was at the water's edge in an instant, giving Oscar a stern nudge. "Away now, Oscar. Get back from the edge. Chippa said it's not safe."

"But I-" He began, and then seeing Marlowe's unyielding eyes, he backed away and sat down just as Chippa let go of his tail and plopped down on his bottom, trying to catch his breath.

"What is that song?" Oscar asked, looking down at Chippa.

Chippa stretched his arms up in the air and rubbed the ends of his ears as he closed his eyes. "'Es a fresh water mermaid. She 'es singing to the stars. You has to stay on land. You 'es on land and she 'es singing, she 'well sing you to sleep. You 'es 'en the water and she 'es singing, she 'well sing you down to the depths of the pond, and you 'es drowning."

Oscar gulped. Chippa opened one eye and looked at him curiously. "You listen, she 'well sing each of you a 'defferent song. 'Defferent dreams for everyone." He wagged one paw at Oscar then. "But stay away from the water."

Oscar nodded and went to where Jynx was laying and watching him. He snuggled in beside her and she gave his head a nudge. Sophie and Montgomery curled up side by side, Tao slept on her own in a meditative position, Marlowe returned to sleep near Alice, and Bailey sprawled out on his back with his paws splayed out, and his head tilted back so far that his forehead was on the ground.

The trees around them gradually moved their branches inward, encircling the group closely. Jynx looked about warily and turned to Chippa. "Are you doing that?" She asked with a tone of suspicion.

He shook his head. "No. 'Esn't me. They 'es circling around on their own. Like a big hug. They 'es doing 'et because they wants to protect us."

Jynx gazed at the trees again in wonder, and then closed her eyes and purred as quietly as she could. Tao joined her purring, and it blended in with the hushing sounds of the breeze through the boughs of the trees, and the distant mermaid's song.

Chippa contemplated all of them and set his paws on his knees with a quiet sigh. "They's all sleeping and I'm waked up." He stood up and surveyed the campsite to be sure that everything was all right, and then he wandered off in search of things to eat, and see, and do.

Marlowe snapped awake, scanning their clearing. The sky was beginning to lighten; it was nearly morning. His attention shifted sharply to a snuffling sound on the other side of Alice. He stood up and saw Chippa sniffing the ground and running his paws over it. His ears were perked straight up, and he growled deep and low.

At the sound of Chippa's deep growl, all of the cats awoke and stared at him.

"What is it?" Jynx asked, going to his side immediately. The Inkling was searching the ground around Alice's bag.

"Chippa left to go find Tinder Root to eat while cats 'es sleeping. Chippa came back, and Chippa knows seashell compass 'es stolen!" His voice was razor sharp. The group was surprised; for the first time since they'd met him, he sounded dangerous.

Jynx looked up at Marlowe. "He's right. I can smell something too, but I've never smelled it before."

"That's not much to go on." Marlowe sighed. "Almost everything in Corevé is a new smell to us."

Oscar looked worried. "Chippa's speaking in third person again. This can't be good."

Alice awoke and sat up on her leaf bed. "What's going on?" She watched the cats as they all began smelling the air and the ground.

Bailey answered her. "Chippa thinks that the seashell compass was stolen while we slept."

Chippa grumbled and growled deeper with his nose to the ground on a scent-trail that led away from Alice's black bag. "Chippa knows the seashell compass 'es stolen!" He snapped.

She gasped and reached down for her bag. Yanking it up quickly, she rustled through it over and over again, and then finally set it on the ground and dropped her face into the palms of her hands.

"He's right. It's gone." She dropped her hands into her lap and looked up at her cats. "I can't believe this. How irresponsible of me to have left my bag on the ground like that. I should have had it up beside me the whole night. I promised to protect the shell compass, and all of you, and now look what's happened. I feel absolutely wretched about this!"

Chippa suddenly stood straight up, his eyes locked on something at a distance that none of them could see. In an instant he bounded off through the grass and around the pond. None of them had any idea that he could move as quickly as he did.

Tao stayed behind with Alice, sitting dutifully by her side as she worried over the lost compass. The rest of the cats followed Chippa swiftly, and when they caught up to him, they saw just in time that he had disappeared behind a short waterfall that fell from a wide stream leading into the pond.

Oscar took a few steps toward the edge of the pond and the side of the waterfall that was about two feet shorter than him. "Where did he go? Should we follow him?"

Marlowe's voice was serious. "No. We couldn't fit behind that waterfall anyway. We don't know where he's gone. We must wait here."

They didn't have to wait long. Chippa came rolling and tumbling out of the waterfall, splashing water all over the cats and the pond. He was wrestling with a diminutive figure in a mossy dark green tunic, who looked like a really big fairy. It was only a little smaller than Chippa, and it had wings of water.

Chippa growled louder than he had when he was sniffing the thief's trail out, and the little female he was tussling with was shrieking right back at him. They both had a tight grip on the seashell compass, and were kicking, and twisting, and pulling all at once.

Jynx launched forward, her growl rumbling like thunder. She hissed violently, arching her back and screaming as loud as she could. All of her hair went on end, and her tail bristled out into the size of a tree.

The little figure that Chippa was wrestling with cried out in horror and let go of the shell, falling backward on her bottom as she gawked up at Jynx in shock. She scooted herself backward with her hands and feet like a crab until she reached the water's edge, never taking her eyes off of the huge, angry black cat before her.

Chippa stood up in a huff and waved his paw in the air, causing a big wave to swell up from the pond and crash down over the little figure, carrying her back out onto the water. She shrieked again and pounded the surface of the pond with her fists, as she stood waist deep in it close to the waterfall.

Jynx lowered the front of her body to the ground and Chippa hopped up onto her shoulders. All of the cats gave the little female dirty looks and flips of their tails as they strode off.

Oscar looked up at Chippa, who was closely examining the compass, and whose face was still contorted with anger.

"What was that, Chippa?" He asked with a buzz of anticipation; the excitement of the chase and the fight still coursing through him.

Chippa didn't look away from the compass. "'Et was a vile water sprite! She 'es wanting to keep 'thes, thinking 'et's a trinket. Wants to play 'weth 'et. Wants to keep 'et. Thief water sprite!" He glared back over his shoulder calling out the insult toward the end of the pond far behind them. The water sprite was long gone. "Stealing 'et 'en the middle of the night, sneaking 'ento the sleeping place. Fights Chippa. Vile sprite!" He grumbled a bit more.

They reached Alice, and Jynx lowered her upper body to the ground once more so Chippa could get down easily. He waddled over to Alice and handed the seashell compass to her. "You 'es having 'et again. You 'es leading us."

"You're entrusting me with it again? Even after it was stolen?" She asked quietly.

He nodded to her. "'Es not Messus P's fault vile sprite stole 'et! Sprite was wicked! You 'es the Chosen One. You 'es the only one. Les go. We has to get 'Thes One."

She gave him a smile, feeling somehow redeemed, and stood, pulling her bag up onto her shoulder. She planted her hat on her head. "You mean Henderson?"

"Yes." He gave a nod and then knelt down in the soft grass as the group gathered around him. He drew his paw in a circle on the ground and a bright orange trail followed everywhere he traced, looking exactly like his footprints when he lit them up. He drew a map of the forest they were in, and the fairy lands at the center of it. On the opposite side of the forest, he drew a few mountains and put a big X in the foothills between them.

"'Thes 'es whole forest we 'es 'en now. Fairies 'en center, and fires 'es up north, so 'es fastest to go 'round the bottom, through Green Forest south of fairies, then we can go north again to base of mountains. That's where 'Thes One 'es. That's Quiri's there." He shuddered slightly in mentioning them.

With a plan set, they headed into the Green Forest, going around the southern end of it, just as Chippa had explained. It didn't take them long at all before they reached the edge of the woods. They saw meadows and fields to the east, and towering mountains and volcanoes to the north.

The volcanoes were spewing forth molten lava and smoke; much worse than they had been when the company had gotten out of their leaf boats after coming off of the river.

Chippa wrung his paws and shook his head; his eyes filled with worry and fear as he groaned quietly.

"'Thes 'es not good! 'Es the earth crystal. 'Es getting out of control!" He whimpered as a great cloud of black smoke poured from the tallest points of the volcanoes. It billowed upward and spread through the air, darkening the skies over the mountains.

Oscar grew uncertain. "Are we going up to those smoking mountains?"

"They're volcanoes darling," Alice answered kindly, "and yes, I believe that we are. Is that right Chippa?"

Chippa groaned again and pointed his paw toward the foothills. "'Thes 'es where the Fairy Queen 'es saying the Quiri birds 'es gone."

They peered at the foothills, and Tao stood up on her hind legs for a moment to get a better look. "I see them. I see some of the Quiri birds. They're circling over that dark forested area, set back into the foothills."

Chippa scowled. "That's 'et. That's where we has to go."

Alice took a deep breath and lifted her chin resolutely, leading the way. Montgomery leaned down close to the ground to let Chippa climb up onto him, and they continued after Alice; Marlowe at her side.

The emerald meadows faded into wide fields of darkened dirt, littered with stones, and the appearance of the trees began to change. They had been bright, full, and lively near the forest, but closer to the foothills, the trees grew tall and shadowy, with twisted old limbs bearing only random, weakened leaves here and there. It seemed they had traveled into a forest graveyard, and were walking amongst the skeletons of what used to live well.

All of them closed in nearer to each other, and to Alice, as they walked, keeping their eyes and ears at attention and on alert for any misstep. The haunted looking trees began to grow taller and thicker as they reached the foothills, and when they arrived at the edge, they all stopped and looked up with disheartened, incredulous dread.

The ominous sky above had darkened with smoke and soot from the volcanoes, and the sunlight had fallen far back behind it, unable to get through the somber black billows. The air was uncomfortably warm, and the vague stench of sulfur wafted about on what little breeze there was to be felt.

"Those are huge trees. Big, awful, scary trees." Bailey murmured in a low voice as he stared up at them. They were all dark wood; so dusky that they were nearly black, and they towered upward toward the sky, wide from their bases all the way to their branches.

The strangest thing about them was that they had grown upward wrapped around each other in a massive tangle. Every tree was connected very closely to several other trees, and the whole thing looked like a great shadowy maze that stretched as far to each side as they could see.

"There's no way that we can navigate into that thick growth. It's like a wall." Marlowe concluded, studying it all closely. "There's no way in."

Oscar looked at Chippa. "Can't you move the trees?"

Chippa pressed his paws together before him and shook his head. His voice was quiet. "I doesn't think I can move those trees. They 'es too big, too tight, too much close together."

"Then we go up into them." Montgomery stated flatly. "That's the way in. We go up into the branches and work our way through. We can do that. Those birds are probably nesting in the top branches anyway. It wouldn't do us any good to try to get into the trees at this level, if the birds are up at the top."

Alice sighed heavily. "How am I ever going to get up into those limbs to rescue Henderson?"

Sophie nudged her shoulder gently. "Ride me. Hold on to my diamond collar."

"Are you sure?" Alice asked in amazement. "I wouldn't be too much for you?"

Sophie smiled a little and shook her head. "Not at all. I'm bigger than any horse I've ever seen. You would be light as a feather on me."

Alice considered it, looking from Sophie back up to the dense labyrinth above them. She wasn't sure that she believed Sophie; cats and horses had very different bone structures, and weight wouldn't be distributed the same on a cat, but she knew there was no other choice. "All right then. I'll do it."

Sophie knelt as low as she could go, and Marlowe did his best to help Alice get onto Sophie's shoulders, and sit in the hollow between them. He gave Sophie a stern look as she stood back up.

"You be extremely careful with her." He admonished.

She gave him a subtle nod. "I'll be careful with her. I promise."

Oscar took Chippa onto his back, and the little Inkling and Alice both held on tight as the cats leapt up the sides of the wooden titans, clawing their way to the snarled jungle at the top.

When they were all safely up on the limbs, they shared a few glances and padded silently along the giant wooden coils, sniffing and listening as best they could, trying to find any hint or clue as to where Henderson might be.

Distant shrieks from the Quiri birds echoed throughout the dimly lit cavernous tree tops, and the cats bristled at the sound of them. They continued on silently, searching every place they passed. Twice they saw smaller Quiri birds flying through the tangles nearby, and the cats ducked into obscure crevices and holes. Their hearts pounded, and they all tried to control their breathing.

Alice slid her handkerchief from her bag, and dabbed at the beads of dew on her forehead. The further they went into the gloomy Quiri fortress, the more stifling and hotter the air became, and the less it moved. There was no breeze, and no fresh air to breathe. There were no sounds of a living forest; only the creaking and shifting of the old wood in the treetops far above them, where the branches were so tightly woven together that only dim light managed to filter through.

The scream of a Quiri bird not far off startled them, and Oscar slipped as he was navigating a difficult branch. Chippa cried out softly, leaning in and holding tighter to him, but Oscar regained his footing just as Montgomery reached for him. He gave a nod of thanks to the old cat, and they let out a silent breath of relief.

"That was close." Oscar sighed in a whisper.

A moment later, the Quiri bird they had heard swooped in on them; giant wings beating the air like deafening war drums, and the cats arched and reared back; their claws out as they hissed and growled menacingly. Chippa tumbled from Oscar's back as Oscar stood up, and he landed on a wide limb, scrambling about in terror.

The huge bird eyed the cats keenly, and they could see how crafty and smart its mind was. In a split second the bird stretched out one of its claws and closed it around Oscar. Oscar clawed and wriggled, trying to get free, but nothing he did was going to loosen him from the vice-grip of the Quiri bird.

"Oscar!" The cats and Alice cried out. Sophie had shared one glance with Marlowe, and leapt away from the fight, hiding herself and Alice in a crevice within the twisted limbs of the branches they had been walking along.

The other cats tried to get close to the Quiri bird to free Oscar, but every time they drew nearer to it, the bird squeezed its claw tighter, crushing the kitten. The bird shrieked loudly, and Marlowe glared furiously at it.

"It's calling out to the other birds! It's calling for them to come help capture us!" He cried out.

Chippa looked around and realized that there was no way out of the situation for any of them. He whined once with fear, but then he scurried over to the base of the tree limb that the bird was nearest to, and planted his paws on it, murmuring intently as he kept his eyes locked on the fowl.

New branches sprouted up instantly from the big limb beneath the Quiri, where he hovered and beat his wings against the air. The branches grew quickly, racing upward, thick with leaves and limbs, and in a flash, they formed a tight cage around the bird.

The Quiri bird didn't realize what was happening in time to make a getaway. It began to panic as the branches encircled its body, and it dropped Oscar from its claw, trying its best to get out of the cage. The branches continued to grow and enclose it, and moments later, the bird was completely engulfed. There was no sight of him, and only a muffled sound that could barely be heard.

Oscar landed silently on his feet and air gushed from him as he coughed and sputtered, getting his breath back. Jynx and Marlowe went right to him and made sure that he was all right.

"I wouldn't have made it if Chippa hadn't thought so fast and saved me." He said quietly as he gave the little Inkling a lick. Chippa closed one eye tightly and wiped at the spot behind his ear where Oscar had gotten him.

"Well done, Chippa." Montgomery said as Sophie reappeared with a relieved Alice. "Quite clever!"

"We need to get out of here. I don't know if the other birds heard their mate here, but we can't take the chance that they did, and that more of them may show up to attack us. Let's get out while we can and go find Henderson." Marlowe spoke in a low voice as he eyed all of them. He headed further into the mighty tangle of branches, and the company followed.

It felt to them that they had traveled a long while, but they finally reached the center of the Quiri

Fortress. There were bird's nests as big as the boat that they had sailed in from Mari Village.

They were thankful that the nests were empty of birds, though they were filled at the bottoms with long wide feathers in brilliant colors, and large bones that had been picked clean of any meat that had once been on them. Alice looked away and closed her eyes for a moment in fervent hope that Henderson was still alive.

At one end of the nests, just a little farther off from them, Alice saw crude cages made of the tree branches. She waved her handkerchief silently in the air to get their attention, and all the cats looked at her as she pointed toward the cove of wooded prison bars.

Moving together, they made their way to the cages. In that area, the branches had grown so close together that they had nearly formed a platform floor, though it was bumpy and gnarled in many places.

Alice leaned forward and whispered in Sophie's ear. "Please let me down here."

Sophie bowed low and Alice slid off of her carefully. When she had her footing, she reached up and stroked Sophie's face lovingly. "You did so very well my darling girl. Thank you." Sophie gave her a tender nudge.

Turning in place, Alice studied the cages. Some of them were built so that they were stacked; one on top of another, to great heights reaching thirty or forty feet. There were bigger enclosures that were single spaces from the floor to the ceiling at the top of the canopy, and Alice wondered what could be kept in such a big cage.

From where they had stopped at the mouth of the cavernous area, she saw that there were three dark canyons of cells that stretched out in a trident shape before them, and all three avenues were lined with cages. She knew that if Henderson was alive, he could be in any one of them.

Alice waved at the cats. "We're going to have to split up to find Henderson."

"I'm staying with you." Marlowe intoned immediately.

"We can meet back here." Alice instructed. Everyone agreed.

The individual prisons were every size imaginable, and there seemed to be more of them than anyone could even count. The cats separated into three groups, and each group made their way along the corridors of limbs and branches, searching everywhere for their lost butler.

Alice grasped tightly to a branch beside her for balance as she stepped along. She hadn't noticed that the branch she was holding onto was in fact part of the door of a massive cage. She did not see the creature that was lurking in the black shadows of the cage.

It watched her and suddenly lunged toward her, hitting its enormous head against the cage door, very near where Alice was gripping the branch.

The powerful thud startled her, and she gasped, staring in disbelief at what was looking back at her. It was the gigantic head of a blood red dragon. Its wide, golden eyes were steady on her, and she planted her hand on her heart as it pounded heavily in her chest.

The beast lowered its head cautiously; its gaze locked on her, and a soft cry sounded from its snout. She looked from the beast's eyes to its nose. The dragon's snout was wrapped tightly with a thick vine, so that it could not open its mouth at all.

"Oh dear... oh... my goodness. Just look at you." She bit at her lower lip as she raised her eyes to meet the dragon's gaze again. "You poor thing. How on earth did they manage to get you in here? Look at you! Trapped! Tied up. Why it's a disgrace!"

Marlowe, who was the only cat with her, hissed quietly, but didn't dare to growl. "Leave it be."

Alice ignored Marlowe. She was growing angrier by the minute as she considered the size of the animal before her, and how horrible it must be for it to be caged up as it had been. She could easily see from where she was that there wasn't room in the cage by half for the beast.

The cats appeared at her side from almost out of nowhere.

"Are you all right? I heard you..." Jynx began sniffing at her worriedly. Alice rubbed the cat's ear and gave her a gentle smile.

"I'm fine my dear, but this fellow isn't. I'm going to have to get him out." She narrowed her eyes at the cage and headed for the lock at the door.

It was then that the rest of the cats looked up and saw what it was that Alice intended to free.

"You're going to do *what?*" Sophie objected in panic.

The cats were horrified. The dragon looked at them and then at Alice and shook his head, grumbling and growling deep in his throat, but she held her hand up and spoke directly to him.

"Now calm down. You don't need to feel upset. I'm going to try to help you. I feel so sorry for you, trapped there in that cage like that. I can see from here that you have wings and it must be terrible to be stuck in there with no room to spread them and no way to fly." She spoke in a soothing voice and the dragon watched her closely.

"We're here to rescue a friend of ours. The Quiri birds captured him and stole him away from us, but I'm going to free you, too. You shouldn't be here. I don't want you to die, and I can see right now that if I leave you, you'll never make it out of here alive. You want to live, don't you?" She went on, going to the lock and eyeing it curiously.

Reaching into her purse she dug around in the depths of it, mumbling softly. "I know I have at least three or four in here… I never leave the house without… now where did I… AHA!!" She called out a bit too loudly, and then looked around with wide eyes.

"I've found one!" She whispered to the dragon as she brandished a knitting needle in her hand. "Just you wait. I'll have you out in a jiffy."

She poked the knitting needle into the lock on the cage and wriggled it about. Marlowe rushed to her and pressed himself against the door of the cage.

"You can't do this! What are you thinking? That's a dragon!"

Montgomery and Sophie were right behind her; both of them protesting as well. "This just won't work!" He said, and she nodded worriedly.

"You can't let a dragon loose!"

Oscar pushed his nose into one of the small openings of the cage. "Are you a real dragon? I thought dragons were only in stories! You're really big!"

Jynx closed her teeth hard on the nape of his neck and dragged him back away from the cage.

"Don't get so close to the dragon's cage! Do you want to be killed? Stay back here!" She snapped at him. He pouted and dropped his head a bit.

Alice turned to look at her cats. Bailey was staring up at the beast in the cage, too dumbfounded to speak. Tao was watching silently beside Bailey.

"I can't believe you! You all think I'd leave this poor thing locked up in here? Well I won't! He deserves to be free, just like everything else. I'm freeing him, and I don't want to hear another word about it!"

She looked back at the dragon who was watching all of them with a somewhat confused expression on his face.

"You're not going to kill us if I free you, are you? No. I know you won't. You'll behave yourself and fly off, and that will be that."

Alice dug at the lock and it finally clicked. She pulled it off, and everyone moved back as she worked to swing the door open.

The dragon hesitated for a moment, and everything was still between them for the space of a breath. No one moved, and everyone watched. He took a few hesitant steps forward, and when his head was out of the cage, he lowered it down to the ground beside Alice, and looked at her sadly.

"You need that wretched vine taken off of you, don't you. Well I'm sure I have something in my bag for that. Just you wait a moment."

She dug around again, as the cats began to back off a short distance, though Marlowe was right beside her with every single hair on his body standing on end. She pulled a pair of gardening shears from the bag and edged up close to the beast, reaching out gently to pat him.

"Now, I don't want you to worry. I won't do anything to hurt you. I'm only going to try to help you, and cut this vine off, so you behave yourself and be good. I'll have it off in no time." She smiled and gave him a nod, and the dragon just watched her.

Sophie whined softly. "Please don't!" She whispered as she stared in horror.

Alice went to work, carefully cutting at the thick vines until one by one they snapped and broke, falling away.

When the last one was gone, the dragon pushed himself up swiftly and turned his long neck back and forth, swaying almost like a great snake.

He opened his jaws as far as they would go and then pulled his great body from the cage, shaking out his legs and arms, opening and closing his claws, and unfurling his colossal wings. The sound of them opening up was like thunder crashing in a storm, and every one of the cats shrank back. Chippa, who had been standing beside Tao, holding tightly to her leg, fell over backward and fainted.

Alice held her breath and stared as the dragon, having stretched as much as he could in the cavern of the tree branches, swung his massive head low again, bringing it back down to Alice and looking directly at her.

He spoke, and his voice was powerful, deep, and low, coming from far within him.

"I am Diovalo, of the fire dragons of the northwest. You have saved me from this certain death, and I owe you a life debt. I will serve you until it is repaid. I am at your service."

Alice waved her hand lightly in the air. "Oh now don't you worry about that. It was nothing at all. You're free as a bird now... or... eh... free as a dragon, I suppose. So, no debt owed to me. I'm just glad that you're out and you'll be all right. You can be... on your... way... if you like."

She stammered at the end, feeling the intensity of his gaze seeping into the core of her. His wide, golden eyes told her that he had meant what he said.

"Dragons do not ever offer themselves as freely as I have." His low, smoky voice filled the air around them, reverberating through them.

Alice's heart beat swiftly, and she took a deep breath as she gazed at his unblinking eyes.

"You're more than welcome to come along with us, if you like. I'm not about to argue with a dragon. There's not really any sense in that, is there? No. Well then..."

She cleared her throat and looked away from him back at the cats. "Has anyone found Henderson?"

They shook their heads sadly, and stared silently at the titan behind Alice.

"Is this Henderson you speak of the friend that you seek?" Diovalo asked in the same deep, smoldering voice.

"Yes." Alice answered, turning back to him.

"He is a human, like you?" Diovalo confirmed.

"Yes." Alice replied, looking at him hopefully.

"He is at the end of this corridor." The giant beast turned with some difficulty, and narrowly made his way through the passage they were in until they came almost to the end of it; a distance from the cage that the dragon had been in.

There, in a small cage near the floor, was Henderson. He was sitting, curled with his knees drawn up by his shoulders; his eyes staring off into nothing. It was only a shell of him.

"Good gracious! Henderson! What have they done to you? OH! Poor dear!" Alice rushed to the cage and wrangled with the lock until it clicked. She yanked the door open. He blinked and raised his head, looking up at her and the cats in a daze.

"Can it be? Is it really you? I've imagined this moment so many times that this doesn't seem real. I... I must be dreaming again."

He shook his head and looked away. Alice reached her hands into the cage and locked them around his arm, practically dragging him out.

"You're not dreaming. Now come out of that wretched hole at once! We must get you out of there, and all of us out of this place before we're discovered." She began to dust his black suit off at the arms and he gaped at her in wonder.

"My heavens! It really is you!" He had barely uttered a word before all of the cats were pushing to get to him and nuzzle him.

"We're here, and we're so glad to see you!" Bailey cried out blissfully. "We do have to leave though. Those horrible Quiri birds might come at any time!"

Henderson shuddered and looked around sharply. "They're monstrous. We had better go immediately. You cannot imagine the terrors that they cause."

His jacket was a bit torn at one shoulder where the sharp talons of the bird that captured him had cut, and he looked a little worse for the wear, but he was all in one piece, and he was generally uninjured. Alice gave him a close going over and decided that he was fine to travel.

"Right then. Let's go. We're headed east by southeast, if I've read the compass correctly." Alice checked the seashell.

"I can carry all of you if you'd prefer to fly out of this prison." Diovalo suggested in his fathomless, bass voice.

Henderson was aghast. He babbled, and stared, and tried to speak, but no words came.

"Yes, thank you, that would be quite helpful!" Alice nodded happily.

Diovalo lowered himself as close as he could to the ground. Henderson somehow found his wits, and helped Alice climb onto the back of Diovalo's neck, just behind his enormous head.

The cats argued and fussed; especially Sophie, who threw a fit until it was suggested by Jynx that she should stay behind. They finally made their way with Chippa and Henderson, up onto Diovalo's back and into the hollow areas just behind both of his wings.

"It's a good thing I have such thick armor." The dragon said smoothly. "I can feel the claws of these cats digging into it." He chuckled softly, and it sounded like distant thunder rumbling.

"Now it is time to leave this dismal place." He stood firm and flared out his wings as much as he could. The noise crashed and echoed throughout the halls of cages and beyond.

With a booming and mighty roar, he swung his head from side to side, shooting a powerful arc of flames from his throat; directing it at every bit of wood around them.

Everything that the dragon fire touched disintegrated immediately. Alice held on firmly to him, stunned at what she saw before her.

The treetops and wooden walls around them fell away, and they found themselves looking up at the darkened sky, with a horizon of sunshine in the distance.

"No wonder they had your snout all tied up! You'd have destroyed their whole fortress!" She cried out in giddy amazement.

He pushed back on his thick legs, and launched himself into the air. His wings beat powerfully as they lifted off and began to fly.

The cats howled, and Henderson screamed. Chippa held on tighter than he ever had in his life; his eyes clenched shut.

Diovalo broke free of the trees of Quiri Fortress, and circled over it once; blasting it with dragon fire, and incinerating much of the area where they had been, though it wasn't even a quarter of the full dark woods. Then he soared higher into the air, away from the volcanoes and the Quiri birds who erupted out of their burning nests, screaming in rage. The dragon left them behind so quickly that they had faded to nothing in minutes.

Alice gave a last look over her shoulder at the smoking dark woods nestled into the foothills of the volcanoes. She felt triumph course through her. She had done it. She, and the cats, and Chippa, had not only gotten there and saved Henderson, but they had rescued a real living dragon, and she was flying right through the sky on him with her family.

Alice looked ahead, and with her bag on her shoulder and her umbrella cane hooked over one elbow, she punched her fist into the air as the other hand held tightly to her hat, pinning it to the top of her head.

"Woooo hooooooo!" She called out loudly, and she heard Diovalo laugh as he flew eastward to the meadows beyond the Green Forest.

Chapter Ten

Aridan

Even grown to the size of large horses, all seven cats, plus Henderson, did not take up much room on the back of the dark red dragon they were flying on.

Diovalo was gargantuan when he had stretched out to his full size, and opened his wings to their entire span. Half of the cats and Chippa were tucked into the hollowed out space behind one wing, while the rest of the cats and Henderson were huddled up together in the hollow behind the other wing. There was less wind there, and it was easier for them to hold on.

All of them were wide-eyed and silent, except for Chippa, who was curled into a ball and holding on with a death grip, refusing to look at anything.

Sophie wailed loudly, crying pitifully, without stopping, but most of her complaining was lost in the rush of the wind.

Diovalo flew them over patches of tall wavering trees, whose leaves shivered and danced in the wind, and sunny green meadows dotted about with flowers and bushes. He soared over streams and rivers, and at long last, he came to the end of the pastoral, picturesque emerald lands below.

Up ahead of them, Alice could see an endless stretch of badlands, where rock and sediment had formed impassable canyons and towering monoliths.

Nothing grew there, save for tiny scraggly tufts of desert sage. There was only a slight variation in the shades of brown and beige all throughout the landscape, all the way to the horizon.

The dragon circled over the last tired meadow, partly green and partly brown. It looked as though it were trying desperately to hold on to the better pastures just beyond to the west, rather than succumbing to the desolation of the badlands to the east. A small stream trickled along through the modest growth, and a thin stand of trees half-clothed in brittle leaves, stood so near to the water that they almost grew out of it.

Stretching his thick legs out, with the huge claws on his feet arced, Diovalo touched down gently onto the ground.

His passengers disembarked, and Sophie went straight behind the trees and threw up. Bailey stumbled around a few steps, and Tao laid down and went into meditation immediately.

Oscar hopped off of Diovalo with wide eyes and a ragged coat, and after a few moments of gathering himself, he went over to the dragon and looked him right in his big golden jeweled eyes.

"Can we go again? Can we please? I think I won't be scared this time! I can do it! I want to go again!" His orange and red striped fur was sticking out in every direction, as though he might have just come out of a hurricane.

"Now Oscar, we've flown enough for one day. We need to rest. It's been a very long day, and the night is coming. We'll see what comes tomorrow." Alice patted him sweetly and tried for a moment to comb through some of his fur before she waved her hand at it dismissively, and gave up.

Jynx was licking her paws and washing her ears when Sophie practically crawled past her. "Hey Soph, you've got a little bit of… something… around your chin and whiskers there. What is that, yesterday's lunch? You might want to tidy that up."

Sophie lurched, and glared half-heartedly at Jynx.

"Awe, you're still sick? Going to go throw up again? Poor princess. Dragon flights are first class. Didn't you know that? All that *speed*, and going *up* and *down*, and *left* and *right*; why that's just part of the fun." Jynx gave Sophie a half raised brow as Sophie dove for her spot behind the trees again.

Henderson was still up on top of Diovalo. "We've landed now, come on little one. Come along… it's time to get down."

"Not getting down! Not moving! Chippa 'es not even opening eyes!" Chippa's face was buried in his arms, muffling his answer. The little Inkling was still locked into position in the hollow behind the dragon's wing. He wasn't budging.

Henderson sighed. Reaching down, he gently closed his arms around Chippa and lifted him up off of the dragon's back. "Come on now. I've got you. No need to worry." He intoned softly.

"NO!" Chippa cried out, and then flung his arms around Henderson's neck so tightly that the man could barely breathe.

Henderson made his way down carefully from Diovalo's back, and when he was on the ground, he knelt down on it and bent over so that Chippa's feet could touch terra firma.

The moment Chippa felt the grass under his paws, he let go of Henderson's neck and flattened himself belly down on the ground, with his head turned to the side. "Chippa 'es never leaving 'thes spot. Never moving again. Chippa 'es staying right here."

Henderson held his hand to his throat and coughed a few times. He gave his head a little shake and stood up. Pulling his pocket watch from his vest, he gasped, blinking in surprise.

"Good heavens! It's long past time that Madam should have had her medication. I've got that." He pulled his bag from his shoulder, and opened it up, digging into it.

"You still have your bag?" Oscar asked, coming up to sniff at it and sit with Henderson.

Henderson looked up at him, slightly miffed. "Of course I still have it. Everything we need is in here. I may have lost my hat, but the bag never left my body."

"How do you know it's time for Alice to take her medication?" Oscar asked, trying to poke his nose closer to the bag.

Henderson took two medicine bottles from the bag, two teacups, two saucers, two packets of tea, a small bag of sweet biscuits, two teaspoons, and a few lumps of sugar. Lastly, he pulled out a small, metal kettle.

"I've got my pocket watch set on London time. That way I know when Madam should have her medication. That, and it keeps me somewhat grounded in this… strange place." He looked around miserably for a moment.

"I know that somewhere very far from here, it is time for tea in London. I know that across our great city and in homes and farms over the countryside, many of our countrymen are sitting down to have afternoon tea. It gives me some semblance of order and normalcy. I need that right now. After everything that I have been through, I can tell you... I am in *dire need* of a rather strong cup of tea."

Henderson went to the trees and broke off a few branches, stacking them clumsily in a little pile. Taking two sticks, he tried his best to rub them together to create a spark, and Diovalo watched him with considerable humor for a while before he spoke.

"It's Henderson, isn't it? May I help you? I come equipped to start fires." Diovalo chuckled, and the rumbling deep in him made them all look up in surprise.

Henderson nodded and backed far away from the little pile of wood he'd been working at. "Yes, yes... it's Henderson. I'd certainly appreciate that, thank you."

Diovalo gave a slight cough, and a short stream of fire shot from his snout, setting Henderson's wood pile ablaze in an instant. Diovalo lowered his head onto his front claw, and gave Henderson a small smile.

"Well! Well that's... that's ideal, really; isn't it! Brilliant!" Henderson stared at the blaze in surprise. "I'd better get water for tea."

He went to the stream and hesitated, looking back at Chippa before he dunked the kettle into it. "Chippa, is this water safe to drink?"

Chippa didn't move or even pick up his head to look at Henderson. "Yes." He muttered weakly.

Henderson filled the pot and went to work making afternoon tea for himself and Alice. "I'm sorry I have no treats for all of you cats. It's a miserable tea, isn't it?" He murmured dejectedly.

Alice smiled. "I think it's lovely. The cats are all right. Except perhaps Bailey, but he'll survive."

Bailey had been sitting near Henderson, watching him with a forlorn expression. "I miss afternoon tea." He said quietly.

Tao went to him and curled her tail around him momentarily, as she stepped past him toward the stream. "I'll get some fish for us, and you'll feel better then." She gave him a smile and went to the water's edge.

Henderson gave Alice her pills, and Marlowe, who was beside her where she sat on a large rock, finally seemed like he might start to relax, somewhat.

"Are we all here?" She asked, looking around at the cats.

"We're all here. Sophie's still retching behind the trees and bushes, but she's around." Jynx smiled pleasantly.

When everyone was seated around the fire, Chippa forced himself to belly crawl over to the cats and lay near the flames.

Alice sipped at her tea and gazed up at Diovalo, who had arced his body around all of them in a crescent shape.

"Diovalo, you may not realize it, but none of us has ever seen a real dragon before, except perhaps Chippa. There are no dragons where we're from. We didn't even know that dragons existed." Alice began conversationally.

"Chippa knew." Chippa said quietly as he stared at the flames, still lying on his belly with the side of his face pressed to the grass.

"Now that I can see you out here in the open and get a good look at you, I must tell you… you're absolutely magnificent. I've never seen anything quite so exotic and beautiful in my life!"

Alice and most of the cats admired him. Sophie was laying on her side with her eyes closed.

Diovalo would have fit comfortably in a professional football field in a stadium, he was so big. He stood on four legs; his back legs were thicker and slightly shorter than his front legs, though all of them were built of solid muscle. He had three forward toes and one rear toe on each claw at the end of his legs, and they were as nimble as fingers. His body was massive; round and heavy, with a long neck, and a long tail that ended in the shape of a sharp spade. If he had driven his tail down into the ground, it would have split the ground as far down as he pushed.

His head was wide at the sides and his round, golden jeweled eyes were set on either side of it. His snout reached almost to a point, and some of his fangs at the front of his mouth extended past his fiery red skin.

He was covered in thick scales that were blood red at the top of his body along his spine, turning a lighter red and fading into orange around his sides and toward his belly. His wide, round belly was as golden as his eyes.

The dragon gave Alice a sleepy sort of nod. "I am beautiful, even among other dragons." Diovalo told her truthfully.

She gazed at him in fascination. "Tell us about yourself and your life please. We know nothing whatsoever of you."

He lifted his head and looked back at her. "You have saved my life; I will indulge you."

He began as he shifted his eyes to the horizon. His deep, smoldering voice sounded around them, and it seemed to the others that he was actually looking back into the past, as his gaze took in nothing before him or around him, but rather focused on a distance that they could not fathom.

"I come from Siang. It is a land which lies northwest of where we are now. Directly north of Mari Village, though at quite a long distance. There are different kinds of dragons; Sea Dragons that live in the sea and who go surging through waves, and Earth Dragons that reside in the ground in vast winding tunnels, and great subterranean lairs.

Then, there are Fire Dragons which live above ground in a very special place almost impossible to get to. I am a Fire Dragon. We dragons have mostly stayed in Siang where the low mountains are." A dark expression came over his countenance, and his voice sharpened somewhat.

"We all live free, or at least we did. There is an evil sorceress who has been capturing the Fire Dragons, and no one knows why. No one knows anything about her. She has managed to capture most of my kind. I eluded her for a while, but then she found me and used her dark magic to subdue and restrain me. I was eventually captured as well."

Diovalo narrowed his eyes and stopped speaking for a moment, but no one who was listening said a word. Sophie finally opened her eyes and stared up at him, taking in everything he said.

"She has a fortress at the top of Mount Jaiath, the biggest of the peaks in the Ring of Fire, which is to say the region of volcanoes here. She imprisoned me in a cage near there. I found a way to break out of it, but when I did, I knew that I could not return to Siang, for she would certainly capture me there again, so I flew south. I slept one night in a big cave, and a few Quiri birds came in, sacrificing themselves. They knew I'd eat them, and I did. There is a toxin in Quiri birds that I did not know about. Eating them filled me with it, and I lost consciousness. When I awoke, I found myself in the cage that you rescued me from. They were going to return me to the evil sorceress."

He looked at Alice then. "You saved my life; not from the Quiri, but from the wicked one in the northeast who is determined to enslave me."

Alice smiled and folded her hands together, her cheeks warming slightly as she blushed, and looked back up at him. "Well, you're here now, and you're safe with us. At least, as safe as we can keep you. I'd like to say that it wasn't anything at all to help you, and I was certainly glad to do it, but I can see that it was important indeed. You may call me Alice."

Henderson scoffed and looked sharply from her to Diovalo. "Madam! I hardly think that's-" He began, but Diovalo lowered his head and brought it close to both of them, eyeing Henderson coolly for a moment before he turned his hypnotic gaze to Alice.

Henderson clamped his jaw and pressed his lips together in a tight, thin line. Chippa giggled at him, covering his mouth with his paws as he looked at the three of them.

"Alice, then. You have my earnest gratitude." Diovalo spoke quietly.

She knew that it was something that he did not do easily; serving them, letting them all ride on him, and staying with them, but she could see that he was dedicated to it, and she refused to shame him by making slight of what he felt he owed to her.

"You are welcome, and we are glad to have you here. Thank you for taking us away from the Quiri." She beamed at him, and reached over to pat his snout.

Alice spent the night sleeping against Marlowe, who curled around her, and Henderson slept leaning on Bailey, who insisted on it. All of them were encircled by Diovalo, who slept with his snout to his tail. Chippa didn't sleep, but rather went out foraging for things to eat with dashed hopes of finding any Flame Trees for Tinder Root.

When morning's first light was new, Henderson made tea again, and Alice checked the seashell compass. It was still directing them east by southeast.

"Where are we going today?" Diovalo asked Alice as he watched her reading the compass.

"I'm afraid it's going to be a long journey. We're headed out over the badlands there." She indicated the barren earth immediately to the east of them. Her attention turned skyward, and she frowned.

"It also looks as if it might not be an easy ride. Those gathering clouds are rather dark and menacing." She turned her head and saw that the impending storm seemed to reach as far around them as she could see.

Chippa was standing at her feet. He knit his fluffy eyebrows. "'Es the cloud kingdom. 'Es going out of control because elements 'es all wrong." He shook his head as his big, black eyes took in the view of the sky. "'Es going to keep getting worse." His voice conveyed the enormity of his sorrow. His heart was breaking when he spoke. "We has to 'fex 'thes soon."

"We'll fix it, Chippa. Don't you fret. We'll fix it all right." Alice reassured him, reaching down to rub his back a little.

Oscar wound himself around Diovalo's front legs, weaving in a figure eight. "May I please ride up front this time? On your neck? I won't fall off. I'll hold on tight. I want to see everything up ahead. I couldn't see much from where we were behind your wings. Is that okay? Can I ride up on your neck please?"

Diovalo looked down and tried to take a few steps to move away from the large kitten, but it seemed that everywhere he tried to place his claw, Oscar was too close. The dragon could not find sure footing, and finally stood up on his back legs.

"Little one, you cannot get so close to my claws! If I mistakenly step on you, I'll crush you. You must stay beside me or behind me, but not in front of me, and not between my legs or near my claws." His voice was stern, but not too sharp.

Jynx was there in a flash. "Oscar, get out from beneath his feet. That's not a safe place for you. I know you like him, and I know you want to be friends with him, but you need to keep a distance. He's much bigger than you are. Now come away from there."

Oscar dropped his head and padded over to Jynx, raising his eyes to meet hers. "I just wanted to ask him about riding on his neck where Alice was yesterday."

"I know what you wanted. You're not doing it. Alice will probably be there again today. She needs to see where we're going, and you need to stay back behind his wing with me and the others where it's safer. I'm not going to have you falling off of a dragon and plummeting to the ground because you were too curious about something. Who knows if you'd land on your feet. Now get up behind his wing with the rest of us." She frowned at him.

"And I love you." She added in a softer voice.

His dejected pout brightened. "I love you too, Jynx." He smiled as he headed for the dragon's wings.

Alice rode on Diovalo's neck, just behind the thick shield around the crown of his head, where she had been the day before. They flew for a long while over the badlands. The ground seemed gloomy, and the grim and foreboding clouds that grew heavier just above them diminished their spirits somewhat.

The air was thick with moisture, to the point of being oppressive, and though there was constant wind, it did nothing to alleviate the nearly stifling pressure they found themselves in.

Sophie buried herself into the deepest part of the hollow of one of Diovalo's wings, and Chippa was tucked reluctantly in the hollow of the other wing, almost underneath Bailey. After a long and silent ride, they finally descended back to the ground.

They had reached the farthest end of the badlands, and before them spanned an endless barren desert. Great sand dunes swept high out of deep valleys, shifting themselves and moving upward to the sky.

All that could be seen in any direction, besides the badlands behind them, were the rolling and vaulted titans of drifting sand before them.

The whole company was tired, and everyone slipped down off of the dragon and stood on the ground, stretching and taking in what lay ahead.

Chippa didn't hug the ground as he had the night before, but he did stay very close to Bailey as the fat pink cat plopped down on the ground staring in dismay at the desert.

"What is the compass telling you, Alice?" Diovalo asked, watching her as she pulled it out to read it.

She considered it carefully. "We still need to go southeast." She said, lifting her head and looking out over the dunes. "That way."

Diovalo sighed, and it sounded like a rushing gale of wind. "I cannot go with you. Dragons cannot cross the desert. The sands are inhabited by giant desert snakes, and those snakes kill dragons. It's one of the few things in this world that can kill a dragon. They're as fast as lightening, and if I am detected, there's almost no chance that I'd make it out alive. All of you would be killed with me as casualties, though you wouldn't be in any danger of an attack without me."

He moved his head very close to her and lowered his voice so much that she was certain she was the only one who could hear him.

"I will wait for you here. It will be safer for you this way, but I owe you a life debt, and for that reason, there is a bond between you and me."

He reached his front claw up to one of the scales underneath his jaw, where his head and neck met. He dug carefully beneath the scale, and produced a small glass bottle. The dragon set it in Alice's open hand, and she stared at it. It was very warm to the touch.

The container was made of old glass; older than she had ever seen. It was shaped in a sphere, though there was a small neck at the top of it. It was capped off with a cork, and around the bottle was a thin maze of a strange looking chain that covered the rounded part of it, as well as the cork. She could see a thick, dark red substance inside of it. Alice tilted the bottle one way and then another, and saw that the substance moved slowly back and forth.

"What is this?" She asked, looking back up at him.

"That is my blood. It is a precious gift; far more than you could imagine. This will bind us irrevocably. Wherever you may be, if you need me, you have only to hold that and call out to me, and I can come to you. I can find you, no matter where you are."

His eyes narrowed. "I am sorry. I wish that I could go with you over the desert, but I cannot risk all of our lives for the sake of the crossing. My life is still yours, and it will be until I have repaid you. Be safe, my friend. I'll be waiting here for you." He spoke in earnest. She gave him a nod and slipped the priceless bottle into her bag, zipping its pocket closed.

"I'll be back for you. You're a good one, Diovalo. Very good. I'm so lucky and glad that I met you." She told him with a smile as she reached her hand to his snout and gave it a gentle rub. "Hide away in the edge of the badlands there. I don't want you too close to the desert snakes."

He agreed, and said goodbye to the cats and Henderson, before walking to a nearby canyon and vanishing into it.

"Where's he going?" Oscar asked worriedly. "I thought he was our dragon! I thought he was coming with us!"

Alice rubbed Oscar's ear. "He can't come with us from this point forward, but we will come back for him, because he is our dragon. Now, let's get everyone together, and get going. It looks like we have a desert to cross."

None of them looked forward to trekking over sand dunes, but with Alice and Marlowe in the lead, that is exactly what they did. Slowly and carefully, they made their way step by step, plodding along over the deep sand.

Alice held onto Marlowe's coat, and he helped her navigate the first big dune. They took it at a sidelong angle, knowing that it would take longer to get to the top of it, but hoping that traveling at a gradual angle, rather than a steep and direct one, might make it easier on all of them, especially Alice.

After what felt to them like an eternity, they reached the top of the dune; a sharp ridge that snaked along for a good distance before it dropped down into a chasm.

They were able to see for a long way off, and as far as the horizon, it was nothing but sand dunes and ravines stretching out forever.

"We're never going to make it! And all that sand is going to get into my beautiful fur! It's going to make it dirty and heavy! You know, I just had my paw-dicure right before we left London, and my feet are simply *ruined*!" Sophie sat down, moaning plaintively.

Alice bit at her lower lip. She knew that Sophie was right about more than her fur and her feet. Alice might be healthy and strong for her age, but she had no delusions that she would be able to make it across the vast desert that spanned out before them.

"We're already this far, Sophie. We've got to try." Alice replied quietly. She reached her hand into Marlowe's fur, closing her fingers around it. "Well, shall we-"

Alice's words were stripped from her tongue before she could breathe them into existence. The ground began to shake and crack, as a loud crashing sound filled the air, and all of them cried out as they lost their balance and fell, tumbling down the far side of the dune that they had just climbed.

Over and over they rolled, down the steep desert wall; arms, legs, tails, paws, and fur flying as sand sprayed everywhere. Growls, cries, and screams sounded out, and they thumped and bumped all the way to the bottom of the abyss in the shadow of the dune.

The ground shook hard, and trembled still, and all of them tried to hold tightly to it, hoping for some kind of balance.

After one long last rumble, the ground quieted and stilled. All of the company were flat out in the sand, panting and looking around worriedly.

"Are you all right? Everyone here? No one hurt?" Alice cried out as she tried to search out the cats, Henderson, and Chippa.

"I 'es okay." Chippa answered miserably, as he spat sand out of his mouth and shook it off of his tail feathers and fur. He sat up and focused on the others.

"I'm filthy!" Sophie pouted.

"We're okay." Marlowe replied, getting up. Bailey was a bit further away, and Oscar was nearer to him than to the group.

"Henderson? Are you alive?" Montgomery asked, giving his coat a shake.

"I'm all right. Just tossed a bit." Henderson managed to groan as he pushed himself up from the sand.

Alice blew grains from her mouth and wiped at her face. "Oh! This is awful! If I wanted sand in my teeth I'd go to the beach!"

"Let me guess." Jynx intoned dryly as she turned her gaze to Chippa. "The earth crystal is out of sorts?"

Chippa nodded and buried his face in his paws. "Yes! Yes, 'et 'es the earth crystal. We 'es 'en so much trouble 'ef we 'esn't finding the Blue Fire Crystal soon! Everything 'well break!" He began to sniffle and weep into his paws.

Tao went to him and nudged him, rubbing her head against his, gently. "We'll find it, Chippa. We'll find it soon. Draw up the courage in yourself, and if you cannot, then seek courage in all of us, and in the knowledge that we have come so very far already. We will get to it, and we'll return it to Mari Village. Have faith, little one."

Chippa sighed and snuffled a little, and then wiped the tears from his face onto Tao's leg. She only watched him and said nothing more. He finally stood up and gazed about.

"That was 'en earthquake, but I doesn't see cracks. We must be careful where we 'es going." He went to Alice and reached his hand up to her pocket, digging into it. She waited as he found a ginger sweet, and stuffed it into his mouth. His saddened and worried look lightened some as he chewed on the candy.

The cats, Alice, and Henderson all gathered together and dusted themselves off. Bailey looked off toward the direction of the next dune and groaned loudly.

"Oh no... no... what is that?" He asked in a pained voice, obviously not wanting to really know the answer. They all turned to look at what had caught his attention.

A huge cloud of dust and sand swirled wildly over the dunes, going up and down, and though it was moving erratically, it was definitely headed straight for them at an alarming speed. The closer it got to them, the bigger it seemed to grow.

"It's a tornado!" Henderson cried out, and he dropped to his knees, burying his head in his arms.

The rest of them panicked and turned their faces downward, closing their eyes. Alice pushed her face in Marlow's fur, and all of them huddled together as closely as they could.

The sheer scream of the winds around it was deafening; sounding like a freight train headed right at them. Just as it was about to reach them, the towering funnel of blasting winds and sand quieted, and the dust and sand settled.

They all hesitated a moment, and then raised their heads and looked at where the whirling cloud had been. It was gone, save for a small puff of swirling grains that wound around a short, fat little man with sand colored skin.

He stepped out of the sand cloud, and it vanished. He was standing on nothing but air, a few feet above the ground.

The small man was bare chested, wearing only a short, cropped satin vest that matched a flowing pair of satin bohemian harem pants, belted around with a thick sash of the same exquisite material.

On his head he wore a deep blue turban, and at the center of it, a great ruby sparkled and shone. There were big golden hoop earrings in his ears, and wide golden bands encircling his wrists.

He crossed his big arms over his chest, and regarded them all with a stoic expression on his chubby face. The man twitched the thick, black moustache that covered his upper lip and drooped down past his round chin.

"Who is that?" Oscar asked wide-eyed, as his tail fluffed out defensively.

Tao frowned and peered closely at the being. "I believe that is a djinn, my young one. I did not know they truly existed. I believed them to be a fable, but I should have realized that at the heart of every fable or lie, there is a seed of truth."

"What's a djinn?" Oscar continued, keeping his eyes on the exotic, unusual little man.

"It's a desert genie." Tao answered quietly.

Chippa growled low and deep. "'Es not good." He grumbled.

"I am Mendax!" The little man announced with a booming voice. Everyone stared at him, except Chippa who continued to growl as he glared at him.

"What are you doing in my desert kingdom of Aridan?" He demanded.

Something deep inside of Alice snapped at that moment. She had had it. After everything they had been through, the last thing she wanted to do was answer to some strange little desert man about her business.

She marched right to him and planted her umbrella cane firmly in the sand, making it sink down a few inches.

Looking directly at Mendax, she reached her hand up, straightened her tattered hat, and lifted her chin resolutely.

"We are on a quest to find a stolen crystal, if you must know, and that is no concern of yours." She didn't want to sound rude, but she was completely out of patience.

Mendax narrowed his beady black eyes and considered what she had said to him. "What crystal?" He asked curiously, looking with great suspicion as though he already knew.

"The Blue Fire Crystal that was stolen from Mari Village. We must go this way and cross your lands. It is east of here, and we must get it back." She stated firmly without hesitation. "If we do not get it back, this whole world will destroy itself!"

He peered at her. "The only thing east of here is the high desert."

"Well then, that's precisely where we're going." Alice announced flatly.

Mendax continued to gaze at her, considering what she had told him as he lifted his hand to his moustache and pulled gently on one end of it in deep thought.

"I shall take you there, then."

Before any of them could respond, he opened his arms and drew his hands in a circle before him. All at once, the company found themselves in the center of a spiraling cloud of sand, being taken up in a gust of wind so strong that every one of them was airborne.

Everyone but Mendax cried out in terror. Alice clamped her hat to her head with one hand while the other hand flailed about, and her legs stretched out behind her.

Henderson had a hold of Bailey's tail as he flew, and Bailey's four paws were spread-eagle outward. Sophie clawed at the air to no avail, and the rest of them tumbled and turned, as the air and sand whipped around them.

They were all flying in the middle of it, but it was like centrifugal force, and none of the sand touched them. It was a vacuum in the funnel, and no sound they made could be heard; every yell and cry was ripped from their mouths the moment it was released.

Chippa clung to Montgomery's leg with both of his arms and legs wrapped around tightly, as he buried his face in the old cat's glittering sea blue and green patchwork circled fur.

As they had lifted off of the ground, they could see through the wide opening in the bottom of the funnel cloud that there was another earthquake happening.

The sand shifted and the ground shook, and a moment later it split wide open; the earth had broken in two, leaving a seemingly bottomless abyss right where they had been only a minute before.

Mendax watched it, then looked at all of them reeling around him, and he threw his turbaned head back and let out a roaring laugh that somehow echoed throughout the funnel, though no other sound was heard over the rush of winds.

The spinning dust cloud took off. It zigged and zagged over the dunes, sweeping up and over them and then down again as if it was riding on waves in the ocean.

There was no illumination in the center of it, only a dimness allowed by the light being pulled in at the top of the funnel and reflecting through the bottom of it.

There was no way for any of them to know how much time had passed between the moment that Mendax had swooped them all up in his cloud, and the moment that he set them all down on the hard, flat, rocky surface where he finally landed.

CHAPTER ELEVEN

THE ILLUSIONARY PALACE

The sand and wind fell away, just as it had when Mendax had arrived at the base of the dune when they met him, but all of the cats, Henderson, and Alice, did not step lightly through the air the way that Mendax had. They all dropped to the ground in heaps. Mendax roared with laughter again.

Groaning and moaning, they pushed themselves to their feet. Oscar tried to stand too soon and stumbled sideways from dizziness; falling over again. Bailey looked back at his tail, where Henderson had just let go. Henderson closed his eyes and made himself sit up.

Montgomery nudged Chippa, who was still holding tight to the cat's leg with his eyes closed. "We're out of it, little Inkling." He murmured.

Chippa shuddered and slowly opened his eyes, looking around miserably. "When Chippa goes home, Chippa 'es never flying again."

"That goes for me as well." Montgomery agreed.

Alice sat up and dusted herself off, straightening her coat, and trying once more to tidy her hat on her head. "Are we all here? Everyone all right?" She asked for the second time since they'd entered the desert.

Everyone answered, and she sighed with relief and turned to look at Mendax, who was watching them with great mirth.

The wind around them blew hard and strong, and Alice narrowed her eyes at the desert genie. "Are you doing that with the wind?"

He shook his head, and his smile faded. "No, I am not."

Chippa tried to stand up and immediately fell onto his bottom. "No, 'es the air crystal. 'Es getting out of control." He grumbled tiredly.

"We have traveled for a day and a night. You are at my borderlands. This is the high desert." Mendax told them seriously. "This is where I leave you."

Alice stood up fully and examined the area. She felt stable again, and she had never been more relieved to be on solid ground. There was one last, great sand dune that connected to where they were, and where they were stole her breath right out of her.

The company stood on a solid rock plateau that connected to the highest end of the last dune. On the other side of the plateau, not far from them, the solid rock ended in a sheer cliff that plummeted straight down several thousand feet to the floor of the desert.

None of them dared to get too near the edge of the cliff, especially with the wind whipping around as it was, tugging and tearing at them.

"I do not know where the crystal is, but I do know that there is something very different here in the high desert than has ever been seen here before. Something is… wrong. For a short time now, no living thing will come here. Everything that once lived here has fled and vanished. This place is nothing more than an empty shell now." Mendax noted soberly.

Alice's heart picked up its pace, and she wanted to ask the djinn a hundred questions, but he waved his hand and crossed his arms over his chest. Sand and dust began to swirl around him again, and a moment later his twister was spiraling out over the dunes once more, vanishing into the distance.

"Oh! How horrid!" Sophie gasped, looking down at her fur as she stood up. "I'm a wreck! I've never been such a mess!"

"You've never looked better." Jynx intoned evenly as she shook sand from herself.

Sophie's long silver and lavender fur was tangled and bushed out in every direction; much like what Oscar's was most of the time. She wept and wailed softly as she tried to get it all back into place. Montgomery went to her and helped her groom.

"At least your Star Flower garland is just fine. Nothing happened to that. Look, it's even glowing still." Montgomery comforted, giving her a nudge. She smiled at him gratefully.

Bailey moaned as he stood up. "I'm so sick that I may never eat again." Henderson blanched in surprise, but said nothing.

Alice dug into her bag and pulled out the seashell compass, giving it a close look. "We go east." She said with as much determination as she could muster.

Looking back at her family, she shrugged a little. "If I've figured it right, we still have two days left to get the crystal returned before the full moon. Look at it this way. We got across the desert safely, and in much better time than we'd ever have made it if we'd walked."

"*If* we'd have made it. The ground would have swallowed us right there if that djinn hadn't picked us up." Montgomery sighed somberly.

"Mendax 'es bad." Chippa grumbled as he reached his paws up and combed his small fingers through the fur on his ears, pushing out the grains of dust and sand.

"Well, whether he's good or bad, he brought us here, and if I'm reading this compass right, I think we're getting closer to the crystal. So off we go." Alice urged them on. She began walking, and they followed her in line.

Except for the wind that howled all around them, pushing and pulling at them, there was no other sound. They did not speak to each other. They only walked along in silence; all of them wary, all of them watching. Chippa rode on Oscar's back, and held on to the orange and red striped fur that was much more on end than usual.

Tension gripped them, and anxiety burned their hearts and minds. Their journey had become much more difficult than they had imagined it would be.

The wind continued to blast them without cessation. The rock plateau they traveled across was mostly even, though not smooth, and it went on and on; emptiness as far as they could see.

There was nothing but grey and black mottled stone beneath their feet, and heavy, grim clouds fattening overhead and filling every part of the sky. The wind rushed wildly all over the plateau, whipping against it brutally.

Alice studied the compass, glancing down at it every once in a while to be certain that they were all going in the right direction. She pressed her lips together in a thoughtful line now and then, wondering how far they would have to go.

The pearl in the compass had been at the inner edge of the shell for the whole journey, pointing a far distance away, but it had begun to move somewhat, going back from the edge toward the center slightly. It made Alice wonder if the crystal was much nearer to them than it had been before.

After a long while, Montgomery stopped, and four of the cats and Henderson stopped behind him.

"Alice!" He called out into the howling wind, and the cats in front of him called to her until, through their chain, his message reached her, and she turned around. She walked back to him, and everyone crowded in a circle about them.

"What is it my dear?" She asked, reaching her free hand up to pet him. Her other hand clamped her hat down to her head.

He narrowed his eyes and gazed over her shoulder. "I saw something a moment ago. It was a flash of light."

Alice leaned closer to Montgomery.

"Where was the light?" She asked loudly.

He lifted his chin, pointing his nose a short distance from them. "Just there, not far in front of us."

Alice opened the compass and looked at it again. "I think we're very close now! Perhaps it was something!" Hope began to course through her, and the weariness of the journey dissipated as she realized that they might very well be able to get to the Blue Fire Crystal.

Oscar piped up, and she could hear the same optimism in his voice that she felt. "Maybe it was light reflecting off of the crystal! Maybe it's out here on the rocks!"

"That's absolutely ridiculous, Oscar." Sophie snapped. "Why would anyone steal it only to leave it out here on the rocks?"

"Because no one would ever walk all the way out here in the middle of nowhere to get it. It seems smart to me to hide it in plain sight." Oscar shot back just as Jynx was opening her mouth. She gave the kitten a bemused smile, which played at the corner of her mouth as she closed it.

"Well, let's look for more light! Maybe we'll be lucky and see it again." Alice redirected their focus, rubbing the side of Montgomery's cheek.

They peered around, searching for any sign, but they didn't have to look for long. Light began shimmering in many places before them, and at first they were confused by it, but then as shape began to gradually form beneath the light, they realized that they were looking at a reflective wall; almost like a mirror. Many more appeared, connected to others, and moment by passing moment, a great building emanated out of nowhere, like a mirage coming to life.

It was octagonal shaped, and each mirror-like wall was a dark amber color, reflecting the desert around it and the gathering clouds in the sky above.

The high and wide walls were each connected by dark gray stone pillars that came up from the rocky plateau and were topped off with turrets that had pointed roofs.

The walls stretched upward, flat and sheer, all of them leaning inward at a slight angle so that the roof of the structure was smaller than the bottom.

At the pinnacle of the structure was another octagonal shaped piece, but it was made of dark wood and had the appearance of a large lookout, or central guard tower. There was a narrow opening all the way around the upper half of it. It was capped off with a pointed roof that sloped downward, reaching out over the edge of the walls it covered.

"Can you see anything inside of that tower at the top?" Alice asked the cats.

"Tao has the best eyesight." Jynx remarked, looking at her.

Tao shook her head. "No, I can't see anything. It's an open air space and if anyone was there, we might be able to see them, but I don't see anyone or anything."

On the wall just to the right of them, a massive arched double door appeared. It was made of the same dark wood as the guard's tower at the top of the building.

"Do you see any guards at all? Any people or anything?" Alice asked apprehensively.

"I see no one," Tao answered stonily, "but I have the strongest sensation that we are being watched."

"I feel that too." Jynx added, and the rest of the cats and Chippa agreed.

"I doesn't trust 'thes." Chippa furrowed his fluffy eyebrows and scowled at the ominous fortress before them.

Alice studied the compass again and sighed heavily. "Well, I'm sorry to hear that, because I have a sneaking suspicion that the Blue Fire Crystal is in there somewhere."

She eyed the cats, Henderson, and Chippa. "We've come this far. Let's keep going. I'm not keen about going through the front door there, so perhaps if we walk around the building, we can find another way in."

Everyone agreed reluctantly and followed her, save for Marlowe, who was at her side. She held on to his collar as they walked, uncertain of what might lay before them, but sure of their strength together.

They rounded the first pillar and saw that the wall beside them looked exactly the same as the wall they had just passed by.

Stepping carefully, they made their way to the next pillar, and came around it to see the same was true again. Except for the farthest wall with the giant doors at the front of the structure, all of the walls looked the same. Nevertheless, they kept going, and when they had gone around half of the building, Alice noticed a nondescript, simple door set into the bottom of one of the pillars between the walls.

"Look at that!" She exclaimed quietly as she pointed her hand out toward it. "I wonder if we can get in that way. It looks like all of you might fit, too."

Henderson rushed forward and stayed her gently. "Oh no, Madam. We have no idea what's beyond that door. Please, I'll go first and let you all know if it's safe to go in."

She gave him a nod, folding her fingers together. "Thank you, Henderson. We'll wait here."

With a swift glance back at them, he pushed the door open, walking slowly and stealthily into the dark passage behind it. A few minutes later, he came back and silently waved at them, and one by one, they all entered.

In through the door they went single file, and as Montgomery came at the end of the line with Chippa before him, the door slammed closed sharply, and latched. Chippa and Oscar both growled low, and eyed everything suspiciously as they made their way along the passage.

It was a narrow hallway with a high ceiling, and it was dark. There was dim light from somewhere overhead, but none of them could see what might be giving it off. The walls were black; swallowing what little light there was, and even the soft sounds of their passage through the space.

They moved slowly and cautiously, and came at last to the door at the end of the narrow hall. Henderson opened it, and they all filtered into a large, round room. The floor was black, and everything in the vast space above them was black; they could see no ceiling or corners, and the room might have gone up forever for all that they could tell.

Bright lights suddenly shone on them, and they discovered that they were standing together in a circle of mirrors. The mirrors were each about three feet wide and ten feet tall. There were several of them side, to side, to side, forming the circle around them.

"Where did the door go?" Oscar asked in a thin voice, turning his head this way and that. "We just came in here through a door, and it's gone. It's all mirrors now, and there's no door."

"Of course there's a door!" Sophie shot out irritably as she looked around; turning once and then twice. "It was right over… it was…" she paused, "…it's gone." She murmured.

"This is the strangest thing!" Henderson breathed out, confounded. "Why, I was just in here when I came to check before, and there were no mirrors. It was just a stone room... there were no..." He walked forward and reached his hand out toward one of the mirrors, and his own reflection, "No mirrors." He finished in a soft, puzzled voice.

Just then the mirrors began to turn slowly; each of them rotating in place, going around like a revolving door. They turned at different speeds; some slower, some faster, and where there should have been black space behind them as they turned, there were only more mirrors, and more reflections of everyone in the room.

Oscar took a few steps forward, tilting his head curiously. "Marlowe, I thought you were next to Alice. How did you get over there by Jynx?" He asked, staring ahead of him and seeing that Marlowe was not where he had been standing.

"I am standing next to Alice. I'm not near Jynx, Jynx is over there with Bailey, can't you see that? What are you looking at?" Marlowe questioned, watching Oscar, but then he saw Oscar off to the side, and then off to another side.

"These are reflections, Oscar dear. We're seeing reflections of each other turning in all of the mirrors, so it makes it seem as though we're in different places than we... than we are..." Alice trailed off, turning in place and gazing at their shifting images. "Marlowe is right..." She reached her hand out to touch him as he stood right beside her, and her fingers grasped at nothing but air.

"Jynx?" Oscar called out, and Jynx tried to walk to him. She could see him standing right in front of her with the mirrors turning behind him, but when she reached him, it was only his reflection.

"Oscar?" She called out. "I… I thought that was you, where are you?" Jynx turned in place; her eyes searching wildly. Oscar's reflection turned in the mirrors and then it was gone.

"Montgomery?" Sophie cried, looking dizzily at all of the spinning mirrors.

"I'm here!" He answered reassuringly. "Let me come to you. This is so confusing!" He padded over to her and discovered that it was only her reflection, and that she wasn't actually standing in front of him at all. "I can see you… you're in the mirror, but… where are you?"

"Tao!" Bailey called out. "Oscar! Marlowe!" He sat down and watched them all trying to walk to each other, but it was only reflections, and the mirrors kept rotating. "Alice! Henderson!" He cried piteously.

"Where 'es everyone?" Chippa whimpered as he held his paws to his mouth and turned in a circle trying to find them. "Cats! Messus P!" He pleaded softly, but he couldn't see anything other than their images in the spinning mirrors.

One by one, the looking glasses stopped turning, and each one of the company discovered that they were in the room alone, surrounded by mirrors.

Chapter Twelve

Dangerous Delusions

Sophie gave her head a shake and looked about. She could see herself reflected, but no one else. She turned slowly and breathed a sigh of relief when she saw that there was a door at one place among all of the mirrors.

"There's the door! I knew it was in here somewhere. Did you all go out the door and leave me again? How could you do that?" She pouted, walking to it and pressing her paw against it. It opened, and she passed through the doorway.

Sophie was greeted with the soft, dulcet tones of a harp playing delicately, and a cool ocean breeze caressing her face. She stared in utter amazement. The room she found herself in was enormous.

It looked to her as if it had come from some Egyptian dream; the floors were honey gold and white marble, as were several slender columns that rose from it to a lofty arched ceiling. There were people here and there throughout the room; all of them dressed in white flowing robes, all of them looking downward with pleasant smiles, focusing on various tasks that they were doing.

In the middle of the room a lotus shaped pool was sunken into the floor, with a fountain rising up several feet from the center of it. Flowers floated on the surface of the water, washed here and there by the gently falling sprinkles from the fountain.

Potted plants and trees dotted the walls, and were set about at every corner and nook of the room. On one wall to her right, there was a large golden bed covered with fat pillows and satins, and beside it there was a table with a tray of small fish, and a bowl of cream.

At the farthest end of the room there was no wall. Instead, there were tall arches that led out and down a few steps to a low balcony that overlooked an endless, sunny ocean. Long, sheer white drapes hung down the sides of the arches from the ceiling to the floor, and they billowed softly at their centers as the breeze filled them.

Sophie sighed in bliss. "I'm in a palace!"

Two of the people dressed in white came to her, and ushered her into the room, giving her a soft cushioned mat to stand on while they carefully brushed out her fur. She closed her eyes and purred happily, reveling in the indulgence.

When she had been fully brushed out, she was taken to the great bed, and she stretched out on all of the cushions there. The bowl of cream was brought to her, and she lapped casually at it while the people petted her, rubbed her ears tenderly, and fed the small fish to her one at a time.

"This is heaven!" She sighed in ecstasy. "I never want to leave!"

Marlowe discovered that he was alone in the room of mirrors as well, and seeing that no one else was around him, he bolted for the door as soon as he saw it. Pushing it open with his head, he hurried in, and the door closed behind him.

He stopped short and looked about in confusion. He was standing in between two grey walls that led a short distance and stopped at a cross hallway, where another grey wall stood. There was no ceiling. It was the same black, empty, cavernous space that had been in the room with the circle of mirrors. The grey walls reached a height of about twelve feet.

He padded down the corridor slowly. "Hello? Anyone?" He called out, listening closely as there was no other sound that he could hear, save for his own voice.

"Marlowe? Is that you?" Alice called from somewhere up ahead of him.

"Yes! I'm coming. I'll be right there." He answered back. He went to the end of the passage and stopped, as it formed a T to the hall he was in. He could go left or right. He looked both ways and was stunned to see that both directions appeared to stretch out for an incredible distance.

"Alice!" He raised his voice a little. "Which way did you go? Where are you?"

He looked left and there was nothing, then he looked right and again saw nothing but the hall. When he looked back to the left, he saw her standing a far distance from him, where she hadn't been just a moment before.

"There you are!" He breathed with relief and began to trot quickly to her. He went further and further, and though he had his eyes on her, after a while he blinked and saw that she was no longer there.

"Alice!" Marlowe cried out. He turned his head, looking around, and saw that there was another hallway near where he thought she had been standing. He sniffed at it, and was certain he could smell her. Marlowe poked his head further into the space. "Alice?" He called loudly.

"Here! Just here!" She answered back. Her voice echoed ahead of him, not far away. He went down that hall, seeing that there was an end to it. When he reached the end, he found that he could go left or right again.

Following his nose, he went left, and didn't go far before he turned a corner and discovered that he had come to a dead end. He turned around and went back the way that he had come, but the walls weren't in the same place as when he had passed by them moments before.

"Alice?" He asked in a worried voice.

She peeped her face around a corner far up ahead of him. "Here I am. Come on! Catch up!"

He rushed to her, but when he got there, there was nothing but a flat gray wall. Turning and looking around, he saw an opening in the wall opposite him. He went that way and found more corners and turns ahead.

Winding his way through the labyrinth of halls, chasing Alice's voice and seeing her just a little too far ahead of him every once in a while, he finally became frustrated.

Marlowe stood up on his hind legs, stretching as far as he could to look over the top of the walls he had been going through.

What he saw pierced his heart and made it sink down through him to the floor. It was a maze so big that there was no end of it in any direction. There was nothing beyond it but blackness to the sides and up above him; nothing at all. There was only the maze of gray walls as far as he could see.

"Marlowe! Come along, please hurry! I'm waiting!" Alice called to him.

He looked down at the hallway where he was standing and saw her off ahead of him. With a sigh, he went back down on all fours and hurried toward the last place where he had seen her, hoping that he could find her.

"Hurry! I need you!" Marlowe heard her cry out, and giving his head a shake, he launched into a run, determined to get to her. He raced down the hall, and around another corner, and down more halls and corners and backed out of dead ends, and kept on going, and going, and going.

Bailey moaned pitifully when he discovered himself alone in the mirrored room. He stood up and padded around, sniffing at the mirrors, trying to see if anyone had gone behind them. There was no trace of any of his family.

When he saw the door, he felt enormously relieved. He pushed his way through it, and only made it a few steps before he stopped in wonder. He had come into a great banquet hall. It was the grandest banquet hall he could have ever imagined; completely filled with more tables than he could count; all of them covered in food.

At every table there was some different kind of delectable cuisine. One was overflowing with hot steaming dishes, another had cool offerings. Yet another had sweet treats, and another was filled with many kinds of meats. There were cheeses and seafood, gravies and creams. Breads and pies, soups and dairy dishes. Everything that he ever could have wished for, and more.

"Oh thank heaven! I've been starving for days!" Bailey gushed as he hurried to the first table and began to gorge himself on the food there.

He went from one table to the next, trying everything, and sometimes going back to where he had been for seconds or thirds, and so he went, table to table, eating all the way.

Tao left the mirrored room through the door, and discovered that she had walked into an immaculate Zen garden. She'd never seen the likes of it. It was carefully and thoughtfully designed with pathways delicately turning through it, places where sand had been meticulously raked, or other spots where stones had been laid with precision. There were plants and flowers in various places. Three waterfalls bubbled and flowed into a wide reflecting pond, and birds chirped harmoniously overhead.

She walked slowly through all of it, taking her time, and finally saw a bamboo deck over the reflecting pond. On the deck there was a prayer mat, and she sat on it. Taking in the encompassing beauty once more, she breathed in and closed her blue eyes, going into a peaceful meditation.

Jynx left the mirrored room in a rush, looking for her family. She bolted through the door as soon as she saw it, and when it closed behind her, she froze. There was nothing; nothing but pitch black darkness.

It was near total sensory deprivation. There was no sound. There was no light to see anything. There was no scent to follow. There was nothing but the floor beneath her feet for her to feel, and nothing else.

Jynx called out, but the sound of her voice did not seem to travel far. "Hello! Alice! Oscar! Someone!"

She waited. There was no answer. She didn't know what could be around her in the darkness, but she slowly put one paw out in front of her, and when she felt the floor beneath it, she took the step.

"Hello?" She cried out again.

The faintest sound of the mew of a kitten reached her ears. It made her heart race. "Oscar? Where are you?"

"Jynx!" She heard his soft cry. "Jynx I can't find you! Where are you?"

His voice sounded far away. She lifted her chin and tried to smell him, but there was no trail or scent. "I'm here! Can you hear me?" She tested the other paw against the floor and took one more step, not able to see anything at all.

"Jynx!" Oscar's voice was a little louder, and she was sure that it was coming from the left side, up ahead of her. One cautious step at a time, she went in the direction she had heard him.

"Oscar! I'm coming! Where are you?"

"I'm here! Jynx hurry! I'm so scared! I can't find you!" Oscar cried desperately. He sounded so small, as he had been when Alice had first brought him home and Jynx had immediately loved him.

She stopped in her tracks and turned her head. The direction of the sound of his voice had changed. It was coming from the right side of her. "Did you move? Oscar, don't move! Just stay right where you are, and I'll come to you! Call out and I'll find you! But don't move!"

He mewed again and again. "Jynx please hurry! Help me! I'm lost and I'm scared!" His voice was suddenly much further up ahead of her. She tried to find her way faster through the blackness.

"I'm coming!" Jynx called out, searching in vain. She began to trust that the floor would be in front of her even though she couldn't see it, and she picked her speed up to almost a run as she tried to follow the kitten's voice. The floor shifted suddenly, and she stumbled and fell.

Jynx pushed herself back up and peered through the darkness engulfing her, straining to get a glimpse of anything at all, but there was nothing. She continued onward, slowing her pace, and kept crying out for Oscar, but she could not find him.

When Oscar left the room with the mirrors, he went through the door and stopped short, turning around in a sudden panic to go back, but there was no door. It had vanished. He discovered that he was in an enormous cage.

He was no longer the size of a horse. Instead, he was a tiny kitten again, as small as he had been when Alice had first found him alone, starving, and frightened in the park.

Oscar stood on a cold, gray concrete floor. A big steel cage surrounded him like a jail cell. The silver bars went up high to a ceiling he could barely see.

He carefully poked his face in between the bars and tried to look around. It was a dimly lit room, with one single bare light bulb hanging from a cord on the high ceiling above.

There were other cages around him, like a dog pound, but there were no animals in them. It was only him, alone in the room. Oscar paced back and forth and began to call out.

"Jynx! Alice! Marlowe!" He cried as loudly as he could. The kitten paced along the wall of the cage for a while, calling out the names of all of the cats, but silence was his only answer.

Finally he turned to see if there was anything in his cell that he could use to escape. There was nothing. No water, no food, no bowl, nothing but him on the cold, gray concrete floor.

Oscar cried out until his voice was nearly gone; becoming raspy and thin. When he knew that it was no use, fear began to take him over and he felt as he had when he was a lost kitten. Trapped; a prisoner orphan with no family, no home, and no one else in the world. An icy chill swept through him.

The kitten huddled in the back corner of the cage; his fur on end as he tried to stay warm and keep some kind of hope, his eyes wide with fear. Every now and again he would cry out softly for one of the cats, or Alice, or Henderson, but there was no sound except his own quiet woeful mew.

Montgomery made his way through the door leading out of the mirrored room, and was shocked to find himself in a dark, dank, back alley in London.

It was puddled with cold, stale water, and there were old, stinking pieces of rubbish and trash scattered about.

He turned back, but there was no door. There wasn't even a wall; it was just the alley that seemed to stretch on forever. Looking down at his feet, he saw that his monocle was on the ground before him and the glass in it was shattered; broken out of it in little slivers of pieces.

His fur was matted and filthy; caked with mud and grime. He tried to shake some of it loose, but it only worsened as he moved. He took a few steps and stopped, realizing that there was nowhere to go.

"Sophie! Alice! Marlowe! Where are you?" Montgomery called, but his voice was scratchy, and the sound of it echoed off of the old stones and cement, coming back to him only to strike the reality into his heart that he was alone.

He felt hope and determination begin to whither in him. Lost and alone, grungy and tattered, he sank down close to the ground and dropped his eyes to his paws.

"You're a disgrace! Look at you! How dare you let anything like this happen!" A deep, strong voice boomed behind him. Montgomery jumped, and spun around to look up. For a moment he was relieved.

Standing over him was Lieutenant General George Perivale, wearing a full military uniform. Montgomery had never been so happy to see his old master, than at that moment, but the look on George's face stifled his hope and relief; snuffing it out almost immediately.

George was shouting at him angrily; something his owner had never done when he was home and alive.

"What an absolute shame and embarrassment you are! I'm appalled! How could you do this! How could you let it all come to this! Here you are filthy and disgusting, hiding back here in this wretched alley! You've let down the countries of England *and* Corevé! You've let down the whole of the Perivale family! You are a coward!" George raged at him furiously.

Montgomery felt his heart shrivel as the harsh words broke over him, ringing in his ears. "You are a coward!

You shall henceforth never be allowed back into any home again! Live out your days in shame! Coward!" George blasted him over and over again.

The words reverberated around and through him, pelting him like heavy stones, filling him with immeasurable shame.

He looked away from George, and pressed his forehead to the wet stones beneath him, cowering in misery.

Henderson stepped through the door out of the mirrored room and blinked when he saw that he was standing in the parlor at home.

He hesitated and then turned to look behind him. He knew he'd just gone through a door, but when he turned, he saw that it was only the house. There was no room full of mirrors behind him.

He realized that somehow they must have come home in the same sort of strange, magical way that they had left London and wound up in Mari Village.

Henderson sighed with relief and straightened his coat, gazing at the room in front of him again.

Neither Alice nor the cats were in it. He frowned as he realized that all of the furniture and the portraits on the wall were draped in black cloth, as though the house was in a period of mourning for the death of the owner.

His heart picked up speed, and he turned to leave, but there was no door behind him; it was only the wall continued where there ought to have been a door.

He looked around again and saw that there was a door at the opposite end of the room. He hurried through the room to the door, and pulled it open. It led straight into another room in the house.

"Madam? Bailey? Marlowe? Sophie?" Henderson heard the door close behind him, and he turned back, but once more there was no door, it was just another wall. Again, there was a door at the opposite end of the room, and again he moved toward it hurriedly and pulled it open.

It led to yet another room in the house. All of the rooms were familiar; they were right, and everything looked just as it should, except for the bizarre door placement, and the black drape all over the furniture and the portraits. He went through the door, and the wall was there behind him again.

Henderson began to run as his heart pounded, flying through each room, calling out for the cats and Mrs. Perivale, and finding no one home but himself.

Fear chilled him as the worst suspicions began to cross his mind. The only reason that black would be draped all over the house, would be if Mrs. Perivale had died.

Henderson kept going as fast as he could, entering a room only to have it close off behind him with a wall and only give him one way out; going forward, constantly forward and never back, from room, to room, to room. There was no upstairs or downstairs. There was no way outside. There was only forward, and there was no one home but him. He kept on going, hoping that he would find any of his family in the next room, or the next after that.

Chippa was stunned, when he pushed through the door leading out of the mirrored room, to find that he was standing in the clearing at the center of his village. He turned in a circle and saw that he was home. There was no door, and there was no room; only the lake in the distance, and Mari Village around him.

Chippa dropped his paws, and frowned. "Where 'es everyone?" He asked loudly, perking his floppy ears up on point. "Messus P? Cats?"

At first there was no answer; just the birds singing in the distance, and the sound of the water against the shoreline at the bottom of the hill. Chippa walked further into the clearing and looked all around.

"'Es no one home?" He called loudly; his gaze searching all of the windows in the homes, and the pathways through the village. There was not another Inkling in sight. He had never seen Mari Village deserted before.

At least, he thought it was deserted. The door of Bayless Grand Mari's home opened, and Jika Mari stepped out. He looked a little bigger than usual, and he was dressed in his warrior gear, carrying his spear.

He slammed the door shut and strode toward Chippa menacingly. "Look who 'es come back... alone. Failed!"

Chippa frowned and planted his hands on his hips. "I 'es not alone. I 'es not failed!"

Jika nodded slowly as he came close to Chippa, glaring down at the much smaller Inkling. "You 'es alone. There 'es no one here but you and me. You 'es failed because you 'es pathetic! You 'es failed because you never does anything right!"

Chippa lifted his paws to his mouth, holding them there as fear crept into his heart. He wasn't sure if he was alone, but he was beginning to suspect that Jika was right.

"I 'es doing one thing right! I 'es right about the Chosen One!" Chippa retorted, though not with much emphasis. He felt the strength in his heart begin to weaken, and his courage dissipate.

Jika raised his voice. "You 'es right about that one thing, but you 'stell failed! They 'es not here. Crystal 'es not back 'en temple! You 'es an embarrassment and a shame to all the tribe! You should be leaving and never coming back!"

Chippa's eyes flooded with tears as his body trembled; he was so afraid that Jika was right. "I 'es not a shame! I has a purpose 'weth the cats and the Chosen One! I has value!" He tried to insist, but his voice was weak, and the tears in his eyes spilled over, dropping to the dirt at his feet.

Jika shoved his chest in Chippa's face. "You 'es failed! Chosen One 'es gone! Nothing 'es here anymore! Everything 'es destroyed! Village gone! Everyone gone!"

Jika slammed his paw into Chippa's chest, shoving him backward. "'Es all over, and 'es all your fault! You must leave! You must go and never, never come back!" Jika shouted at him. "Fail! Shame!" He yelled cruelly, glaring furiously at Chippa.

Chippa shook his head, wishing it was all wrong and it would go away. He backed off from Jika a step at a time, but Jika came at him, and fear washed over Chippa.

He turned and ran toward the lake, but he knew that Jika could follow him and stop him if he tried to take the boat. He went to a giant old tree and bent down close to the roots, digging swiftly with his front paws.

Chippa dug deep into the dirt to find a place to hide away from the bully Jika, and from his own unending failures. He dug and dug, deeper and faster as he crawled further into the hole, burrowing downward.

Alice realized that everyone was gone, and she stood alone in the room full of mirrors. There was no door. There was no way out. There were only the mirrors. She held her hand to her heart as she wondered where her family had all vanished to.

The darkness was still above her. The floor at her feet was still black. The lights around the upper edges of the mirrors still shone toward her, and all she could see was herself reflected back.

Slowly her reflections began to shift and change, and as she watched, each of her reflections in the mirrors around her morphed into a younger version of herself. It was as if time was falling away from her year by year in each mirror.

Alice saw herself slimmer, and with fewer wrinkles; with brown hair again, with no spots or aging. She saw herself standing taller and more erect. She saw who she used to see when she looked in the mirror. All about her, in every mirror, was a different version of herself in younger years.

They all smiled and waved at her in a friendly way. She stared at them. "Come!" They called out to her. She could hear her own voice; her younger, more youthful voice. "Alice!" They called out to her. "Come closer! Come near to us!"

She took a few steps toward them, and stopped. They beckoned, and waved, and smiled. "Come!" They urged her.

"Come with us, and you will be this way again! You can be any one of us again! Step close to the mirror, and touch our hands! Touch your own hands! You can live just like this, in this younger body again! Think how useful you used to be when you were younger. You could be useful again!" They coaxed her.

Alice bit at her lower lip. It felt like it had been a long time since she had been useful. "Who... who are you? What are you doing?" She asked, trying to figure out how she was looking at herself in younger years.

"We're you! Alice... it's you. You know that. Come to the mirrors Alice. Choose one of us! Remember all that you once did! Think of George! You could have another full life! You don't have to be old and useless anymore... you could be young and free again! All you have to do is come to the mirrors and choose one of us!" They smiled and waved their hands at her, pleading with her to come to one of them; any of them.

Alice took a few steps toward one of the mirrors, in which she had been in her forties. Her son had been young then. Her husband had been home most of the time. She had been so happy in those years.

She felt tears stinging at the back of her eyes, and she began to reach her hand out to the glass before her, wishing with much of her heart that she could have that time back.

"Yes! Yes Alice! Come! Touch the mirror! Touch your own hand in the mirror... your younger hand, and you will be in that life again! Closer!" The younger version of herself called out to her, holding her open palm against the inside of the mirror.

Alice reached out to touch it, but just as she was about to press her fingers to the glass, she stopped.

~ 233 ~

She saw the juxtaposition of her old and aged hand against the reflection of her younger hand, and her younger body, and her younger face. She saw the great differences before her, and she drew her old hand back.

"I know what this is… this is some kind of… trick! This is an illusion! This is some sort of temptation meant to keep me from my real purpose here!"

Anger grew swift and strong within Alice. "You will not deceive me!"

Alice ripped her umbrella cane off of the crook of her arm and pointed it toward one of the mirrors. "I am more useful the way that I am now, than I ever was at any of these younger ages, because I have a lifetime of experience!"

She rushed forward and struck the mirror in front of her with the sharp point of her umbrella cane, and the mirror shattered. The shards of it evaporated into thin air, rather than crashing to the floor, as she turned to the next mirror.

The reflections of her younger self begged and pleaded for her to stop and take her younger hand. Alice was done listening to them.

"I have a lifetime of wisdom!" She charged at the next mirror, and then the next, shattering all of them as she went along; shouting at them louder as she moved. "And I don't want to live another whole life all over again! That's the wisdom that comes with age!"

Chapter Thirteen

Shattered Illusions

Sophie downed another fish, and gazed out of the open arches in the breezeway to the balcony overlooking the sea. She frowned somewhat, and narrowed her eyes. Sophie loved being pampered, but there was something bothering her at the back of her mind.

None of the other cats were around. Alice and Henderson weren't around. She was bitterly disappointed in the guilt that began to wash through her, wishing it would go away; but she couldn't deny it.

Sophie knew that there was a greater responsibility to her family, and to the world of Corevé, and that even though she was having the time of her life, there were more important and pressing things that she needed to attend to. She hated to admit it, but it was no time to think of herself.

Wondering silently how she could find a way out, she decided not to disrupt any of what was going on around her.

Sophie stretched lavishly, and slowly stepped down from the bed, taking her time walking around the room, pretending she was just curious about it, and getting a little walk in.

She discreetly eyed the whole place as she padded leisurely through it, making a point of not drawing the attention of anyone else in the room.

Finally, she found what she was looking for. It was a humble wooden door that would never have been in a palace such as the one she found herself in. She knew that it had to be a door back to her family.

Glancing once over her shoulder to be sure that no one was looking at her, she moved silently to the door and pressed it gently with her paw. It swung back and she slipped through it as quickly as she could.

Sophie found herself standing back in the great black room, except that all of the mirrors had been shattered and broken, and Alice was standing alone in the room, huffing and holding her umbrella cane aloft.

Marlowe had run farther and longer than he ever thought he might be able to. Alice continually stayed a distance ahead of him; never near enough for him to reach, while constantly calling out to him, beckoning him forward, onward toward her, though he never got to her.

He began to realize that she was moving far too fast. His Alice did not move as quickly as the Alice whom he was following. He finally stopped and looked around. There was a dead end to one side of him, and yet another long narrow hallway to the other side, where Alice was standing and calling out to him.

Knowing that he had to find another way, he turned toward the dead end and crouched down, tucking his chin low.

With every bit of strength in his body, he flattened his ears back and vaulted forward, bashing the top of his head into the gray wall. He crashed through it with tremendous force.

Giving his head a shake, he raised his chin. He was standing in the black room, where Alice and Sophie were both staring at him.

Marlowe rushed to Alice with a cry, and sniffed closely to be sure that it was her.

Alice wrapped her arms around his neck, and buried her face in his fur for a moment, comforting him. "We're here, don't you fret my dearest, we're here."

Sophie nudged his head and he gave her a rub in return. "You're both all right?" He asked worriedly.

"We're okay." Alice answered. "We just haven't seen the others. We have no idea where anyone is."

They began to call out as loudly as they could for their family, name by name, hoping that the others could hear them and find their way back.

Bailey wasn't even halfway through the beautiful banquet hall, when he stopped and sat down to have a think.

He had eaten practically everything he could find on every table, and he realized that the more he ate, the hungrier he seemed to feel. He knew that he should have been laid out flat in a food coma by then, but he had never felt so ravenously hungry in his life.

The tables where he had gorged himself had somehow been replenished with the food he had eaten, and he began to wonder at that as well.

No one had come in and cleared away dirty dishes. No one had brought new food; it had all just reappeared, as though he had never eaten it or touched it at all.

Frowning with contempt, Bailey stood up and lifted his chin, looking around the room. There was no way out. It was only him, and the tables of food.

His family was gone; Henderson especially, and he was alone and starving. His stomach rumbled, and he began to feel sick and sad.

Dejectedly, he lay down and rolled onto his side with a listless groan. It was there that he saw something strange on the floor, not far from him. It was a wooden trapdoor. Old, dark, simple wood. There was a big round ring on it.

He made his way over to it, and it occurred to him that the trapdoor might very well be the only way out of the room, since the door on the wall had disappeared.

Grabbing the ring with his teeth, he gave the door a hard tug, and it opened for him. It was dark in the space under the trapdoor, but he was willing to try anything to get out of the banquet hall.

Bailey tried to jump through the door headfirst, but as he was getting through it, it began to shrink very quickly, and he could feel himself getting stuck. He scrambled and struggled, and clawed his back feet on the banquet room floor as his upper body was hanging and dangling down into blackness.

Bailey pressed his front paws against the underside of the banquet floor, and wriggled and pushed as much as he could, until finally he popped through the doorframe. It closed fully as soon as he was out of it, and he landed with a thump on his bottom, blinking in surprise.

Sophie scoffed in a friendly way, teasing him lightly as she went to him. "I guess cats don't always land on their feet, do they?" She gave him a nudge, and Alice went to him and rubbed his head all over with her hands.

"My poor darling, are you all right?" She asked, looking him over.

Bailey nodded. "I'm fine. I'm just starving."

Sophie smirked. "He's fine."

Tao opened her eyes and blinked a few times. She gazed about slowly, and sniffed at the air. She knew that something wasn't right. Lifting her chin, she peered at the sun shining overhead. She realized that it hadn't moved. She knew she had been sitting in the Zen garden for a long while, and yet no time had passed around her.

Standing up from the mat she had been laying on, she breathed in the air deeply, and the staleness of it made her fur stand on end.

Tao began to understand that she was in some kind of a holding cell. Some place made to make her forget what was going on elsewhere; some place made to distract her, rather than enrich her.

She hurried down the path from the pond to the walls around the garden sanctuary. The walls reached up more than twenty feet, and the only thing over them was a square of blue sky with a few puffy white clouds dotted over it, and the sun, shining down warmly and not moving.

Tao ran the full length of the four walls enclosing the garden; scanning them for a door or a window; any way out that she could find, but there was nothing. She walked back to the bamboo dock and sat on the mat, contemplating her situation.

Tao knew that where there was a way in, there was also a way out. She thought about how nothing was moving above her, and that there was no way out that she could see.

Slowly, she leaned over and looked at her reflection in the pond where the bamboo dock was. She saw her face and body, she saw the sun, sky, and clouds, behind her.

Tao realized that the only thing that was real in the Zen garden was her. She was her only way out. She considered it for a long moment, and then with a graceful arc of her body, she leapt suddenly from her position, diving straight into her reflection in the pond.

There was no splash. It wasn't water. It was almost like a mirage or curtain; something that only seemed to be there, but wasn't.

Her front paws touched down on the hard black ground. She'd landed safely and looked up quickly, seeing Alice, Marlowe, Bailey, and Sophie.

"I'm sorry... I seem to have been gone. I'm here now. Are you all right?" Tao asked, taking in their faces with concern.

"We're fine." Sophie answered, sniffing around at the frames where the mirrors had been broken. There was no glass, but the frames still stood where they had been.

"I'm starving." Bailey groaned as he sat back on his bottom.

"Where are the others?" Tao asked with concern.

Alice rubbed Tao's ears and face as she hugged her. "We don't know my darling. We were separated. The four of you are the only ones who've made it back. We're trying to find a way out so that we can look for everyone else. I'm so relieved that you're all right!"

Marlowe perked up his ears. "Some silence please, I think I can hear Oscar."

Every one of them listened closely. The faintest mew of a kitten sounded at a great distance. Marlowe called out loudly.

"Oscar! It's Marlowe! If you can hear me, I want you to try to find a door. Look for a door, and follow my voice! These places we were in are traps. Try to find a way out!"

They fell silent again and listened. "Marlowe! I hear you!" Came a scratchy, thin voice.

Oscar hadn't moved from the spot at the back of the cage where he was cowering. When he heard Marlowe, he slowly pushed himself up and began to look around again.

There were no doors that he could see from where he was, but he thought that maybe if he could get a better look, he might be able to see if there was a door beyond the other cages.

Oscar's heart lightened with hope to hear the older cat's voice. He plucked up a little courage and went to the bars on his cage. He had peeked through them before, but then as he stood there, sizing up the space between the bars, he wondered if there was a way that he could fit through them.

He poked his nose tentatively in between two of them, and then closed his eyes and pushed forward. He could feel the pressure against his whiskers and face, but it was only a slight pressure, so he kept pushing. Before he realized it, his whole body had slipped right through the space.

Expecting much more resistance from the bars than there actually was, the force of his final push made him tumble and roll once, and when he lifted his head and looked around, he saw that he was back in the black room with Alice, Marlowe, Sophie, Tao, and Bailey.

"You're here!" Oscar gasped, rushing to Marlowe and rubbing his head against him. Alice went to the massive kitten and comforted him, scratching her fingers behind his ear and patting him.

"I was so scared! I was in a horrible place! So all alone." He told them sadly and quietly.

Alice looked right at him. "Well you aren't there now, and I'm beginning to wonder just how much of this around us is even real. You're back with us, and you're safe. That's all that matters. Now we need to find the others."

Oscar's head shot straight up, and his eyes searched the room. "Where are the others? Where's Jynx and Montgomery? Where's Henderson and Chippa? Jynx!" He cried out, searching the room, walking here and there to sniff for her.

"We've looked. We don't know where they are." Tao admitted with a solemn voice.

"I have to find her!" Oscar vowed resolutely. He walked slowly along the angles of the black wall that formed the room, smelling everywhere, trying to detect her scent. "Jynx! Where are you? Jynx!" He called out again.

Oscar looked up at Alice and blinked. "You said you were wondering how much of this place is real…" He trailed off. "What if we find the parts that aren't real?"

The kitten turned his face back to the wall and began to press his forehead to each panel as he passed it, testing them to see if they were really there, and really solid.

He had been surprised that the bars of his cage weren't actually solid bars, and that the whole time he had been imprisoned there, all he had needed to do to escape was to push his way through them.

Each panel did not give as he passed it, so he continued onward, going to the next panel. The room was octagonal shaped, just like the outside walls of the building they were in; giving the room both a circular and an angular look.

Oscar was just over halfway around the room, still pressing his forehead to the panels, still calling out Jynx's name, when one of the panels seemed to give way, and he pushed his head and half of his body through it.

"Oscar!" He heard Alice yell out. The back half of his body was still in the black room with them, but the front half of his body was in some other place where there was nothing but darkness. There was no light; there was no sound. There was nothing.

"Jynx!" Oscar called out as loud as he could, trying with futility to look around him, blinded by the blackness.

"Oscar!" He heard her call back. "Oscar where are you?"

"I'm here! I was lost, but I found everyone, and now I'm here to find you! I can't see you; it's too dark in here! Follow my voice! I'm waiting for you. I know how to escape. Can you hear me?" He called to her, grateful that Marlowe had done the same for him when he had believed that there was no way out.

"I can hear you! Keep talking. I am coming to you!" Jynx answered back. She knew that it had to be him. The whole time she had been in the black nothing, following his calls to her, he had not said anything like what he was saying to her just then. She knew that it was finally real.

"I'm here Jynx! Follow my voice! Keep following my voice!" Oscar cried out as loud as he was able to.

Moments later he caught her scent; just as he had learned to do in the darkness of the heart of the mountain they had sailed through. "I smell you! You're close!" Excitement flooded through him. The next thing he knew, he felt her face against his.

"I'm here little one, I'm here. Thank goodness I've finally found you. I've been looking all over for you." Jynx heaved a great sigh, thinking to herself that she had never felt such relief in her life.

"Thank you for coming after me. I wouldn't have found my own way out of here." She admitted quietly.

"I would always come for you." Oscar beamed happily.

"I'll always come for you too." She answered. "Now, you said you know how to get out?"

"Yeah, stay right by me. We're already there." He grinned as he led her through the strange wall that wasn't really there. She walked out with him, and they were both in the room with their family again. Everyone welcomed Jynx back, and even Sophie gave her a small smile.

"That's Henderson!" Alice said suddenly, stopping for a moment and looking around. All of them were silent again as they listened, and she began to look all over the room.

"I can hear him too!" Bailey piped up, getting to his feet and lifting his nose in the air. "But I can't smell him. He's not close enough."

"Where did that door come from?" Alice asked curiously, eyeing an old wooden door in the wall. "That wasn't there before... but then, everything here keeps changing, doesn't it?"

Alice walked over to the door and called out to him, raising her voice. "Henderson! Henderson can you hear me?"

"Madam?" She heard him call back. The cats perked up.

"That's him!" Oscar buzzed excitedly, hurrying to Alice's side.

Alice reached her hand to the doorknob and turned it, pulling the door open. There was nothing but the black wall behind it. She frowned and closed the door. "Well, I thought that would work." She sighed and her shoulders slumped.

Thinking for a moment, she bit at her lower lip and reached for the door handle once more, giving it another turn, and opening it again. Henderson nearly crashed into her arms. She took a few steps back as he rushed into the room and stopped short, panting and out of breath.

Henderson blinked at all of them in astonishment. "You're here! My goodness... what a nightmare! What a horrible..." He paused as he gazed slowly, taking them all in. "I'm so grateful to see you all, truly. Where are Montgomery and Chippa?"

Just then there was a soft scratching noise, and a panicked cry. They all looked up to see Chippa falling through the air, tumbling downward from the dark recesses, far above.

In a flash, Jynx shot her paw out and pulled him to her carefully, swiping him right out of thin air. She set him on the ground, and he sat in a tiny ball for a moment, and then slowly uncurled and looked up at them.

The fur on his face was wet with tears, and he looked more miserable than he had been even on Diovalo's back.

"You… you 'es all here? I was 'en Mari Village… 'et was bad! I was digging to get away, and I digged… here." He frowned in confusion.

"It's all right, Chippa. We're back together and we're staying together." Alice told him as she went to him and rubbed her hand over the soft fur on top of his head. She reached into her pocket and found a ginger chew for him, giving it to him as she comforted him. "You weren't really in Mari Village. We've all been in different illusions. It was a trick."

Chippa frowned darkly as he chewed. Alice stood up straight and looked at her cats and Henderson.

"Now… we have got to find Montgomery! Where on earth is he?" She asked, gazing at the perimeter of the room. The door that Henderson had come through was still there. Narrowing her eyes thoughtfully, she went to it and tried the door handle.

Alice opened the door and saw nothing, and closed it. Waiting a moment, she opened it and saw a brick wall. She closed the door. Opening it again, she saw the black wall, and closed the door. She continued to open it and close it, over and over again, as she became more and more agitated.

"He has to be somewhere. He isn't gone and vanished into thin air!" Alice opened the door again and again, and each time it was something different, but it was always nothing.

"Montgomery!" She called loudly. "Where are you! Come back this instant!" She insisted as she yanked the door open once more.

Instead of a wall, there was a long, dark, dank alley that dead ended. It was made of crumbling bricks and concrete; paved with broken old cobblestones. It was strewn about with tattered bits of rubbish; wet from rain, and puddled with dark water.

Alice peered hard into the dim alley, and waved her hand behind her without looking. "Henderson, come here please and hold this door for me."

Henderson was there right away, looking into the alley from behind her. He reached for the doorknob to hold the door open, and she walked in, heading slowly toward a large, furry mess of a ball at the end of the alley. It was dirty, and its coat was matted as it lay huddled in a corner, not moving.

It shivered, and she heard it groan miserably. Alice touched it gently, and the animal slowly turned its head and looked up at her.

"Montgomery!" Alice gasped, reaching both her hands to him.

"I won't go with you." He moaned in devastation. "Leave me here."

Alice stared at him. "What? What are you talking about? Of course I'm taking you with me!"

"No, you can't." Montgomery insisted. "I've failed you!" He paused a moment, and then continued as she stared at him.

"George was here. He was right here with me. He was furious with me for letting the family down; for letting you down, and the mission; for failing at everything. He was right. I have no business staying with any of you. I have failed you all, and I deserve to be left here to rot. George called me a coward, and he was right!"

Alice was appalled. "Why, that's an outrage! How could you ever believe such a thing! George loved you! You were his own! Why, he's the one who brought you home to live with us to begin with! You were our first cat! There isn't a bit of truth to what you experienced here. You've always been brave and loyal, and George and I have always been so proud of you! Don't you even think on this nightmare! It was an illusion; like everything else in this wretched place!"

Alice glared around at the alley. "Now, you come along with me and get out of here! The others are waiting! Look, there's Henderson just there, holding the door for us. Let's go!"

Montgomery looked past her shoulder and saw the door, and Henderson in it, and beyond him, he could see the other cats looking for him and calling out to him.

With a great sigh, he pushed himself to his feet. Alice took his collar in her hand and walked with him like she was leading a horse down the alley, and through the door.

The moment that Montgomery came through the door, and Henderson closed it sharply behind him, Montgomery saw that he was whole again, and clean. He was as he had been before. Even his monocle was back in place, and shining. He wept quietly in relief as Sophie went to him and nuzzled him.

"You're all right, and you're back, and that's all that matters. Whatever happened in there; just let it go and forget it. It wasn't real. You're here now. Focus on that." She spoke tenderly to him. He nudged her back, and gave her a little smile.

"Thank you my old friend." Montgomery murmured softly.

Just then the room went pitch black, and they all cried out, huddling together tightly so that none of them could be lost again.

A bluish white light shone down from some high place, far up in the darkness of the ceiling, creating a circle of light on the floor at the very center of the room. In the center of the circle of light, sitting on the floor, was the Blue Fire Crystal.

CHAPTER FOURTEEN

TRUTH

Chippa tried to run for the crystal, but he couldn't move. Turning around, he saw what was stopping him, and wailed loudly.

It was another Inkling. A strange looking Inkling. Chippa glared hotly at him. "What 'es you! You 'es not Mari! You 'es no Inkling!"

The Inkling began to shimmer and shift as it changed, transforming into a tall, narrow figure of a man. He wore a black suit with thin white stripes, and coattails.

On his head was a top hat which was black on one half, and white on the other. A white mask covered part of his face, concealing his forehead, and part of his nose and cheek, but the rest of his face was pitch black, though it wasn't flesh of any kind. It was a shadow, more than a face.

In one hand, covered in a black glove, he had a long black cane with a white tip. He held onto Chippa's tail with the other white gloved hand, and he didn't let go.

The man chuckled softly, and looked at the gathering. They had circled at a distance around the crystal. He strode, dragging Chippa with him by his tail feathers, toward the center of the room near the crystal, and he spoke. His voice was deep, and it echoed all over the room, seeming to come from everywhere simultaneously. Chippa wriggled and howled furiously.

"So you've made it through my Illusionary Palace, and now you think you're going to take the Blue Fire Crystal." His evil laugh reverberated throughout the room.

"Well, you can't get something for nothing, you know." With that, he let go of Chippa. The little Inkling bolted for the crystal, but as he did, a long wide sword fell point down from the source of the light in the ceiling, heading straight for the blue gem.

Chippa yelped and moved quickly out of the way after nearly being shorn in two as he reached for the element stone.

He scowled and eyed the sword, which hovered in the air above the Blue Fire Crystal. Chippa circled his quarry. As he moved back away from it, the sword rose back up a bit, but anytime he drew nearer to the crystal, the blade came back down again. He growled angrily in frustration.

The shadowy man laughed wickedly. "Now you see the price you must pay to retrieve the crystal. You'll have to die to get it."

Chippa kept circling, drawing near and backing up again as the sword moved up and down, dependent upon his proximity to it. Chippa tried desperately to find a way to get it. His eyes never left the crystal and the sword.

The cruel man walked to Alice and stared at her silently for a long moment, before speaking. "You are the Chosen One." It was a statement rather than a question. "I expected someone else."

Alice narrowed her gaze at him coldly. "Oh, you'll find that I'm full of surprises." She lifted her chin and tried to glare back at the place in his mask where his eyes should be, but weren't. "And who are you?"

"I'm the Illusionist." He answered simply.

Alice narrowed her eyes at him. "You sent all of us into those horrible places."

"I did indeed. Did you enjoy them?" He mused with a shallow laugh, as he turned his head toward the cats.

The cats growled fiercely. Chippa was still solely focused on the crystal and the sword, and was growing more frustrated at his predicament with each passing moment.

"You have to admit, even though each of them was an illusion, there was still truth at the heart of them all." The Illusionist contended evenly as he returned his attention to Alice.

There was silence for a moment as they realized that he was right. He set the end of his cane on the floor in front of him and placed both of his hands; one gloved in white, and the other in black, on its head.

"You'll find that I'm full of surprises as well, and here's one for you now. You have three seconds to get the crystal before I take it, and disappear with it forever." He laughed, and his voice rang out around the room, encircling all of them.

"*There was no truth at the heart of mine!*" Montgomery shouted bitterly. Alice looked over the shoulder of the Illusionist and saw that Montgomery was directly across from her, on the other side of the room. The expression on his face, the anger in his eyes, and the determination in his voice chilled her, and she froze.

In a split second he bounded forward, leaping toward the light and the crystal, in an elegant arc.

~ 252 ~

Alice screamed at the top of her lungs, thrusting her hand outward as Montgomery landed at the center of the room, pushing the crystal out of the light. The sword plunged down, sinking into his body.

"*NO!*" Alice screamed as her heart broke, and all of the cats echoed her cry.

Chippa wrapped himself around the crystal and raced off with it to a dark spot behind Jynx, where he hid.

The Illusionist laughed loud and deep, throwing his head back as the cacophonic sound ricocheted off the walls at a deafening volume.

Alice tore her eyes away from the sight of Montgomery laying in the brilliant light, with the sword lodged erect in his body, as his lifeblood pooled around him.

Sophie, Oscar, and Bailey rushed to him as Marlowe, Jynx, and Tao kept their eyes locked on the Illusionist.

Alice glared at the figure before her; her face stony with fury. In a flash, she snatched a long knitting needle with a sharp point at one end, out of her black bag. Without even blinking, she turned the point of the needle toward the Illusionist, and buried it in his chest.

His laughter was suddenly silenced as his body shattered and broke into countless shards of every size, just as the mirrors had done, sending splinters in every direction. Every one of them disappeared.

Alice gasped and looked down. On the back of her hand, just between her thumb and forefinger there was a deep cut. Blood began to pour from it as she watched.

Henderson yelled for everyone to look out, and they all lifted their heads to see that the Illusionary Palace was disappearing around them; all of it breaking into pieces like a shattered mirror; just like the Illusionist. Every bit of it disappeared like it had never existed.

A few moments later, they were all standing outside in the howling wind and pelting rain, with darkened skies looming overhead. The sword was gone right along with everything else, but Montgomery was still laying on the rocky plateau as his life spilled from him. The cats, Henderson, Chippa, and Alice went to him.

Thunder crashed, and lightning zig-zagged all over the sky. The ground shook and trembled, and the gusts of wind around them threatened to carry them all away.

Henderson unbuttoned his overshirt and pulled it off of himself, leaving only his undershirt on. He tied the material as best he could around the wound in Montgomery, doing everything possible to stop the bleeding, which had worsened when the sword disappeared, leaving the wound wide open.

"Oh dear heavens no! Montgomery…" Alice wept as she looked at him and ran her hand soothingly over his face. "What have you done?" She whispered to him.

"I have done what needed to be done. I acted with bravery and courage. There was no truth in what the Illusionist showed to me, and this is the proof of it. We have the Blue Fire Crystal, and the Illusionist is defeated." He sighed and closed his eyes.

"We have to get him out of here." Alice stated adamantly. "He can't be up here in all this." She waved her hand at the horrible weather around them and the shaking earth beneath their feet.

Chippa went to her side and tugged on her coat. She looked down, and he held up the Blue Fire Crystal to her with both paws.

"So much trouble for this thing…" She said quietly as she took it from him carefully, and tucked it into her bag. As she did so, she remembered the secret vial hidden in the inner pocket of her bag. She unzipped the pocket and pulled out the glass bottle of Diovalo's blood.

"What is that?" Oscar asked, looking up at her with tears in his eyes.

"It might be our only way out of here, if Diovalo can somehow make it across the desert. I know he shouldn't try to do it, but we have no choice. I refuse to lose my Montgomery here."

Alice looked at her oldest cat, who lay weakening, surrounded by his family. Sophie had her face nuzzled into his neck and she wasn't moving.

Alice looked back at the vial for a moment and took a deep breath. She reached her hand up far over her head, and cried out with all of the volume she could muster. "Diovalo! Diovalo come! I need you!"

The dark blood in the vial began to glow vibrantly with a fiery red light that suddenly shot up into the grim sky like a beacon. She held it aloft and minutes later, Tao; who was peering at the horizon searching for the dragon, spoke out.

"There he is! I see him!" She nodded in a northwest direction over the great sand dunes of the Aridan desert.

Everyone watched closely, as the great dragon sped across the sky to them. Not far behind him, long streaks shot up out of the desert dunes, aiming right for him.

"What are those things coming out of the sand?" Oscar asked in bewilderment.

Alice groaned. "I think they're giant sand snakes. We have to hope with everything in us that none of them reaches Diovalo, or they'll kill him."

Oscar gasped and they all stared in desperation as Diovalo made his way toward the beacon, shining so brightly from the vial in Alice's hand. He narrowly escaped two giant sand snakes, and finally set his claws down on the stony plateau, as the winds picked up even more; blasting around them wildly.

"Elements 'es out of control!" Chippa cried out to them, his words nearly stolen from his mouth by the gusts whipping around them.

Henderson and Alice were trying to figure out how to get Montgomery off of the ground and onto Diovalo's back, when Chippa stopped them.

"I can try to use the air!" He offered with a bit of confidence. I 'well try." He looked uncertain, but more than willing.

Chippa rubbed his paws together, and then pushed the air between him and Montgomery. Everyone watched in amazement as the air lifted the big cat off of the ground. Chippa walked with him, concentrating as hard as he could as he moved Montgomery through the air, and gently settled him into the hollow behind Diovalo's wing.

Alice, Marlowe, and Sophie sat with him, while Henderson went with Chippa, Bailey, Tao, and Jynx to the hollow behind Diovalo's other wing. Jynx looked at Oscar sternly.

~ 256 ~

"Okay Oscar, you can ride on the dragon's neck. Just hold on tight and don't fall off." She narrowed her eyes at him, and he grinned at her wide-eyed as he bounced where he stood.

"Really? I get to ride on his neck? Thank you!" Oscar raced up to the spot just behind Diovalo's head where Alice normally sat, and he curled his kitten claws tightly around the scales there.

As soon as everyone was nestled in, Diovalo lifted off of the ground and flew westward, doing his best to avoid the desert dunes, and the giant sand snakes.

When he'd gone far enough clear of them, he turned northward and flew for a long while through the screaming wind and pounding rain, amidst streaks of lightening, and rolling thunder.

At long last he touched down at the edge of the Green Forest, in a wide meadow. The clouds were thick and dark there as well, and lighting shot across the sky, but there was no rain. The wind gusted, but with much less force than it had in the southeast on the plateau.

Chippa worked just as carefully to get Montgomery down off of the dragon as he had in getting him up onto it, and he brought the old cat to rest in a thick, soft, patch of grass beside a cool silver stream.

Chippa looked up at Diovalo, who brought his head down close to the group. "Can you save him?" He asked hopefully.

Henderson spoke for all of them in their confusion. "How could Diovalo save Montgomery?"

Chippa turned to glance at them all. "Dragon tears 'es powerful healing."

"Don't try to save me!" Montgomery breathed out with labored effort. "I have used the last of my nine lives being as brave and courageous as I have ever been, and as I have always tried to be." He blinked his eyes slowly. "I could ask for no greater honor than to save all of you; my family. My dearest ones."

Sophie wept. "Please don't go! Stay here! I need you to stay here. Let Diovalo heal you! We have to try something! Anything! You can't leave me, Montgomery!" She pleaded and begged, but he gave his head a little shake.

"No my dear, it's my time to go. We must all go at some point." His breath grew thin and shallow.

"No! Montgomery, whatever will I do without you?" She whispered through her tears.

Montgomery gave her a little smile. "Carry on, and fight the good fight. Evil cannot ever win."

Sophie pulled her glowing fairy garland off of her neck and placed it around his head, arranging it on him. "Every one of my heartbeats, all of my life, will whisper your name." She choked out through her tears. He looked at all of the cats around him, and Alice, and Henderson.

"Thank you, Henderson, for taking such excellent care of me all of my life." Montgomery gazed at him through heavily lidded eyes. Henderson nodded and turned away from him, standing alone, and weeping.

"Thank you, Alice, for being all that you have been to me throughout my years with you. I wouldn't trade a moment of it. I love you all." He sighed again, and closed his eyes. Alice stroked him tenderly.

As her fingers moved through his fur, he disappeared, and there was no trace of him left behind;

not even the garland. All of them gasped and looked at each other.

"Where is he?" Alice entreated Chippa. "Do you know? What just happened?"

Chippa blinked his big, black eyes sadly, as tears rolled out of them. "I doesn't know. He 'es gone, that 'es all."

They all knew that for certain. Montgomery had passed away and left them, vanishing into thin air.

Alice reached for Marlowe and Bailey, then Tao and Jynx, as they all wept and held tightly to one another, but Sophie walked away from them in silence, and went to the edge of the meadow to a stand of trees, where she sat alone with her head bowed.

After a while, Alice rested on a big rock and looked at her family. One short than they had been when they arrived in Corevé. She shook her head and wished that it had gone differently. It was a high price to pay, and she wondered if it was too high a price.

She felt a wet drop on her hand, and when she looked up, she saw that Diovalo had shed a few tears. They fell one by one onto her hand; big and thick. They dissolved into her skin, and where the cut had been, she saw that it was healed almost immediately.

More drops began to fall all around her, and she looked up again, but it wasn't tears from Diovalo. The clouds above had begun to spill out their raindrops to the ground below.

Marlowe padded to Sophie's distant spot, and he sat beside her without a word. She wept for a while, and he stayed where he was, silently, at her side.

When several minutes had passed, she finally spoke. "We've been friends nearly all my life." She began, only just loud enough for Marlowe to hear her. "He was only a couple of years older than me when I came to live with Alice. We've fought, and been close friends, and lived together since I was a kitten."

Marlowe listened, and said nothing.

"I have no idea how I'm ever going to go on without him. I feel like... like I've just lost part of myself. I don't really think I'm of any true use to the family. Not in a practical way. Montgomery was the only one who ever saw any value in me."

She let out an ironic sort of laugh. "I know I'm shallow and vain. He was just able to see past all of that, and find some true worth in me, and now that he's gone, I feel like that worth in me is gone with him. Does it stop existing in me if he was the only one who saw it?" She asked, without really wanting an answer. She was sure that she already knew the truth.

Marlowe spoke gently. "You have a big and caring heart, and in those rare moments when you let it show, and when you use your considerable courage and strength, nothing ever stops you. Never doubt that you are needed and loved in this family."

Sophie blinked at him in surprise, but leaned over and gave him a nudge. "Thank you." She whispered.

"He isn't gone from you, Sophie. He never will be, as long as you can remember him. All you need to do is close your eyes and look back over a lifetime of memories. Everything about him will be there, and you can find him and treasure him anytime you want to. He will exist within you as long as you remember him." Marlowe's voice was filled with compassion and comfort.

Sophie nodded. "I feel so much pain and loss right now, but I think you're right. He's so much a part of me that he will always be with me."

"He will always be with all of us, my friend." Marlowe answered.

Raindrops began to fall thicker and faster around them. Marlowe looked up doubtfully at the threatening skies above. "The rain is getting worse. You should come back to our camp."

Sophie lifted her face and let the raindrops fall all over it, rolling back off of her forehead and down her cheeks.

"Not yet. I want to let the rain wash away this heartbreaking sadness. This rainstorm you see crying out over us from the sky is just what it feels like in my heart right now. I wish he had stayed. I wish with everything in me that he was here."

Marlowe gave her a gentle nudge. "Bleed out your sorrows then, but come back soon." He turned and left her.

The rain grew worse, and the winds picked up. The earth began to tremble, and the volcanoes to the north spewed forth fire and smoke. The world around them was falling to pieces.

Sophie made it back to camp just as Chippa was doing his best to create an air bubble around them to protect them from the elements. He managed it, and they were kept dry from the driving rain, and sheltered from the growing winds. Sophie did not speak to anyone, and the others only shared a little conversation before they all tried to get some sleep.

Chapter Fifteen

Full Circle

None of them slept much, and by the break of dawn they could see that there was no sense in staying where they were. All of the elements had grown even more uncontrollable during the night.

Chippa had to relinquish the protective air bubble, and as they were readying to leave their camp, the winds were so bad that they could barely hear each other speak.

They climbed onto Diovalo, and Alice sat at his neck just behind his head. It was a rough take off for him as they left the ground; for the powerful gusts that twisted and turned past them. They finally got into the air, and Diovalo started flying over the Green Forest.

They saw the White Song Forest below; a pristine white circle in sea of varying shades of green. It felt like forever ago to them that they had walked through it and seen the Fairy Sway.

As they were flying over the western side of Lyria, the wind screamed around them. It had grown so powerful that it had begun to tear limbs off of big trees, and rip smaller trees right out of the ground.

All kinds of things were flying past them, from flurries of small leaves and twigs, to much bigger leaves the size of their silver leaf boats, and even tree limbs the size of logs.

Diovalo did his best to avoid all of it, but one of the biggest trees that was whipping around in the gusts through the air, smashed into his left wing and he faltered.

The great red dragon tried to keep flying, but he was injured too badly, and they began to jolt unevenly downward out of the sky, heading swiftly to the ground in a wide spiral.

Chippa picked his face up from where he'd had it buried in Bailey's side, and looked around.

"What 'es 'et?" He cried out loudly. Henderson leaned close and yelled in Chippa's ear.

"Diovalo is hurt. Something hit his wing, and he can't fly. We're landing... or crashing." He answered worriedly.

Chippa panicked. He peeked out past Bailey where he had a better view of what was going on around him. There was no hope for it. Henderson was right; they were going down.

Staring for a long moment, Chippa looked at Henderson. "What wing 'es 'et? I can try to help!"

Henderson pursed his lips a moment and pointed at Diovalo's left wing on the other side of his back. "That wing. On the other side."

Chippa whined and pressed his paws together, wringing them for a minute, but Diovalo skewed again in his downward turns, letting out a mighty roar of pain. Chippa knew that he had to do whatever he could to help; no matter what it might cost him.

The Inkling moved forward, inching himself along the dragon's big scales as quickly as he could; holding on tightly while the wind rushed around his ears and tail, blasting at his fur. His fingers and toes on every paw were locked fast around each scale as he clamored across the dragon's back to his other wing.

~ 263 ~

The cats all watched him in horror; terrified that he might fall off or be blown away, but after long, tense moments, he made it. The cats tried to help him into the hollow behind the injured wing, but Chippa shook his head at them.

He moved right past them, and out onto Diovalo's wing. Step by step he made his way across to the spot where Diovalo had been injured. For one moment, Chippa looked down. The dizzying height and steep spiraling pattern made him cringe and shut his eyes tight, but after a deep breath he opened them again, and moved his paws over the front edge of Diovalo's wing.

The dragon looked back at him, and Chippa nodded to him. He had caused the air to push upward beneath Diovalo's wing, lifting and carrying him, so that as long as Diovalo's wing was extended, they could soar without him having to move it.

Chippa remained on Diovalo's wing, making sure that the air cushion he had made beneath the dragon continued to work as he wanted it to.

Just as all of them were feeling reassured that they'd be all right flying, the thick clouds overhead grew too heavy, and rain began to pour over them much harder than it had the night before.

Lightning raced through the sky as the ground shook and rumbled beneath them. The winds howled and raged, while smoke and lava began exploding from the volcanoes at greater heights. Still, they flew onward; all of them holding on to Diovalo for their lives.

After what seemed like an eternity, they saw that they had crossed over the Sea of Tranquility, and the lake that washed up into it. Beyond that, they could finally see Mari Village below them. Diovalo and Chippa carefully brought them down into a wide meadow at the far northern edge of the village, where there was space for the dragon to land.

The Inklings were in a sheer panic; all of them rushing around the village at the sight of a dragon coming in, but as he drew nearer, they could all see Chippa standing on the edge of his wing. The whole village stopped and stared as the great dragon touched down.

Alice and her family came down off of Diovalo, and she wrapped her arms around Chippa tightly, when he made it to the ground. He hugged her in return, and she set him on the grass, just as every member of the village arrived at the field; all of them gaping in amazement.

"Chippa!" Alice cried out loudly. "We never would have made it without you; especially getting back here! You've done a tremendous job! You've saved us all, and you are a hero!"

The little Inkling grinned widely, and wiped at the corner of one eye. Bayless Grand Mari and Oppa Mari came through the crowd of Inklings to the dragon, and the company.

"You 'es back!" Bayless Grand Mari exclaimed in wonder, "and you brought a dragon?" He stared up at Diovalo, who winced in pain.

"We has the Blue Fire Crystal!" Chippa called out, and then he turned to Oppa Mari, the healer. "Diovalo 'es the dragon. He 'es hurt. Please heal 'et!" He implored, and she looked from him up to the dragon's wing where he pointed.

"Of course!" She answered, and she went directly to work. The dragon only eyed her cautiously for a moment before lowering his wing to her so that she could help him.

"The village 'es damaged some, but not so bad as the rest of Corevé." Bayless Grand Mari told Chippa. "We 'es been protecting this place from the wild elements, but we can't do 'et for much longer! We must hurry!" He urged, waving his paws at Chippa.

Chippa took Alice's hand and she walked with him to the Element Temple near the clearing. She took the Blue Fire Crystal from her bag, and gently set it back on its pillar with the other crystals. Then she set the seashell compass on the pillar at the center.

Everyone looked up hopefully; eyeing the horizon to the east, and the world around them, desperate to see the end of the chaos.

Following one final great upheaval of all of the elements, they all died down in peace and calm, as if sighing in relief, and finally relaxing.

Alice looked down at Chippa. "Is it done?"

Chippa beamed. "'Et's done!"

He jumped and turned in a happy circle where he stood. "'Et's done! We did 'et!" He chattered and chirped blissfully, and all of the Inklings cheered for them.

"We have something to make sure that this never happens again!" Alice spoke out over the crowd around them. Bayless Grand Mari looked at her in surprise.

"What does you have?" He asked with interest.

Alice took the silver ring from Marlowe's collar. "This was a gift from the Fairy Queen. She told us that if we place it around the element stones here, they will be protected, and nothing will ever be able to separate them again. No one can steal them. They will always be safe."

Bayless Grand Mari looked mightily impressed. "You 'es bringing an important thing. We 'es all very grateful." He nodded to her and bowed. Following his lead, the entire tribe bowed low to Alice, the cats, Henderson, and Chippa.

Alice felt her cheeks grow warm and she giggled a little. Turning to the element crystals, they saw that just as the Fairy Queen had said, the silvery ring expanded until it was just big enough to fit around the stones where they sat on their pillars. It stayed in place; hovering and glowing brightly around them.

Alice sighed with contentment and relief, and walked from the Element Temple with her family. She spoke to Bayless Grand Mari and the tribe again.

Clearing her throat, she lifted her voice so everyone could hear. "The thief was an illusionist. He was able to transform before our eyes. When we first encountered him, he was an Inkling like all of you, but then he changed right in front of us into a kind of man, and when I defeated him, he disappeared altogether. He was the mystery Inkling that went into the Element Temple."

All of the Inklings began to talk about what they had just learned, and Bayless Grand Mari grumbled about how anything could have the disrespect to turn itself into an Inkling.

Chippa raised his eyes to Alice, and waved his paw subtly to indicate that she should follow him. Alice, the cats, and Henderson did so. They went back to

Diovalo, where he had stayed in the field, and they saw Oppa Mari just climbing down from his back.

"He 'es all right. He 'es healed now." She grinned and gazed at them all a little bashfully. "I 'es never healing a dragon before. I like 'et."

Diovalo brought his head down close to her. "I am grateful. Thank you for your kindness and your work."

He looked at Alice, Henderson, and the cats. "I must go back to my home in Siang. I have an obligation to fight the evil that is taking over there, and defeat it. I've learned some courage and strength from all of you. I thought that I could just leave and escape it, but now I realize that I need to stand up for what I know is right. Alice, I still owe you my life; that debt has not yet been repaid, but it will be."

Alice nodded and gave his snout a rub before he stood up and towered over them all, giving his wings a powerful thrust through the air, and then lifting off to the skies. They watched him until he was gone, and Oscar sighed sadly.

"I'm going to miss riding on a dragon." He said with a longing gaze.

Bayless Grand Mari whistled loudly, and called the attention of everyone in the tribe. "Now everything 'es 'fexed, and we has our heroes!" He walked to Chippa and took him by the paw, raising their paws together up in the air. All the Inklings cheered.

Alice realized that the entire village was standing before them, looking at them. Her mind had been on returning the Blue Fire Crystal when they had first landed, and then on Diovalo after that, but now that she was the center of attention, she realized that she wasn't looking quite her best.

She tried to push the loose strands of her white hair back from her face, straighten her tattered hat, and tidy her coat and dress some.

Henderson did the same; giving his few strands of thin hair at the top a quick finger comb, and then tugging at his undershirt and jacket. He looked displeased with the results and sighed wearily, as Alice gave him a smile.

"Don't you fret my friend, we're heroes here, and everyone is going to remember what we did; not what we looked like on the day that we returned." He nodded and gave her a half-hearted smile.

Bayless Grand Mari turned to Chippa. "You has not chosen what your future 'es going to be 'en the tribe. Now you 'es saving all of Corevé and all of us. You 'es choosing any future you wants. What choice does you make?" He asked loudly.

Chippa looked at Alice and the cats, and took a deep breath. Lifting his chin, he spoke so that all of his tribe could hear him. "I learned much on 'thes journey. I know now I 'es wanting to be a healer, and work 'weth Oppa Mari."

There was a stunned silence over the field, and all of the Inklings including Bayless Grand Mari, looked at Oppa Mari. She smiled wide and went to Chippa, taking his paw in hers as Bayless Grand Mari let go of it.

"Then you 'es being a healer 'weth me, and I 'es being very proud to teach you." The dark old Inkling answered happily.

Chippa shouted, "Woohoo!" and jumped a bit in the air. He turned to Alice, Henderson, and the cats. "'Et's because of all of you." He said quietly.

Alice shook her head. "No my dear, it's because of you. You have always been this brave and strong; always this courageous, and now everyone else can see it too. You have great value, and now they all know it."

Chippa nodded, and faced his tribe. Even Jika Mari gave him a nod of approval. He beamed.

"Well," Alice sighed, looking at all of them, "I think it's time for my family and me to go back to our home and our world."

Just then, a soft glowing light came through the air and stopped before them. It was a fairy. She was dressed in silver, and she carried a white leaf that was wrapped around something. They all turned to look at her, and she spoke to them with a small, and pleasant voice.

"I have a message for you." She began. "Because of Sophie's generosity in giving her Star Flower garland to Montgomery while he was alive with you, the Fairy Queen has made an exception for him."

They listened to her in puzzlement, and she continued. "Because of your big heart, Sophie, the Fairy Queen will allow Montgomery to live and remain in the White Song Forest as a guardian of the fairies. All nine of his lives are gone, so he can never leave the forest, or he will disappear forever."

Sophie drew close to her. "Wait… are you saying that he's alive?"

The fairy nodded. "He is, but only so long as he stays in the White Song Forest. You see, when he died, he was wearing your gift of the Star Flower garland. It brought him to us, and the Fairy Queen breathed life back into him once more. It's a limited gift. He can never leave, and you will never see him again, but he will be very well cared for and loved, and I can tell you that he is truly happy. He is youthful and strong. He has made the choice to remain there and live among us. He did ask me to send this to you, Sophie."

The lovely fairy handed the white leaf wrapped package to Alice. Alice opened it for Sophie as Sophie watched with tears in her eyes. They shared a momentary glance with Marlowe. The leaf fell away, and in Alice's hand was Montgomery's monocle.

She and Sophie both stifled a cry. Alice turned to Sophie and the cat lifted her chin so that Alice could fasten it to her diamond collar.

"It's perfect." Alice told her with a smile and a soothing pat.

Alice turned to the messenger fairy. "I don't think I've ever heard of anything so sweet and beautiful. Please give Montgomery our love, and tell him that we wish him well in his new life. He is missed, and he will always be cherished by us."

The fairy bowed low, and then turned and flew off, vanishing a few moments later from their sight.

Bayless Grand Mari looked up at Alice and spoke so that the entire tribe could hear him. "You 'es the Chosen One. Chippa was right. You 'es saved all of our world. No one could have done 'et but you."

Alice smiled and felt her cheeks warm again. "I could never have done it without my cats, Henderson, and especially Chippa."

"You has been given a special reward. A 'geft. Because you 'es saving the Blue Fire Crystal and restoring the balance to the elements, you 'es now having the same power 'weth the elements that the

~ 271 ~

Inklings has. No one else has 'thes 'geft. You 'es a protector." Bayless Grand Mari told her seriously. "Very special."

Amazement flooded through her, and she silently wondered if she'd be able to use her gift in her own world, or only in Corevé. She bowed her head to him slightly.

"Thank you. It has been my privilege to have Chippa at my side, and to do this mission for all of you, and for beautiful Corevé." The Inklings all cheered her, Henderson, and the cats.

Chippa reached up and took her finger in his paw, curling his small fingers around it. "'Es time to go back to your home." He said quietly.

Alice looked around at her cats. "I don't think you'll look like this when we get home, and I will be sorry that you won't be able to talk to me the same way that you do now, but I'll still be listening when you tell me things."

Turning to Chippa, she nodded. "Thank you my friend, for everything. I miss you already, little one." She told him with a loving smile, and then everything went black.

CHAPTER SIXTEEN

REALIZATION

The old grandfather clock ticked away, and Alice opened her eyes. She blinked, and looked about the bedroom. She was in her bed. Sitting up slowly, she tried to figure out how she had gotten there. She had been standing beside Chippa only a moment before.

Turning to look over at the clock on her dresser, she saw that it was only one minute past the last minute she had looked at that clock, before the whole adventure began. No time had passed at all.

She reached up and rubbed her eyes; gazing at the room again. Marlowe was curled up at her feet. He lifted his head and looked at her. It was strange to her to see him in his usual fur coat, such a small and normal size, resting at the foot of her bed.

"Marlowe…" She began quietly. He got up and stretched, arching his back, and then padded silently up the bed to her. "Did… did all of that really happen or was it just a dream?"

He leaned his head down and licked at the back of her right hand as he began to purr. She rubbed the fingers of her left hand over his ears, but then she stopped as he looked up at her, and she lifted her right hand to look at the back of it in the dim light of the room.

There was a faint scar just above her thumb. She gasped. She touched it gently. "It's… it's where I was cut! Diovalo healed that for me. It looks just like it did when we were in the meadow that night and he… he healed it with his tears!"

Alice breathed out in amazement. "It *was* real!" She leaned over the edge of the bed and peered around it to look by the fireplace. Sophie was sleeping in Montgomery's bed, and she had his small monocle fastened on her diamond collar.

"Oh no… my dear, poor, Montgomery." She sighed and wiped a tear at the corner of her eye. More tears began to come, and she laid back down and nestled her head into her pillow, looking out of the window at the night.

Marlowe laid beside her, tucked his paws underneath him, and purred quietly with his eyes closed.

When morning came, she and Henderson were both quiet. They went about their routine as normal; neither one of them speaking about what had happened.

After breakfast, she went to the front door and looked down as she opened it. Marlowe was beside her, gazing up at her expectantly.

"Coming along then?" She smiled at him. She could almost hear his voice in her head, and it made her happy. "Of course you are. Let's go."

Alice strolled with him down the sunny lane to the end of the street where the old church was. Marlowe waited outside for her, and she went in with her chin lifted and her spirits high.

She walked into the reception room and saw Deborah's table set up where it had been the last time she was in, which was only the day before, in Deborah's world.

The young woman was speaking to another older lady. They both turned to look at Alice.

Alice smiled widely at the other older woman. "Genevieve! How lovely to see you here!"

Before Genevieve could reply, Deborah frowned at Alice. "Oh, it's you again, ma'am. I've already told you, there's nothing here for you. What are you doing back here?"

Alice narrowed her eyes and stepped up to the table. "I'm here to teach knitting and defensive skills, and no one could do it as well as me."

Deborah sighed and planted her hands on the table, pushing herself up dramatically as though it was some effort to do so, and it was a great burden for her to have to address Alice and handle her. "Listen, I already told you that we don't need you or want you here-"

Genevieve's eyes went wide and burned dangerously at Deborah. "Do you have any idea to whom you are speaking? This is Lieutenant General George Perivale's wife!"

Deborah gasped, and stared at Alice. "I... I didn't realize that. I'm so sorry."

Alice took a deep breath. "My husband was one of the bravest and strongest men in Her Majesty's service, and you're going to find that I am just as strong, just as determined, and far less patient than he was. Now if you will, sign me up before I contact your superiors!"

Genevieve kept her sharp gaze on Deborah. "I *am* her superior. Young lady, if you wish to keep your position here, you had better get Mrs. Perivale signed up for the Widows of War program, and I would be glad to take any class that she is willing to teach! I'll be signing up for all of them!"

Deborah had her job done swiftly and silently. Genevieve and Alice walked out of the church smiling at one another.

"Do you know, I've always admired you, Alice." Genevieve told her pleasantly. "I'm so delighted that you'll be joining us in our work here. We really do need you! You'll make such a difference!"

"I'm very glad to be of help! I am certain that there is quite a bit that I'll be able to do." She was proud and satisfied with herself that she had returned to the church to resolve the issue. It felt complete to her, and it felt right.

When she and Marlowe walked through the door, Henderson came to her and handed her a message. "It's from Edward." He said with a smile as he turned and left her.

She opened the note. 'We'll come for dinner with you this Friday. I'm so sorry about the call yesterday. We miss you and love you dearly, mother.' She sighed and smiled, holding her hand over her heart.

"He is a good boy." She said quietly as she tucked the note into her pocket.

Later that afternoon, she was sitting in an armchair in the library, knitting a blanket and thinking about all that had happened.

Marlowe was near her feet, and the rest of the cats were curled up around the fireplace. The clock ticked, the fire crackled, and the sounds of the city outside were muffled.

Alice gazed down at the knitting needles in her hands, and the new scar she bore; thinking about them.

Something had stuck in the back of her mind, and she had gone over it and over it, but it just wouldn't go away, and she puzzled at it until something finally snapped.

Henderson walked into the library, and she sprang up from her chair at the same moment. He jumped slightly; blanching skittishly.

"Oh! I'm sorry Madam, if I've startled you!" He gasped; startled himself.

Alice shook her head and held out her hand, looking from him to the cats. "I've just realized something!" She began to pace along the floor as she explained.

"I've been thinking about this, and it didn't make sense until now! The Illusionist was an illusion... he wasn't real. The Illusionary Palace was an illusion; it wasn't real either. So how could I be injured and scarred from something that wasn't real?" The cats all sat up and watched her as she walked back and forth.

"The Illusionist said it, and Tao... you said it too!" She looked at her small Siamese cat, sitting at attention beside the fireplace.

"At the center of a lie, no matter how big the lie, there is usually truth. Everything at the Illusionary Palace was a lie, except one thing, and that was the thing that cut me when I killed the lie! It was the truth! Don't you see?" She stopped pacing and turned to face them all.

They stared at her in silence, waiting. She looked at each of them and sighed. Something bright and red caught her eye; and the attention of Henderson and the cats.

They all looked up to the old glass bottle with a thin chain woven around it in places, sitting on the top of Alice's rolltop desk.

The blood in the vial had begun to glow, bright and vibrant. "I knew it!" Alice cried out as she rushed to her desk and picked up the vial, holding it in her hands. She turned to face her family.

"The seed of truth that cut me... the truth that left this scar on my hand, was that the Illusionist was an illusion! He wasn't the villain! He wasn't the one we should have defeated. He was just a game; an illusion created by the *real* villain; the sorceress who is taking all the fire breathing dragons from Siang. She took the Blue Fire Crystal as well, but we got it back from her. Look at this bottle! It's Diovalo. He's in trouble, and he needs me. He needs us! We have got to find a way to get back to Corevé and help him! We have to save their world!"

...to be continued in book two of the Mrs. Perivale series: **Mrs. Perivale and the Dragon Prince**

The Starling Chronicles

Book One

The Starlings of Ramblewood

By Dash Hoffman

Chapter One
Endings and Beginnings

The rhythmic sway of a heavy old brass pendulum swished in sync with the soft tick – tick – ticking of the timeworn grandfather clock that stood sentry near the front door of the apartment. The sounds filled the silent air, thick with grief and confusion.

The apartment was well designed; beautiful furnishings, lofty view of the bustling streets far below, several large windows that let in sunlight, and city light, and a pretty picture of the world outside, save for that moment. At that moment the skies were filled with dark, heavy clouds that were pouring themselves out onto the earth and everything on it.

There was only one person in the apartment; a young girl of fourteen years old. Her green eyes were puffy and rimmed with red, and her lips were slightly swollen from weeping, though she had cried herself out, and there were no more tears to be had.

A deep grinding noise emerged from the depths of the grandfather clock as the gears whirred and spun, and golden chimes began to ring out; tolling the hour one beat at a time, like a heartbeat, going, going, gone. It was ten in the morning.

She looked at the aged piece, and her eyes stopped on a carefully trimmed square of paper; yellowed at the edges, which curled slightly. She knew the words that were written there; she'd read them countless times, but she read them again, just to see the handwriting of the woman who had composed the letters into words, into a thought shared.

'The irony of time is that it does not exist'

The girl wished with everything in her heart that time did not exist, for if it didn't, things wouldn't change and everything would stay the same, and her mother would still be there with her.

A strong knock sounded at the door beside the clock. The girl's heart skipped a beat, and her eyes flew to the entrance of her home as the handle turned. Her breath quickened as the door opened, but then a flood of relief washed through her when she saw the woman who walked into the room.

The girl was reminded sharply and suddenly of how similar her mother and her aunt looked. Her mother Marleigh had long, dark brown hair with gentle waves in it, green eyes, olive skin, and a sweet and warm smile. Her aunt Vianne was not quite as slender as Marleigh, though she was fit. Vianne stood a few inches shorter than Marleigh, with the same brown hair in big curls that almost reached her shoulders. Her eyes were green as well, her skin olive toned, and her smile which was usually as warm as Marleigh's, was gone that day.

"Jules!" Vianne exclaimed as she blinked back tears and pressed her lips together tightly for a moment, "Goodness, it's been so long since I've seen you. You've grown so much. Come here darling. Come here." She held her arms out, and for the first time since the news had come about her mother's death, Jules felt some lightness in her grief. The sharing of it with someone who loved her mother as much as she did made the pain more bearable somehow.

Jules sprung from the sofa and into her aunt's arms, burying her face in the woman's neck and letting her sorrow flow once more. Somehow there were a few more tears that found their way to her cheeks and chin, before leaving her. They held one another tightly for a long minute, and then Vianne let her go and looked down at her.

"Jules, I know this is terrible timing, but there's something that you have to know. There's someone that you have to meet right now." Vianne looked as serious as Jules had ever seen her, though she hadn't seen her very often in her growing up years.

Confusion furrowed Jules' brow. "Someone I need to... meet?" She asked quizzically. She couldn't for the life of her imagine who it might be; not so soon after her mother's death.

Vianne stepped aside, and Jules drew in a sharp breath of wonder. There, standing behind where Jules had been, was a young boy. He was two inches shorter than Jules, with dark brown hair that lay in modest, gentle curls around his head. He had olive toned skin, and his frame was thin but sturdy. Jules stared at his eyes. They were exactly like hers.

"Jules, this is Henry. Henry..." Vianne took a deep breath and let it out slowly, pacing herself. "This is your sister, Jules." Vianne said nothing more then, and the boy and the girl stood silent as well, staring at one another as the clock ticked ever onward.

"Sister?" He whispered, tearing his eyes from Jules and looking up suddenly at Vianne. "I... that can't be.

You never told me I had a sister!" The confusion on his face matched that of Jules'.

She frowned at her aunt. "Is this some kind of joke? I don't have a brother! How could you try to play some kind of joke like this on me, especially today?" Pain stabbed at her heart again, and she planted her hands on her hips.

Vianne shook her head slowly, and looked from Henry to Jules. "I'm so very sorry. This is no joke. It's as true as can be. You two are brother and sister. I realize this is a shock to you both, but it's true. Marleigh was a mother to both of you, but for your own safety, we separated you two when Henry was born, and you were raised apart from one another. Now... with Marleigh gone, it seems that we have no choice but to put you two together and hope for the best. I'm sure you both have a million questions, but we don't have much time. I'm going to make a pot of tea, and we can talk for a few minutes, but then we have to leave."

With that, Vianne swept into the kitchen; her long, thin, multicolored silk jacket billowing out slightly behind her, almost like a half-full sail. Her sweet floral perfume left a scent in her wake. The clock ticked on in the silence, and Henry and Jules stared at each other.

They were both still for a long moment, but then she took the first few steps toward him, and in response, he began to walk slowly and carefully toward her; one foot in front of the other.

They stopped just before each other, staring into one another's faces and eyes. Jules and Henry had the same green eyes, just like Vianne's and Marleigh's. Her hair was long and straight, reaching to the middle of her back when it was loose, where his was close cropped to his head, save for the wavy curls at his crown. They looked like slightly different mirror images of each other.

She lifted her hand and held it out to him. "I'm Jules... Jules Starling." She said in a soft voice, trying to wrap her mind around what she was seeing.

He took her hand and gave it a friendly shake. "I'm Henry Starling." He answered quietly. They let go of each other and he raised his hand to his chin and scratched it thoughtfully.

"This is so... bizarre." He said in a soft voice, staring at her. "I never knew you existed. I didn't even know that my mother was alive."

Jules blinked. "What do you mean? Where have you been all this time?"

"I live with aunt Vianne. I've always lived with her. She told me that my mother was gone, so I was living with her. She's raising me." Henry pushed his hands down into his pockets. He was wearing a navy-blue button up shirt that was carefully pressed and tucked into his belted pants, and on his feet, he wore dark leather loafers.

It was a smart contrast to Jules' jeans, ankle boots, long sleeved t-shirt, and vest. Her hair was pulled up into a ponytail, and she wore a thin leather-strand braided bracelet that she had made herself.

"My mother..." Jules paused a moment, trying to make herself say the strange words, "I mean, *our* mother, just passed away." She shook her head. "This can't be real. This can't be true! You can't be her son. She never would have let you live somewhere else! She would have had you living with us if you were..."

She trailed off again, still staring at him, still trying to make any kind of sense of it.

"It's true!" Vianne's voice called from the kitchen.

Henry and Jules both looked at the doorway to the kitchen and then back to each other. She lifted her chin slightly. "How old are you?"

"I'm twelve." He answered simply. "How old are you?"

She did the math in her head as she replied. "I'm fourteen." She paused a moment. "I don't remember mom being pregnant, but I guess I wouldn't have noticed if I was a year old and change." She sighed in resignation. There was silence between them again as they regarded each other for another long moment.

He frowned slightly. "I'm so sorry to hear that she's gone; that you've lost her. It must be dreadful for you. I... I'm not quite sure how I should feel, I mean, I've lived my whole life thinking that she was gone. I never knew her, but you've always had her, and I can't imagine losing someone you've always had. I'm sorry." He said again.

Jules swallowed the lump that formed in her throat and nodded. "Me too." she whispered. Then she tilted her head a little to the side; her pony tail shifted slightly. "Do you think this is real? Do you think you're really my brother?"

Henry nodded. "I do. Look at us. It's... it's like looking in the mirror, almost. I don't know how it's possible, but I do believe it."

She shook her head, and her ponytail swung a little. "Then I'm glad." She bit at her lower lip for a moment and drew in a long, slow breath to steady herself. When she spoke again, her voice cracked.

"I thought I was going to be alone in the world, except for aunt Vianne, but I guess I'm not. I guess you're not. I guess... I guess we have each other." She gave him a hopeful look.

He returned a firm nod to her. "We do indeed." He agreed with her.

Before he could add anything else, Vianne called them to the small dining room just off of the kitchen and living room. The strange and tender moment between the newly met siblings broke, and they walked together into the other room.

Tea was waiting on the table; three pretty china cups, sitting neatly in china saucers, set at three places on the dining room table. They each had a cloth napkin, and a cookie. Amber colored liquid in the teacups sent off undulating swirls of steam, and the crisp scent of the tea touched delicately at their noses.

Jules and Henry glanced at each other, and then looked to Vianne, who was standing behind her chair waiting for them. She gave them each a kind half-smile that didn't quite reach her eyes, and they sat.

She poured milk into her tea and stirred it with a little teaspoon. "I wish you two were meeting under better circumstances, I really do. There's just no way around it now." She said in a quiet voice.

"Why haven't we met before?" Henry asked, giving her a narrow look. "I've spent my whole life with you, thinking my mother was dead already, and never knowing I had a sister in this world. I would have preferred to grow up with them both, not that I'm ungrateful to you for raising me, but they are my family. Or..." He paused with a disappointed look, "they were."

Vianne sighed, and Jules felt a surge of relief that Henry had pressed again for more information about them and their strange beginnings. She felt just as he did, that they should always have been together from the beginning.

"You've been kept apart so that you would be safe. Marleigh and I didn't want to do it, but there was no choice in the matter, really. It was the best way to protect you." She sounded tired. Vianne lifted her teacup and took a long sip of her brew.

"How could keeping us apart keep us safe?" Jules questioned suspiciously. "That doesn't make any sense. What would we need to be kept safe from anyway?" She had never in her life felt that she was in any danger.

Vianne set her cup back in the saucer and touched both of her forefingers to the rim of it as she spoke, without raising her eyes to look at either of the children.

"You needed to be kept safe from the same people who killed you mother. We thought that separating you and raising you apart would give you a better chance. We were right, I think, but now that my sister is gone, you both need to stay with me; as close to me as possible. It's the only way." She was quiet then, as both Henry and Jules stared at her.

Jules tried to find her voice, and after several long moments, she was able to speak just above a whisper. "Killed? She was killed?"

Vianne looked at her with a pained expression. "They didn't tell you that?" She asked in a soft voice as she reached her hand out to her niece. "I'm so sorry. I thought you knew that. Who told you?"

Jules swallowed hard. "There was an officer at the door this morning. It didn't look like a regular police officer, but he said he was a special investigator. He just said that she…" she nearly choked saying the words as tears stung at her eyes again, "that she died at work. He said someone would come for me, but he didn't say who. He told me to wait here, so I did. Then you came."

It had been the worst morning of her whole life, and the only thing that had improved it was the arrival of her aunt, and the boy who was sitting across from her watching her with sorrowful eyes.

Vianne shook her head slowly. "I'm so sorry, honey. I thought they told you."

"They?" Jules frowned slightly.

"I mean he." Vianne looked away and waved her hand dismissively. "Well, we need to look to the immediate future for now. You'll be coming to live with Henry and me right away. I have a room ready for you. You'll just need to pack your things, and we'll go."

Jules looked down at her tea, staring at it. It had cooled enough that there was no more steam coming off of it. She was going to have to pack and leave her home, just as fast as that, and there was nothing to be done about it.

"I have so many questions." Henry filled the silence with his curiosity, looking from his sister to Vianne.

Vianne gave him a half-hearted smile. "Not today, dear. We will have lots of time to talk it all through. Today we need to focus on the necessary changes and nothing else."

Henry looked back over at Jules. "Would you like some help packing?" He offered kindly.

She raised her eyes to meet his. She didn't know what to say at first, but then she realized that she wanted to have the last few moments of her life in her home where she and her mother had lived together, just to herself.

"I appreciate you offering, but I think I'll just go pack my own things." She tried to sound polite, and she hoped that he would understand.

Henry gave her a nod and a sympathetic look, and she knew then that she was going to like having him in her life. He did get it. He got her, and that was an enormous and helpful relief.

She didn't feel like eating or drinking anything, but she made herself swallow the tea that was sitting before her, and then she excused herself from the table and pushed her chair in.

Giving her aunt a curious look, she said quietly, "What's going to happen to everything here that isn't mine? What about my mom's stuff?"

Vianne sighed and shook her head. "Someone else will come to get it, and we'll go through it later on. We don't need to make all of the changes at once. We'll do it a step at a time, and that will make it easier." She reached her hand out to Jules' and pressed her fingers warmly against Jules' hand.

"I know things are at their darkest now, but that only means that the road ahead has light that will heal you over time. It will heal all of us. You'll survive, and beautiful times will come again. For now, do little things, and the big things will be taken care of as we go along."

Jules nodded and walked through the living room and down the hallway to her bedroom. She stood in the doorway, looking around at her personal space in her home. There was a dresser with a few feminine figurines on it. There were pictures and posters on the walls of places around the world that she had either gone to with her mother, or wanted to go to someday. Most of them were sites yet unseen by her. Dreams of lands to discover.

There were shelves with books; lots of books. Her mother had insisted on homeschooling her, and they had studied almost everything under the sun, it seemed like. She considered taking all of them, but she'd read them each several times, and she guessed that they would wind up at her aunt's house eventually anyway.

She had a few stuffed animals on her bed, and she thought about taking them, but something in her heart told her that her childhood days were done in the biggest way, and that her life would never ever be the same again.

As she looked at the trinkets and toys that were set about here and there in her tidied room, she slowly became aware that most of what she was looking at wasn't anything that she was going to want to keep or take with her. It was all just stuff. None of it would bring her mother back. All of it brought memories to her, but the memories were there whether or not she had the stuff.

The weight of the pain in her heart and the worry on her mind made her need to go light; it made her want to let go of everything that she didn't absolutely have to have.

Taking her shoulder bag, she pushed a few small things into it that she did want to keep, and she pulled a small suitcase out of the closet and filled it with the clothes she would need, and a book she had been reading, 'Journey to the Center of the Earth'. It was written by a man who had the same name as her, 'Jules Verne'. She liked that fact as much as she liked the story.

With a long last look around, Jules held in the sob that wanted to sound from her throat, and she forced her aching heart to keep beating. She took a deep breath and whispered, "Goodbye, old life." Turning away from it, she went out to the living room to see her aunt and her brother waiting for her.

It was the strangest sensation she had ever known; walking out of her home for what would be the last time, locking the door behind her, and knowing that the key on the little braided keychain that she had made would never slip into the lock and open the home up again.

She left with her family, and did not turn around to look back over her shoulder. She was leaving and it was done. All she had was the road ahead of her, and she wanted nothing more at that moment than to keep her eyes on it.

***

They boarded a train in Grand Central Station, and Henry and Jules sat across from one another beside the window. They watched silently out of the glass as the train passed through the chaotic noise of the city, and through the seemingly unending rows of houses set on alternating streets, one after the other.

Finally the boxy houses gave way to patches of trees and wide open land in the countryside, and to long slim fences that rose and fell on the hills that flew past the train.

The day was wet everywhere; from the city to the suburbs, and raindrops that hit the train trailed into long thin lines, seeming to streak into the past right behind Jules, where her own tears appeared to have gone, leaving nothing in her to weep further.

As the train began to pull into the countryside, the dark clouds thinned and then broke apart, and golden shafts of sunlight filtered through them, overtaking them. By the time they were deep into the country, there was no more rain; nothing but a beautiful warm day.

Vianne stood up as the train came to one of its many stops, and the children followed her out of the car and onto the platform. The train station before them was nothing like the loud, dirty, noisy stations in the city. This one was small and made of wood, with a charming old style to it, as though it was from another century and hadn't noticed that the rest of the world had gone racing by into a much moderner future.

Despite her bleak mood, Jules noticed the modest place and liked it. It was cheery and welcoming, and that was a balm to her raw soul.

'*Sea Mist Cove*' read the tidy sign that hung from the sheltering roof over the platform. Jules blinked as she read it, and she realized for the first time that while she had seen her aunt Vianne a handful of times over the years as she had grown, she had never been to her home, and she had no idea where her aunt lived. She had only known that her aunt and her mother would meet up now and then for brief visits.

"Is that the name of the town here? Is this where you live?" Jules asked, turning her eyes from the trim little sign to her aunt.

Vianne nodded and gave her a smile. "It is. It's a spot of a town, but it has everything we need, and it's quite a lovely place to live. Henry enjoys it, don't you Henry?"

He shrugged lightly. "I wish it had a bigger library, but I do enjoy it. We live near the beach on the far side of the cove, so we don't really have any close neighbors. It's really private, which I like, and quiet. I do love walking along the beach at low tide. It's like treasure hunting."

Vianne ruffled her fingers over the brown curls atop his head and laughed softly. "I don't think there's a library big enough for you on this earth."

Henry chuckled quietly. "I think you're right." He turned to Jules then, and held his hand out to take her suitcase. "Can I carry that for you?"

She only held back for a moment before handing it to him. "Thanks." She said, adjusting the shoulder bag she had slung at an angle over her torso. She wasn't used to having help, but as she watched her brother picking up the suitcase, she realized it might be nice to have someone to share her time, troubles, and joys with.

He gave her an encouraging look. "I think you'll really like it here. It's nice. At least, I hope you'll like it here."

Vianne took them to her car, parked near the train station, and then drove them down the road and past the edge of the town.

Sea Mist Cove gave the impression that someone with a fanciful imagination had painted it on a warm summer day in a pleasant mood, and then breathed onto the painting and brought it all to life. There were small shops lining the main street, streetlamps that were elegantly and intricately designed as though from another era, flowers in pretty pots and hanging baskets set all about, and from what Jules could see, the whole town looked clean from top to bottom. There was no gum on the sidewalks or trash on the street. There were no long lines of cars honking at each other or billows of smoke coming from any buildings. It was a sweet town, and it made Jules feel calm and peaceful, which she hadn't expected at all.

Vianne drove them past the community and up and down a few hills until the narrow road turned right, and she turned left, pulling onto a winding lane that led over more green hills and past trees filled with leaves that danced in the ocean breeze.

Jules squinted a little as she looked out of the car window, letting that same breeze wash over her face and tug teasingly at the end of her ponytail. She could taste the sea salt on her lips, and she watched the way the afternoon light danced lambent across the tops of the waves, glittering as if the whole sea were diamonds.

When they came to a crest in the hill, she could easily see why the town had been named as it had. There was a big cove, almost a full circle, ringed with hills that were covered in trees, where the sea came in gently and washed up on a golden sandy shore, and that's where the town was built.

Beyond the cove, just outside of it, the sea seemed to take over the rest of the world, stretching out to the horizon so far that the blue of the water and the blue of the sky appeared to become one.

"Here we are." Vianne said with a tired smile as she came around the last curve and the trees along the road opened up fully into a wide clearing.

An arched sign made of filigree metalwork and looking as though it had been created in the 1800's, stood sentry over the road. There was a word on it, and Jules ducked her head down to look through the windshield of the car to read it just before they passed beneath it.

'Ramblewood'

"What's Ramblewood?" Jules asked, as the home and grounds came into clear view.

"This whole place is Ramblewood. The house, the grounds, the small forest we just drove through, the beach just down the hill there behind the house… this is all Ramblewood. It's an estate, actually, but that sounds so pretentious to me, that we skip that and keep it simple. Ramblewood is home, and that's where we live." Vianne made it sound so matter-of-fact that Jules could almost sense the hominess of it.

As she got out of the car and stood before the home, she drew in a deep breath and gazed in wonder. All of it entranced her from the first view. The house was two and a half stories tall; the architecture all Victorian, and absolutely pristine.

On the first level there was a spacious wraparound porch that ran the length of the house, with arched latticework and a delicately carved railing. There were big windows all the way around it, hung with lace curtains. The front door was at the corner of the house, and that whole corner had a regal and welcoming style to it.

On the second level there was another deck, with a short metal railing, that spanned the length and width of the deck below it. A rounded room came off of one side of the house, with five windows on the second level, and a grandly carved turret, like someone had placed a large dollop of chocolate cream atop the house. Above the front corner of the house there arose a tower, almost in the style of a French chateau, with smaller windows that looked out on all sides, and it was crowned with a small squared deck.

The grounds all around the house were immaculately kept; the green grass, hedges, and trees were trimmed, the flowers and bushes set about just so, and tenderly cared for. It was the finest, prettiest, most exotic and mysterious house that Jules had ever seen. She was astounded at the sight of it.

"This is where you live?" She asked, not taking her eyes from it.

"This is where *we* live." Vianne replied with a kind smile, wrapping her arm around Jules' shoulders. "I know this is the worst day of your life, but tomorrow will be the first day of your new life, and this will be a good home to have a new life in. You will find some happiness here. You will have a family here, and you will be at home here as long as you like. Welcome, my darling. Welcome to Ramblewood."

Ramblewood

Chapter Two
Mysteries

Vianne and Henry brought Jules into the house and they stopped in the octagonal foyer. There were two wide doorways that led off from it; one to the left and the other to the right. Directly across from the big oak front door, there was a broad staircase with a white wooden railing that wound up from the floor in a gradual curve to the upper level.

The floors and steps were all hardwood in lighter tones, glossed to a sheen, though there were colorful Arabian and Oriental rugs over much of the areas. A great crystal chandelier hung in the voluminous space over the foyer.

"I think we'll have a light dinner in the kitchen nook, and then we'll call it a night. It's been a long, dreadful day, and we all need some rest. Henry, you can show Jules around the house tomorrow while I'm at work." Vianne took a few steps toward the staircase. "Let's get you settled into your room, shall we?"

Henry and Jules followed Vianne up the steps, rounding them to the second floor. There was a landing that spread out to a long hallway that was split into a V-shape.

"I thought I'd put you in the turret room." Vianne said, heading down the hall. "There's a nice view of the ocean and the beach from there, and Henry's room is just down the hall in the tower over the foyer, so he's close."

Jules was surprised, and she felt the slightest glimmer of curiosity and what might be the corner of the edge of happiness at being put in such an elegant place.

The room was expansive in the width and height of it, as the turret was open spaced as well, with a twisting spiral light that hung from the center of it. The windows were tall with arches at the top of them and lace curtains over the glass. The bed stood at a wall that was beside a solitary window, and it was covered in a thick, white, cotton duvet, and stacked with deep pillows of varying sizes. A wooden desk was set against the far wall, topped with a stained glass Tiffany lamp, and a brand new computer. The computer seemed like an anomaly in such a classically designed home.

Vianne opened a door in the wall and headed into the walk-in closet, turning on the light inside. "This is all yours. I know you didn't bring much, but I think we'll wind up filling up some of this space with your things, and you can make it your own over time. There's no rush. Just be comfortable now." She left the closet, and opened another door that led to a private bathroom with a claw-foot tub and a standalone shower. White tile lined the floor and matched a white counter and cabinetry in the room, making everything look brighter.

Jules could scarcely take it all in. She stood in the room, looking all around it in awe, and then walked over to the cushy armchair beside one of the windows and sank down into it.

"It is the worst day of my life." She said in a soft tone, looking at Vianne as Henry set the suitcase down on the wooden chest at the end of the bed. "This takes some of the edge off. Thank you for… for everything." She managed to finish as she felt emotion rising in her again.

Vianne went to her and hugged her warmly, holding her for a long moment before she let her go and looked down at her. "Henry and I are going to make dinner. Come down to the kitchen whenever you're ready. It's just to the left when you come off of the stairs."

With that, they turned to go, though as Henry walked out he gave her a lasting glance over his shoulder, and she could see that he looked worried about her.

Jules unpacked her suitcase and stored it in the closet. She wandered around her new room, feeling that she was in a terrible dream. Going to the window, she opened it and a rush of cool ocean breeze danced in the curtains and swept over her, calming her. She closed her eyes as she took it into her lungs.

It had been the strangest day of her life. She had lost her mother and found a brother she never knew she had. Then she had moved to a new home, all in a matter of several hours. Leaving the window open, she went back down the hall and the stairs to the foyer.

Her aunt and brother had dinner ready, and it was simple, and just right for her. They ate a hot soup with soft bread and tea. Jules didn't feel hungry, but the soup smelled and tasted good, and when the meal was over, exhaustion overtook her, and she said goodnight to her family and went to bed.

Jules' sleep was so deep that there were no dreams, or at least, none that she could remember when she awoke in the morning. Before she was fully awake, she could hear the distant crashing of the waves on the sand, and she opened her eyes and looked around the room. It was even prettier than it had been the day before. The sunlight was warm and bright, the day was new, and though her mother was gone, she somehow didn't feel alone.

After a fast shower and dressing, she stepped out into the hall. She saw Henry's door open at the end of the hallway, and she walked quietly to it, hoping he was there and awake.

She peered in, and saw him sitting in an armchair as cushy as hers was, near the window in his room, with a book in his hands and his nose buried in the pages.

"Henry?" She asked hesitantly.

The boy looked up at her presently, and closed the book as a cautious smile overtook his face. "How are you feeling?" He asked, setting the book down on the small table beside him.

"I'm... in a weird place." She answered honestly.

"So am I." He replied. "I made breakfast if you're hungry. I waited for you, so we could eat together if you want to." The corner of his mouth turned up a little and there was a light in his green eyes. He pushed his hands down into his pockets as he watched her hopefully.

Jules felt an unexpected warmth in her heart that began to grow just a bit. She nodded. "Okay. That sounds good. Thank you."

Looking as though he was trying not to be too anxious, Henry walked swiftly across the room, one foot in front of the other, and led her down the stairs and into the kitchen again, going to the nook where they had eaten dinner.

"Normally we eat dinner in the dining room, just beyond those doors," he told her, pointing to a set of pocket doors at the end of the room, "but aunt Vianne wanted to keep it simple. We usually have breakfast in here."

He set out a cheese plate with four kinds of cheeses, grapes, strawberries, honey, and two kinds of breads, as well as a ceramic pot of oatmeal and two dishes of yogurt. "I didn't know what you like, so I kind of raided the fridge for a bit of everything."

He looked uncertain and Jules gave him a half smile. "This looks great, thank you." She sat down with him and he breathed out a sigh of relief.

"Where is aunt Vianne, anyway?" Jules asked as she took the teapot from Henry.

"She went to work." He stated flatly as he buttered some bread.

"Where does she work?" Jules asked, pouring milk into her tea.

He frowned. "That's an interesting question, actually. She works in the garden most every day, but I never see her out there."

Jules blinked in confusion. "Doesn't she have a job?"

Henry looked slightly contemplative. "I... I guess so. She has an office here, on one side of the library. I'll show you that when I give you the tour, but she's not usually in it. She doesn't leave to go to work, except to work in the greenhouse and the garden."

"But you never see her in the garden…" Jules finished for him.

"Right." He answered, chewing thoughtfully on his bite of bread. He swallowed and looked at his sister. "What did… mom… do?" He asked, finding it strange to say the word 'mom'.

Jules felt as if a weight was crushing her heart. She sighed and her shoulders slumped. "She… well, she had an office at the apartment, and she worked out of the office. I'm not really sure what she did. She didn't talk with me about it, she just went to work in there sometimes, and I wasn't allowed in, and when she was done working, she'd come out."

Henry frowned. "So, neither of them really works at an office or a business outside of home."

She shook her head. "I guess not. She was nearly always there. Most of the time she worked at home, but sometimes she said she was working '*out in the field*'. I never knew what she actually did, or where it was. She said it wasn't something she could discuss with me, so I didn't ask, but I always wondered." Jules found herself reminiscing about simple memories that had suddenly become precious to her. "She homeschooled me, so I didn't meet a lot of other kids, but we had outings all the time."

Henry was suddenly piqued with enormous interest. "I'm homeschooled too! aunt Vianne teaches me. It's astounding how much she knows. I don't feel that I'm missing anything I'd be getting at a public school, aside from a group of friends, I guess. I am in some reading groups at the library in town, and I am on a rowing team, so I have a few friends, but we stay pretty close to home. Where did you go on outings?"

"Museums and art galleries, historical places, old battlegrounds and state capitals, things like that." She answered, reaching for some cheese and grapes.

"It's fascinating." He shook his head and picked up his teacup, staring at it as his mind became a whir with the information they were sharing.

"What's fascinating?" She asked, nibbling on some cheese.

He set his teacup down and looked squarely at her. "Don't you see? We were kept apart from each other right from the beginning, but we were raised the same way by sisters. We're both homeschooled, they both work at home, and we are both kept close to them and apart from each other. That's just so... interesting to me. I feel like we've been kept behind a wall. Carefully kept, if that makes any sense. I mean, look at what aunt Vianne said yesterday; they wanted to keep us apart because they had to, until now when there is no choice, and she said she wants to keep us both as close to her as possible. Like she's guarding us from something. Like they've both been guarding us. See what I mean?"

Jules frowned, too. "I do see what you mean. That is strange." She furrowed her brow and thought on it for a long minute. "Why do you think they'd do that?"

He shook his head slowly. "Honestly, I have no idea."

"You live here, is there anything strange or unusual about this place?" She asked, eyeing him curiously as she sipped her tea.

"You mean other than the place itself? It doesn't seem too strange to me; it's home, but I'm well aware that no one else we know lives like we do." He shook his head and shrugged. "I don't think I've seen anything here that's too out of place."

"Other than aunt Vianne working in the garden and you never seeing her there? That's weird." Jules couldn't make it out at all. If she worked there, of course she could be seen working there.

Henry was quiet a moment as he considered it. "I guess not. We study, we go to town, we have meals together, she goes to work in the garden or the greenhouse. Sometimes she comes out looking a bit worse for the wear, and she tells me she's had a hard day of it in the garden, but that's it."

Jules was quiet then for a long moment. "Do you think your life will change much with me being here?" She asked, wondering what kind of impact her presence was really going to have.

He smiled at her. "I hope it does. I'm glad you're here, and I want to tell you, I thought about us all night and all morning. Even though we didn't grow up together, I want you to know that I will always be there for you, no matter what."

Jules felt that her heart had healed in more ways than she ever knew it could. She swallowed the tears that sprang to her eyes. "I'll always be there for you no matter what too. I promise."

They shared a smile and he handed her a fig drizzled with honey. "So what was mom like? Do you mind me asking?"

Jules didn't know what to say at first. She didn't know how to describe a person succinctly. "Mom was strong and smart. She was a really determined lady; it seemed like everything she set her mind to, she did, even if it took a little while. She wouldn't give up on things. She was kind and she tried to be funny a lot, though I didn't think she was very funny, but maybe that was me. She used to read books to me all the time. She'd lay in my bed with me and read stories I hadn't heard yet, or sometimes get back into old favorites, but usually we read new ones. I loved that."

He stared at her, imagining himself in her place, wondering what it would be like for his mother to read a story to him. "It sounds pretty incredible." He said quietly.

"What is it like growing up with aunt Vianne?" Jules returned the question to him.

"It's fun, but she keeps a close eye on me. I don't really mind it; I have no interest in getting into trouble, but it always feels like there's an invisible fence around this home and around me, keeping me back from… from I don't know what." He sighed and gave his head a little shake.

"So mysterious." Jules gave him a little smile. "Maybe we should just go out to the garden and the greenhouse and see what she's up to. Maybe she could use some help out there." She couldn't see why Henry hadn't thought of that.

He shook his head adamantly. "Oh no, we can't. I'm not allowed out there. The greenhouse is strictly off limits."

She pushed her lower lip out as she considered what he said. "Kind of like mom keeping me out of her office in the apartment. So strange."

They continued to talk as they finished their breakfast, and she helped him do the dishes and put them all away.

With breakfast out of the way, he took her on a tour of the house. First through the dining room, which was a sophisticated looking space with dark wood paneled walls and crystal chandeliers, along with a long dark wooden dining table and matching chairs all around it.

Next, he showed her the library, which was good sized, with a thick, soft sofa and a big fireplace. "We always have fires going in here in the wintertime, and I spend a lot of time in here. Sometimes she lets me have tea in here, if I'm in the middle of an important study assignment or a really great book." He gave her a smile and then took her through the library to Vianne's office.

There was a computer on the desk and a printer nearby. There were photos of Marleigh and Vianne as younger women in a frame on the desk. Jules looked around the room and planted her hands on her hips, casing the place with an eagle eye.

Henry paused and watched her. "Do you see anything unusual?"

She twisted her mouth and shook her head. "No, this place is exceptionally ordinary." She frowned a little. "This is an old house, are there any secret doors or anything?"

Henry nodded. "Yes, but nothing connected to this room, and nothing too exciting. They just go to other rooms in the house."

He took her through to the music room, which was the downstairs half of the turret room. There was a baby grand piano near the rounded windows, and there were other instruments set in stands or on shelves throughout the room. A viola, a violin, a saxophone, a harp, a clarinet, a French horn, various drums from around the world, and an ancient looking harpsichord.

Jules gazed about, impressed. "Does she play all of these?"

Henry ran his fingers over the keys on the piano. "We both do. She's taught me to play all of them. We play together nearly every day."

She smiled again and looked at him with tremendous respect. "That's amazing. I only know the piano a bit."

He smiled back. "You'll learn the rest. You're here now with us. We'll teach you." He brightened then and looked at her hopefully. "Would you like to play a piece with me?"

She nodded and they sat down together on the bench at the piano. After a few tries, they had it figured out, and they played a bit of Beethoven together, discovering that they had a shared passion for music, and much more in common than they realized. Jules hadn't expected to find herself feeling happy ever again, but sitting there with her brother at the piano, playing along with him at his side, she realized that she did feel some happiness, and she was grateful for it.

After a while, they left the music room and he took her through the drawing room and back up the stairs. There were other rooms to see there, though most of them were bedrooms. Jules learned that her aunt had collected various treasures from all over the world, from many different countries and times, and they were beautifully displayed throughout her home.

The siblings went for a long walk down away from the house and along the beach, talking about everything and getting to know one another. They found that they had so much in common; much more than they would have guessed, and they found that they each had a good friend in the other, for which they were both profoundly glad.

Jules picked up seashells along the way as they walked, and when they got back to the house, Henry took her to his room and gave her a delicately carved wooden box to put them all in. She took it to her room and set it on one of the small tables near the window. Looking at it, she remembered Vianne telling her just the day before that she would make the room her own and fill it with her own things soon enough, and she rested her hand on the box of sea shells and felt a little pleased. She would make this place her home, a little at a time, and she would be happy there, someday.

Henry and Jules spent the day together, and decided to surprise Vianne with a dinner ready-made for her. They prepared the meal and waited, and the hours ticked by, but there was no sign of her in the gardens, and no sign of anyone in the greenhouse; not that they could see through the panes of it very well, especially from the house.

The dinner hour had passed, and though they were talking and enjoying each other's company, both of them were becoming worried that Vianne had been gone too long. She hadn't even come in for lunch.

Finally, Jules paused in their conversation to say something about it. "She's been gone an awfully long time. I mean, I haven't even seen her today. She should have been in at some point, shouldn't she?"

"I think so, yes. She's not usually gone this long." Henry answered, biting at his lower lip.

"Well, we have dinner ready and I'm beginning to get worried. I know you said we aren't supposed to go out to the greenhouse, but she gave you that rule. She never said a word about it to me; at least not yet, so I'm going to go out there and see if I can find her. I want to at least make sure she's okay." She stood up and headed for the door.

"You shouldn't go! We should wait here for her." He pleaded as he stood up.

"Henry, it's really late and she's been gone all day. I don't mind if she isn't pleased with me for going out there; I just want to make sure she's okay." Jules gave him a solemn look. "You can stay here if you want to, then you won't get in trouble and it will just be me, and I'll even tell her that I didn't know I shouldn't go out there."

He shook his head and pushed his hands down into his pants pockets. "No, that's all right. I'll go with you. I'm worried too. It has been too long."

Together they walked outside and down a pretty path through the gorgeous gardens at the side of the house. There were flowers and trees and bushes of every kind, and even a little pond. Just as they were coming to the greenhouse, which was down a little hill from the main house, Jules saw Henry reach his hand out and touch a beautiful old lamppost by the path.

"That's pretty." She said, looking up at it as it glowed in the golden late afternoon light.

"It always makes me think of Narnia." Henry told her with a grin. "I do love that series."

She smiled and nodded. "Me too." She replied as they reached the door of the greenhouse. They both stopped and hesitated, looking at each other.

"Are you sure you want to go in? I can go in alone and look for her. She probably won't be as mad at me, but you know the rules. Maybe you should wait out here?" She suggested helpfully.

Henry shook his head resolutely. "No, I'm going in with you."

Taking a deep breath she nodded. "Okay then. Let's go."

Reaching for the door handle, she turned it and they walked into the greenhouse together. It was a tall, white framed structure with squares of glass all over it; most of them refracting the light of the sinking sun into rainbows all over the place. Inside there were tables and shelves lined with plants of many different species and sizes. There were a few work benches in the back.

The children walked slowly through all of the greenery, looking for their aunt. They went down one aisle between tables and plants, and reached the end of the greenhouse, then turned and headed back up the other aisle, opposite of the way they'd just gone.

"I don't see her, do you?" Jules asked, looking around carefully.

"No, I don't." Henry answered, wondering how he had lived at the house all his life and never gone inside the greenhouse before, regardless of the rules, but then again, he just wasn't a rule breaker.

They reached the other end of the greenhouse and came back to the front of it again. "She's not here." Jules said with a deep frown. "This is so strange."

Henry raised his brows a bit. "Maybe she went back up to the house while we were walking through here. Maybe we didn't hear the door. It is pretty quiet."

Jules nodded. "Okay. We'll head back up to the house and see if she's there."

She reached for the door handle and stopped, frozen where she stood, staring at it.

Henry saw her and his heartbeat picked up. "What? What is it? What's wrong?"

Jules shook her head slowly and reached her hand forward to the door handle. There, hanging on it, was a long brassy looking thin chain; a necklace, with a pendant at the end of it. She curled her fingertips around it and lifted it from the door.

"This... this necklace, it was mom's." She spoke reverently, holding it up and looking at it with a pained expression.

"Hold on, aunt Vianne's got one just like that." He said, peering at it. He leaned closer and furrowed his brow a bit.

"No, this one was mom's. I know it. She always wore it; she never took it off. What's it doing here?" She asked, her heart pierced with pain anew as she held the precious token in her hands.

Without another word, she slipped the chain over her neck, feeling somehow closer to her mother as she did so, and holding the pendant in her hand.

It was a little 3D brass globe, with detailed outlines of the countries of the world and the latitudes and longitudes engraved into it. Around the globe, at a small distance, was a thin ring, like one of Saturn's rings, forming the equator horizontally around the sphere, and there was another ring just like the first, running vertically around the globe, just like a prime meridian and only intersecting with the equatorial ring. The metal ball inside was suspended within the rings.

"This is mom's." Jules repeated, studying it closely. "I saw her wear this every day."

Henry leaned closer to get a better look. "Oh, you know what, aunt Vianne's is just a little different. Hers is similar, but it has different markings along the two planes around the sphere. Hers is engraved with strange looking marks just here," he reached his finger out and touched the plane, and as he did, there was a flash of white light, and everything around them vanished into blackness.

Chapter Three
New York

The blackness faded almost as fast as it had engulfed them, and Henry and Jules gasped. They stood frozen, just as they had been standing in the greenhouse a moment before, but they were not in the greenhouse any longer.

In the space of a breath, the greenhouse had vanished, and they discovered they were both standing on wet cobblestone. It was a narrow road, encased between two tall buildings about three stories in height each, that were matched by more buildings just a little further down the road.

They turned their heads slowly as they looked around, trying to take in the scene about them and absorb it all. Henry reached for Jules' hand.

"What… what just happened? Are you seeing this?" Jules whispered as they stared at the windows, doors, and shops along the road. "Or am I dreaming?"

"I see an old, old city. Is that what you see?" Henry asked in a whisper.

"I see it. Cobblestone road, brick buildings?" Jules asked him in return.

"Yeah." Henry answered, swallowing hard, though his throat was dry.

"Where are we?" Jules asked worriedly.

Henry spoke in a low tone. "I think the better question is, *when* are we?"

Her head spun and Jules blinked at him. "What?"

"Didn't you notice? There aren't any cars here! Those are horse drawn carriages! Look at the way people are dressed. This looks like what I've seen in books and movies from a century ago! I don't think we're in our time anymore." He groaned quietly.

Jules peered around, and noticed that everything he had said was true. Every female she saw was wearing a long dress, a hat, and gloves, and every man was dressed well in fine coats, with hats, and most had walking canes. There were no cars; there were only horse drawn carriages. There was nothing around them that was from their time.

"Oh… my… g-" Jules started to say, but Henry clamped a hand over her mouth.

"Shh! We need to get out of sight and figure this out!" He breathed in a hushed voice. "We obviously aren't from here. It may be intuition, but I feel like the last thing we want to do is make a scene and attract attention to ourselves."

"You're probably right." Jules agreed, finally turning back to him with wide eyes and a pale face.

Henry looked about quickly and spied an alley closer to the end of the street. "Let's get over there. Quietly. Quickly. We'll be out of sight and we can try to figure out what's going on."

Just as they turned to head to the alley, a man's voice called out, and they froze in their tracks, looking behind them.

To read all of
The Starling Chronicles series,
and many other exciting
Dash Hoffman stories,
please visit the official website:

www.got-moxie.com/bookshelf

or

www.amazon.com/Dash-
Hoffman/e/B06XDMMQTJ

Follow Dash!
Instagram @dashhoffmanbooks
Twitter @readdashhoffman
Facebook @DashHoffmanOfficial

Mrs. Perivale and the Dragon Prince
Journey Blue
The Starling Chronicles
The Wish Weaver
Voyager: The Butterfly Effect

MRS. PERIVALE AND THE DRAGON PRINCE

Alice Perivale saved the world, now she's pleased to make a teacup garden. 73 year old Mrs. Perivale is enjoying time with her grandson when her secret vial of dragon's blood begins to glow brightly, and she fears that things have gone terribly wrong in the magical land of Corevé since she left. Alice loses no time in calling her mighty dragon friend Diovalo out of foreboding, thunderous skies, to land in Hyde Park and whisk her, her six cats, her butler Henderson, and her stunned grandson away.

Armed with stab-tastic knitting needles, her fist high in the air, Alice is certain she's ready to find and rescue the fire dragons who have vanished without a trace. Her task becomes almost impossible when her company is betrayed, her family is pulled apart, and her identity is splintered, but Alice knows that hope is the brightest light in darkness.

How can she help those who need her most when every step takes her somewhere she never imagined she'd be?

Mrs. Perivale and the Dragon Prince is the second book in the enchanting *Mrs. Perivale* YA fantasy series. If you're looking to escape reality for a while with a laugh-out-loud, heart-touching adventure, discover the heroine you never knew you needed today! YA+

The Wish Weaver

Amias and his young friends enjoy simple lives in their village at the foot of the Kamado mountains, though there are circumstances for each of them that they wish they could change; a family member with ill health, a love unrequited, a life debt that cannot be repaid, and more.

A traveling stranger passes through the village and enchants them with a tale of the Wish Weaver who lives far up the mountain and weaves wishes into being. When his friends decide to go to the Wish Weaver to change their lives, Amias determines to go with them, though he is skeptical about anyone granting wishes freely to one and all. Along the journey the friends face tremendous hardships and when their quest takes a dark turn, Amias becomes the only one who might be able to save them all. If he is very clever and very lucky, his sole wish might come true.

This book is written in the style of an old Grimm's Bros fairytale and an Aesop fable. It is light and dark, and there are many moral lessons to discover woven deftly into the story. This tale takes a hard look at choosing what is right over what is easy, at moral value over material value, at self-love over infatuation, and at strong, true friendships.

YA+

Journey Blue

Blue is an unusual girl living on her own in a strange world. It is a place of consistency and method; seamless and cold, and she thinks she knows her world until the day she feels something, or rather someone, pulling at her from far away.

Visions of a mysterious boy intrigue her, and she is unable to ignore the magnetic draw within her to him. Even though Blue doesn't know him, this remarkable girl sets out to find the boy, traveling through what she believes is the monotonous machine of a land she lives in, only to discover that it's nothing at all like she ever imagined.

From giant white turtles and glowing bridges of light to colorful sand dunes and bottles of wishes, Blue's journey becomes a bizarre twist of terrifying danger and delightful fun. With the help of extraordinary and dear friends that she makes along the way, she discovers the highs of happiness and hope, and the lows of fear and sadness.

It isn't all fun and games; dark and dangerous forces come after her, doing everything to stop her from going onward. Her courage and determination are unbreakable however, and Blue refuses to give up on finding the unknown boy, no matter what it takes, how surreal the world around her becomes, or how impossible it may be to get to him. This journey straight out of reality will leave you reeling. YA+

The Starling Chronicles
Book One ~ The Starlings of Ramblewood

Daring and clever fourteen year old Jules Starling has just lost her mother and met her twelve year old bookish brother Henry for the first time. Before she even has a chance to get settled into her new home at Ramblewood with Henry and their aunt Vianne, every part of the real world they know begins to unravel swiftly!

When Vianne goes missing and they begin a search for her, traveling through time by accident is only the beginning of a series of unimaginable surprises and wild adventures for the Starling children. After a dreamlike visit to the Time Palace and a strict warning not to do anything or go anywhere, they are shanghaied onto a fantastical ship by a rogue pirate and a world class crew, traveling through oceans, air, and space.

Their new friends are a tremendous support, but the search for Vianne takes them on a dangerous quest much further than they ever dreamed they could go. Jules and Henry soon discover that they'll have to find courage, bravery, and strength in themselves and in each other if they ever hope to overcome the formidable challenges they must face and succeed in their vital mission!

This is the first book in the Starling Chronicles series, which takes the Starling children on many extraordinary adventures through space and time! YA+

VOYAGER:
THE BUTTERFLY EFFECT

Audrey Bennet and Jude Harper have just lost their dear friend Daniel, but Danny shared an unbelievable secret with them before he passed away. He invented a time machine. After finding it, they decide to leave it untouched and under coded lock and key in Harper's basement, but fate brings about necessity.

Just when they need him most, Danny is there to help them. Audrey is working hard on a case that should not be happening; she's the unlucky police detective tasked with putting an old woman in jail at the insistence of a heartless tycoon.

When she hears Ruth Harrison's story, she knows she must do everything in her power to help Ruth win her freedom, her life, and get back a bit of her past so she can find peace in her future. Even if it means dragging Jude Harper back in time with her to uncover the truth.

This is a tale of enduring love; love between friends, love between lovers, and the strength that it takes to bind them all together. Harper and Audrey discover that everything that happens in every life, no matter how small, can have a powerful effect; a butterfly effect, that ripples throughout the rest of time.

Made in the USA
Monee, IL
04 June 2021